To Tom and Madeleine
with love and best wishes.
Alan

Alf Stone
21/7/24

THE BUTTERFLY HUNTER

A.B. STONE

The Book Guild Ltd

First published in Great Britain in 2024 by
The Book Guild Ltd
Unit E2 Airfield Business Park,
Harrison Road, Market Harborough,
Leicestershire. LE16 7UL
Tel: 0116 2792299
www.bookguild.co.uk
Email: info@bookguild.co.uk
Twitter: @bookguild

Copyright © 2024 A. B. Stone

The right of A. B. Stone to be identified as the author of this
work has been asserted by them in accordance with the
Copyright, Design and Patents Act 1988.

All rights reserved. No part of this publication may be
reproduced, transmitted, or stored in a retrieval system, in any form or by any means,
without permission in writing from the publisher, nor be otherwise circulated in
any form of binding or cover other than that in which it is published and without
a similar condition being imposed on the subsequent purchaser.

This work is entirely fictitious and bears no resemblance to any persons living or dead.

Typeset in 11pt Minion Pro

Printed on FSC accredited paper
Printed and bound in Great Britain by 4edge Limited

ISBN 978 1835740 262

British Library Cataloguing in Publication Data.
A catalogue record for this book is available from the British Library.

To my family and friends, be they near or far.

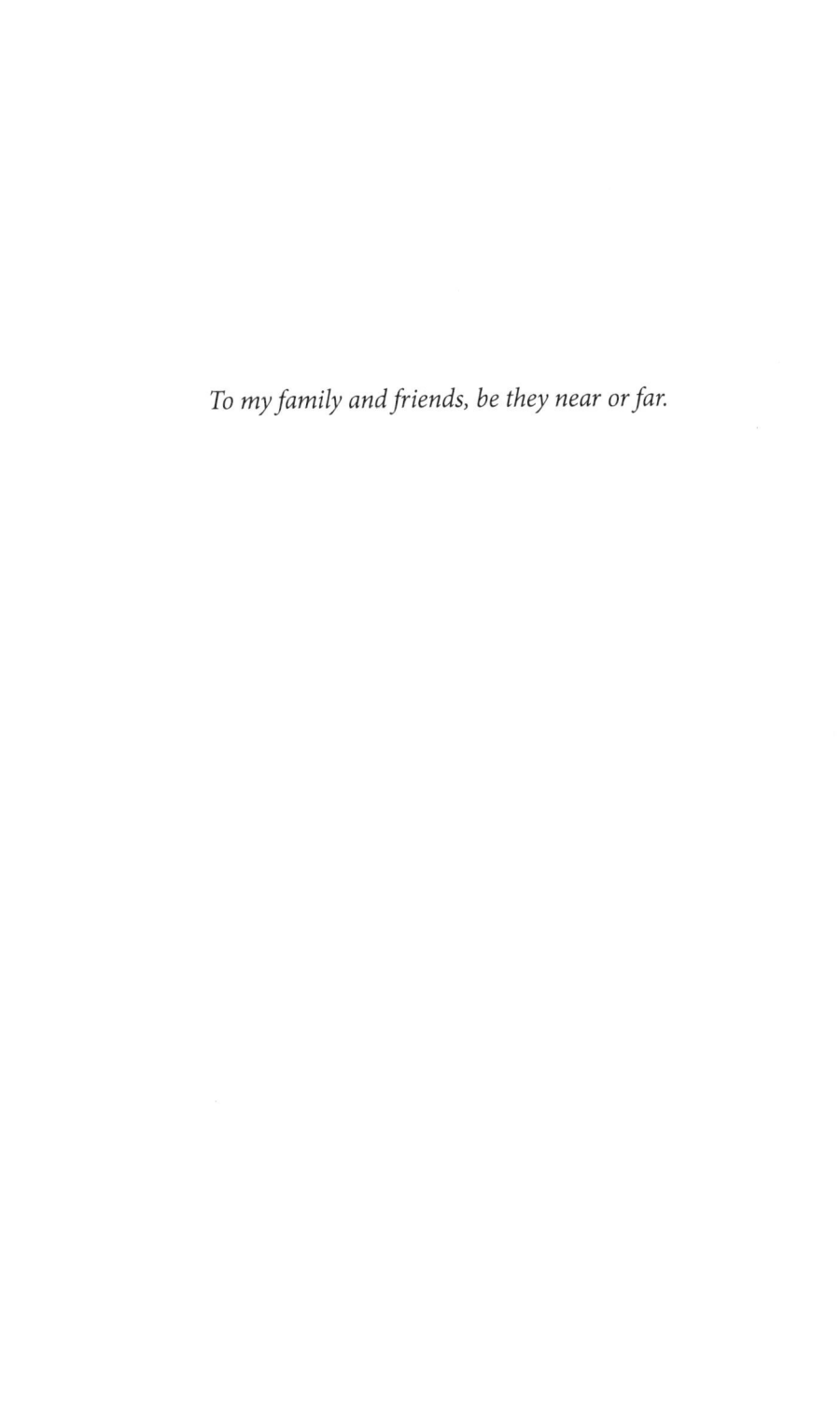

And, though the villain 'scape a while, he feels
Slow Vengeance, like a bloodhound, at his heels

JONATHAN SWIFT

ONE

Manaus, Brazil, 1963

Another sweltering day. The stray dogs are back, lying on their bellies in little groups of two or three, quietly appreciating one another's company like old men relaxing at their club. Women at the roadside market are busy swapping gossip and haggling with the stallholders over the price of papayas and *farinha*. A noisy rabble of men, most of them overweight and shirtless, are hanging around under the big mango tree, drinking beer and playing games with the metal caps off the beer bottles. No one seems to give a damn about the dead body lying in the street.

It made Klara wonder whether stumbling across a corpse in this godforsaken Brazilian backwater was as commonplace as seeing a tramp sleeping in a shop doorway back home in New York. At first, she thought it was the body of an old woman, maybe someone who'd succumbed to the heat. But when she got closer, she found herself peering into the face of a woman of her own age, blonde like herself, and a lot better dressed than the local women. It was almost like looking at her own body sprawled on the ground. She shuddered at the thought. Same build, same height, more or less. Then, she saw the blood. The gunshot wound. She understood immediately. A case of mistaken identity; that's what it was. Tragic for the dead woman but providential for her. *She* was the one those bastards were after, the one they wanted to get rid of, not this unfortunate lookalike who just happened to be in the wrong place at the wrong time. She felt an urge to offer an apology, but she didn't. That would have been absurd. Anyway, she wasn't responsible for what had happened, was she? At least, not directly.

She heard a flurry of wings. A pair of vultures swooped down from the mango tree and alighted on the ground in front of her, their beady black eyes fixed on the corpse. She screamed blue murder at the unholy creatures. They hobbled backwards, hissing defiantly, then spread their wings and flapped their way back into the mango tree. They were still watching her. She could feel it. They were waiting.

New York, two months earlier

In an empty room above the art gallery at the corner of 89th Street and Fifth Avenue, Klara was standing at the window, watching the rain spattering on the glass, half hoping that the man she was supposed to meet there wouldn't show up. Even over the phone his voice had sounded threatening. She'd told herself a million times she'd be a fool to come, but in truth he'd left her little choice. He knew too much about her. About her family. She lit a cigarette and blew a stream of smoke through her nostrils.

A voice behind her made her swing round. She recognised the German accent. It was him.

'So, *Fräulein* Brandt, here you are.' There was no warmth in his greeting – if you could call it a greeting.

He was a lot older than he'd sounded on the phone and walked with a slight limp.

'You sure took your time,' she said. 'I was just about to give you up. And by the way, it's *Miss* Brandt, not *Fräulein*. This is America, you know, not your precious Fatherland. Okay, I came. I'm here. So why don't you tell me what you want?'

The old man raised his hand like a policeman holding up the traffic. 'A little patience, please, Miss Brandt. You please come with me. The others are waiting.'

'What d'you mean? I thought it would just be you.'

'Then you were mistaken.'

He looked harmless enough in his baggy tweed jacket, puffing on his pipe like some old professor, but she didn't trust him an inch. That phone call. He'd alarmed her by talking about things she'd never mentioned to anybody… the nightmare of her childhood in wartime Germany… the father she'd once respected, even loved, but now wanted to forget. How could he have known all that? Then came the crunch. '*Klara Brandt*,' he'd said. 'I like that name. It has a nice ring to it. Certainly preferable to your real name. I wonder if those people in Washington would be interested if someone were to tell them that the daughter of Colonel Hans Friedrich Weber has been living in New York for the past eighteen years under an assumed name. I think they would, don't you?'

That was a week ago. When she'd asked him what he wanted, he said they needed to talk and told her to meet him at this gallery. It wasn't far from the Guggenheim and seemed like a safe enough place for a rendezvous with a stranger. She hadn't reckoned on being left on her own in this shabby attic several floors above the public exhibition space.

'You please follow me,' he was saying. He ushered her into a room at the end of the corridor and gestured towards several people sitting around a table. Someone was wearing an expensive perfume, most likely the woman with the blue-rinse hair. There were four men and two women. None of them could have been a day under sixty.

She flinched when she felt his hand on her arm. 'My friends,' she heard him say, 'allow me to introduce our guest, Miss Klara Brandt.'

Six pairs of eyes turned to look at her. She pulled her coat more snugly around her shoulders. She had the impression they'd been expecting somebody else, someone different, not this young woman with blonde hair and blue eyes, wearing coral pink lipstick. There were a few perfunctory nods and some mumbled hellos. She heard someone whisper 'Klara Weber!'

He pointed to an empty chair. 'Now, you please come and join us.'

There was a hush as she took off her coat and sat down. She looked around the room. It was gloomy. Faded brown wallpaper. No carpet, just bare wooden floorboards. And these curious old people staring at her.

They looked as if they'd just stepped out of one of those dusty picture frames stacked against the wall.

He leant over to her. The smoke from his pipe had a sickly-sweet aroma. 'Let me pour you a cup of coffee, yes?' There was a glass jug half full of coffee on the table and a jumble of white paper cups. In front of him was a black leather attaché case, which he pushed to one side. 'So, Miss Brandt, if you're ready, perhaps we can get down to business.'

What business? she wondered. Who were these people, with their furtive, watchful eyes? Most likely a gang of goddamn fascists operating right here in the middle of New York, scheming to recruit her because they knew her father had been a high-ranking officer in the Wehrmacht. She could see him now, in his smart uniform, clicking the heels of his shiny polished boots as he welcomed important guests to their house in Berlin. But it wasn't just that. He'd been a member of that privileged clique that gathered around the Führer himself, a coterie of the trusted and the faithful. Something to be proud of, then. But not now. *Don't these people know the war's been over for almost twenty years?*

She turned to the man with the pipe. 'Okay, let's talk business then. You can begin by telling me who you all are, and why I'm here.'

He waved aside a lingering cloud of smoke. 'Sorry, no names. You must understand that in our kind of work secrecy is paramount.'

'Oh? And what kind of work is that?'

'Come now, Miss Brandt, I think you must have some idea about that.'

Yes, she thought, a pretty good idea. She'd been lucky. After the war, she'd been put on a boat to the United States, just a child, carrying false papers. She'd been given a new name to sever her from her father's unsavoury legacy. The shadows of her past didn't belong in the new life she'd made for herself, so she'd packed them away in the tightest corners of her mind. The occasional shot or two of hard liquor helped to keep them there. Now, this old man had deliberately roused them.

'Miss Brandt,' he was saying, 'there's something we want you to do for us. You have assumed as much, yes?'

'Have I? Go on.'

'All of us around this table have one single objective, one dream.'

She knew what that was. World domination, that's what.

'It boils down to this,' he continued. 'We need to find a certain man.'

'I see. Who?'

'Someone from the old days. In fact, someone who knew your father.'

'Really?'

'Certainly. This man we want was also a member of the Führer's inner circle. A particularly zealous member, and clever enough to avoid getting captured when the Allies reached Berlin in '45.'

'Well, he's probably dead by now.'

'No. We believe he's still alive, hiding somewhere, even now, as we speak. A living remnant of the Third Reich, no less. A very important remnant. We have to find him.'

So, it was just as she'd thought. A pack of lousy Nazis still dreaming about resurrecting themselves.

He continued. '*Fräulein* Weber...'

She corrected him. 'Miss Brandt.'

'Of course, Miss Brandt. You must understand that I'm not talking about any ordinary war criminal. This man was one of the top-ranking members of that evil gang responsible for death and destruction all over Europe.' He fixed his eyes on her. 'Each one of us here today was a victim of their madness. Every member of our families dragged away and murdered, even the children. Yet, somehow, *we* survived. *You* survived. Why? For what? Think about that.'

For a moment, Klara was confused. Had she got the wrong end of the stick about these people? She lit another cigarette but said nothing.

'Excuse me.' It was the woman with the blue-rinse hair. She'd taken off her thick glasses and was waving them at her. She sounded Polish, or perhaps Czech. 'I understand you were only a child when you left Germany, *Fräulein*, but perhaps you remember what life was like in your country under those people, yes? How old are you now? Thirty-three? Thirty-four?'

'My country? My country is the United States of America, but I know what you mean. Of course I remember. All too vividly. I and my family had first-hand experience of the way those people did things. I wasn't a baby when I left. I was sixteen.'

'Then you should understand why we are here, why fate has spared us. You want I tell you? Listen to me. We have a job to do. A sacred duty. We have to find this man, this criminal, this... monstrosity.' Her voice started to shake. 'Catch him, trap him, grab him... whatever is necessary to bring him to justice.' She raised her eyes to the ceiling and uttered something unintelligible. It sounded like a curse.

'So that's it,' Klara said. 'That's what this is all about. But you're not really going after him, are you? All that was twenty years ago.'

The man with the pipe was shaking his head. 'Miss Brandt, the number of years is irrelevant. This man was one of the most ruthless operators among that entire pack of wolves. He made sure their outlandish ideas were brought to life. How much do you remember about the Nuremberg trials? Those at the top of the heap were tried, and many were executed. But the man we want disappeared, so they tried him *in absentia*. He was given a death sentence, but it was never carried out. How did he manage to get away? We don't know. Where has he been hiding for almost twenty years? We don't know that either.'

'Well, that doesn't help terribly much, does it? Anyway, what's all this got to do with me?'

'Believe me, Miss Brandt, it has more to do with you than you might think. Besides, you're a journalist, aren't you? A story like this—'

'I'm sure that's not why you got me here, just for a story. There's something you haven't told me. Who is he, this man? Doesn't he have a name?'

'Oh, he has a name all right, and it's a name I think you'll recognise. You want to know?'

He pushed his chair backwards, pressed the palms of his hands on the table to lever himself up, and limped across to the window. He appeared to be gazing at something in the far distance. Then he said, 'His name is Walther Schacht.'

Klara froze. A cold shiver ran down her spine. Walther Schacht! She knew that name as well as she knew her own. Walther Schacht! The words rang in her brain like a rattle from Hell. She could feel the hairs on the back of her neck stiffening. Schacht! *He* was the bastard who'd ordered the slaughter of her family… father, mother and her two brothers, all murdered on his instructions. She thought he was dead. All those years. How could he still be alive? Her head was spinning.

'Yes, Miss Brandt, SS-Gruppenführer Walther Ludwig Schacht, a man with almost absolute power. A ruthless administrator of murder.' She had the strange feeling he was speaking in slow motion, through a sort of haze. Suddenly he was standing right next to her, pounding his fist on the table. 'We have to find this man, this fucking… monster. *Do you understand, Miss Brandt?* We must not let him get away with his crimes and live and die a free man. We've got to find him now, before it's too late.'

Klara's head was bursting. *Schacht, alive!* 'My god! If I ever get my hands on that filthy bastard, I'll give him something to remember! Listen, after all these years, you don't really believe there's any chance of finding him, do you? He could be hiding anywhere. You sure he's still alive?'

'Oh yes, he's alive all right. But the question is, where? It's common knowledge that quite a few of them ended up in South America. Mainly small fry, but not all.' He took two staccato puffs from his pipe to try to keep it alight. 'South America is a big place. A very big haystack in which to search for a needle, wouldn't you agree?' He paused. She nodded. 'We've had fragmentary reports from… from certain people we know… that lead us to believe he's holed up somewhere down there. Most likely somewhere in Brazil. Maybe Paraguay.'

'You mean… you don't actually know where he is? Oh, that's swell.'

The heavily built man sitting opposite her stubbed out his cigarette with such sudden force it made her jump. She'd never seen anyone with so black an expression on his face.

'Know where he is?' He spoke with a thick accent that she couldn't quite place. 'If I knew where that fucking bastard is hiding, I wouldn't be sitting here. I'd…' He shut his eyes and shook a fist in the air. He seemed scarcely aware that he'd picked up a paper cup and crushed the life out of it.

The man with the pipe waited for him to settle down. 'So, now we come to the point, yes? My dear Miss Brandt, this is what you can do for us. We want you to find out where *Herr* Schacht is hiding. In what circumstances. In what sort of place. We've spent many years trying to locate him. We're no longer young, and time is running out – for us and for him. This is our last chance.'

She knew they were going to ask her to do *something* for them, but not this. Walther Schacht! Even the mention of his name gave her butterflies. She was gripping the edge of the table with both hands.

'Me? Why me? It makes no sense. Surely you have people specially trained for jobs like this. Professionals.'

'Miss Brandt, two of our agents – yes, professionals – have tried to find him, and failed. Schacht and his minders managed to give them the slip.' He took a box of matches out of his jacket pocket and fussed with his pipe. 'As a matter of fact, one of them didn't make it back. That was unfortunate, but we've lost agents before. It happens.'

Klara caught her breath. 'I don't like the sound of that.'

'That's why it's time to take a different approach. That means you. No one would suspect a woman like you of being a secret agent on a mission. You're more likely to be taken for an American tourist.'

'Are you kidding? You want to know something? There's plenty of people who don't look like secret agents, not just me. So why me?'

'True, but how many of them can speak fluent German, and have the military skills you picked up in the US army?'

'The army? Well, you've certainly done your homework. That was ages ago. I volunteered because I felt I owed something to my new country. Anyway, all that training was pointless. I spent most of my time at Camp Drum, right here in upstate New York, for Chrissakes.'

'Well, you won't be looking for Schacht in upstate New York, that's for sure. And there's something else, something critical.'

'Oh, is there? What's that?'

He was standing directly behind her chair, where she couldn't see him. 'Your intense hate for Walther Schacht.

It's obvious to me that underneath that composed surface of yours, you're burning for justice to be done. I say justice, but the thirst for vengeance can be infinitely more powerful than the desire for justice, isn't that right, Miss Brandt?' He gripped her shoulders from behind. She clenched her teeth but said nothing. 'I'd go so far as to say that vengeance is in your blood. If it were necessary, I think you'd walk through fire to get your hands on Walther Schacht. Isn't that so?' He released her shoulders. 'Don't worry. We'll give him justice. The kind of justice he deserves.' He sat down.

Klara gave him a blank stare. 'I get it. You're asking me to scour an entire continent to track down a dangerous fugitive, a convicted murderer, while doing my best to make sure he doesn't shoot me or strangle me or poison me. Oh, really, is that all?'

'Please, Miss Brandt.'

'And what d'you want me to do if I find him? Shoot him?'

'Certainly not. You'll send us the precise details of where we can find him. Just that. As for what happens afterwards, you don't need to worry. We'll take care of the rest. You remember when Adolf Eichmann was abducted from Argentina, three years ago?'

'Another of those bastards! Of course I do. Who doesn't?'

'Well, we want it to go like that. We want Schacht alive, so he too can testify before the world. So no shooting. You understand? As for abducting him, we'll send the experts to do that. You don't even need to go anywhere near him once you find out where he's hiding.

Just tell us what we need to know, then you come home. That's all.'

'That's it? That's all, really? You just want me to find out where he is?'

He nodded.

'You have other people to do the grabbing?'

He nodded again.

The room fell silent except for the sound of Klara's fingers drumming on the table. She knew all eyes were on her. 'I see. Well, let's assume that I do agree to go along with this, and let's say I find him. How am I supposed to get in touch with you from the middle of nowhere? That's if he hasn't murdered me by then, of course.'

'Telegram. You'll find some sort of tin-pot telegraphist in the most unlikely places. Miss Brandt, please listen carefully. I'm sure you remember the gentleman who greeted you when you arrived at my art gallery, yes? I'm talking about the doorman in the gallery's foyer, in the blue uniform.'

'Him? The man with that ridiculous moustache? What about him? I didn't like the way he looked at me.'

'We call him Eduardo. It's not his real name, of course. This Eduardo isn't all he seems. He's one of our... er... senior associates. For the time being, he's using my gallery as his headquarters. You'll send your telegrams to him.'

'What? To that pompous... peacock? You're joking. Not to you?'

'No. Take my word for it, Miss Brandt, that pompous peacock, as you call him, may look like some sort of Italian gigolo, but that's all part of the game, and he's expertly skilled at it. He's seen a lot more of life than most people, the good, the bad and the unspeakable. He's got all the right connections and will quickly organise whatever action is necessary. Today, his job is to scrutinise everyone who comes into the gallery, for our protection. There are certain people who would dearly love to get rid of every one of us in this room.'

'That doesn't surprise me. And what about that shifty-looking character in the black three-piece suit who practically prodded me into the elevator when I arrived this morning? Is he also one of your so-called associates?'

'Yes, he's one of us, but forget about him. Send your telegrams to Eduardo. You'll have to make your messages as cryptic as you can, just in case they fall into the wrong hands. Eduardo will know what they mean. Remember, our enemies are clever, and we must always bear in mind the possibility that they're watching us. It's hard to say for sure.'

'What d'you mean, *us*?'

'I mean Eduardo, me… you.'

'Well, that's just dandy.'

'Don't worry, we've been playing this game for a long time.' He looked at her in silence for a while, then he said, 'So, now you know what we want you to do. The question is, are you with us or not? We need to know. It's not without risk, as you've already pointed out. I'll be honest with you. Schacht won't hesitate to kill if he thinks we're getting too close. He and his agents will kill anybody, without a second thought. It would mean nothing to them… just a few more deaths. Do what you have to do, but it's best to keep out of his way. You understand?' He waited for Klara to say something, but she didn't. 'Miss Brandt, if you need time to think it over, then say so.'

'Listen. If you're asking me how I feel about risking my life pursuing an old man for crimes he committed all those years ago… Christ! I'll never forget any of those goddamn brutes. And certainly not Walther Schacht. I don't care how old and decrepit he is, the bastard deserves to die, in the worst way possible, justice or no justice. I'll find him.'

'Good, but remember, we want him alive. At least, for a while. After that… well, his execution has been delayed for too long.' He pointed to the black attaché case on the table and pushed it towards her. 'This is for you. Take good care of it.' He held out a key in front of her then hesitated and looked straight into her eyes. 'You're sure about this, are you? No second thoughts?'

'No. None. This has to be done.'

'Right.' He stood up. There was a rumble of feet as the others also got up. 'So, now it's up to you.' He took her hand. 'I wish you the best of luck. We all do. We won't be meeting again until it's over. *Auf Wiedersehen, Fräulein* Brandt.'

She watched him tap the contents of his pipe into an ashtray and fill it with fresh tobacco from a leather pouch. He had some trouble lighting it, but the third match did the trick.

Back down in the gallery's foyer, she found the moustachioed man in the blue uniform waiting for her. Now, she was seeing him in a new light, no longer a strutting peacock but a fox masquerading as one. The image made her smile. He was holding the street door open for her. 'Thank you, Eduardo,' she said.

'You're very welcome, Miss Brandt.' He nodded at the attaché case. 'You be careful with that, now.'

*

She was back on Fifth Avenue, in the world of normal folk going about their daily business. It was still raining. A jogger in a grey tracksuit splashed past her. In front of the Guggenheim, a few people were sheltering under the mustard-coloured awning of a hot-dog stand. She could smell the frying onions. She didn't want a hot dog. She wanted a drink, a proper drink. Her eye landed on a couple of men sheltering in a shop doorway. One of them, smoking a cigarette, turned his head to look at her. He said something to the other, then he too looked at her. She ignored them. She'd long been accustomed to men eyeing her like that. But then she was struck by a worrying thought. Could they be secret agents working for the other side, keeping an eye on Eduardo, watching his every move? She took a good look at them. They certainly looked like secret agents. Jesus! What if they'd been lying in wait for *her*? She felt her fingers tighten their grip on the handle of the attaché case. *No, that's nonsense*, she told herself. They had no way of knowing who she was or what she was up to, did they?

She was still thinking about this when she reached 85th Street. She was halfway across when the snarl of a revving engine made her turn round. She saw a car racing towards her and only just managed to get out of the way as it screeched past, missing her by inches. 'Idiot!' she yelled, waving her fist in the air. 'You ought to be locked up, you crazy maniac!' She watched the car speed across Fifth Avenue and disappear into Central Park, leaving her fuming. 'Goddamn moron!'

The sky had darkened and the wind was blowing the rain into her face. She spotted a brightly lit café. The smell of freshly brewed coffee hit her as she walked through the door. Just what she needed. There was an empty table away from the other customers where she could sit undisturbed. A framed picture of a smiling President Kennedy was hanging on the wall. She found it strangely reassuring. She put the attaché case underneath her chair and gave her order to the waitress. 'Just coffee. Black, as strong as it comes. Oh, and… er… a vodka. Better make that a double, will you.'

She lit a cigarette, drew on it repeatedly, and closed her eyes. She was feeling dizzy. It may have been the nicotine or a delayed reaction to the near miss with that car. Her coffee arrived, and her vodka. She downed half the glass in one gulp then closed her eyes again. Christ! What had she got herself into? She thought about her family. A long time ago. A different world. Her father, a professional soldier, a colonel in the Wehrmacht. One of the conspirators who'd tried to assassinate the Führer in 1944 because they thought he was making a mess of the war and ruining Germany. They'd all been arrested… humiliated… hanged. She'd watched the Gestapo take away her mother and her two brothers. Never saw any of them again. She'd bottled up those painful memories for twenty years and now they'd bubbled over. She felt a helpless rage and cursed the thugs who'd been responsible for all that had happened. The fingers of her left hand found their way to an old scar on her forehead, slightly raised above the surrounding skin. It was a memento of her struggle to stay alive in what was left of Berlin. For a moment, she was back there; a skinny child, cold and hungry, wandering through streets strewn with rubble and broken glass. She took another swig of vodka. Somewhere inside her head something was changing. She could feel the long stretch of years since her childhood melting away, the twenty years which separated *then* from *now*. She felt as if she was waking up from a long, confused dream. *Then* and *now* were simply two parts of the same thing – only this time, now, she was in a position to do something about it. It was at that moment she knew she would risk anything – *everything*, if necessary – to bring Walther Schacht to justice.

Her cigarette was only half smoked, but she stubbed it out and lit a new one. She drank the rest of the vodka and ordered another. She leant over to pick up the attaché case from under her chair, placed it on the table, and brushed her fingers lightly back and forth across the black leather, allowing her fingertips to enjoy the microscopic ridges on its surface. She could smell the leather. She fished out the key from her handbag, unlocked the two latches, and lifted the lid.

A glance inside revealed a batch of documents. She took them out and spread them on the table. Typed sheets listing names, addresses and phone numbers. Maps, some standard printed ones and others hand-drawn, annotated with detailed comments. A memo giving Walther Schacht's physical characteristics, his height, weight, colour of eyes, colour of hair, timbre of voice, style of walking, and so on… twenty years out of date, she was thinking. Probably useless. There was a large sealed envelope made of stiff manila paper. She used a table knife to cut it open and gasped when she saw what was inside: several thick wads of banknotes, held together with rubber bands, a small fortune in hundred-dollar bills. Who could have provided so much money? She hastily returned the envelope and everything else to the attaché case. Then, she noticed a zipped compartment inside the lid. When she opened it, she found two photographs. Black-and-white prints. Two different pictures of the same person, wearing a uniform. Probably in his mid-forties or maybe a bit more. He wasn't particularly attractive: thickset, with a large roundish head and short dark hair receding at the temples. In one of the photos he wore a friendly smile. A nice person to have a cosy drink with, perhaps? Ha! She swallowed what was left of the vodka. In the other photo he looked grim and arrogant, wearing a swastika armband. The photo was stamped *WLS, Berlin 1943*. She stared at the image for so long that it was almost as if Schacht was right there, sitting in front of her, smirking. 'You murdering bastard!' she cried out, and drove her fist hard into his face.

TWO

Lily Wang was arranging her long black hair into a ponytail when Klara sauntered into the apartment. Lily was originally from Shanghai, and, like Klara, she'd been brought to the USA as a child. They'd first met as students at Columbia and had remained close friends. Now, they shared a place on Carmine Street in Greenwich Village. Lily was a couple of years younger than her roommate; attractive, petite and spirited. Her work with a well-known fashion magazine and Klara's activities as a journalist left neither of them much time for anything else. They had their men friends, but there were no romantic attachments on the horizon. They had no regrets about that.

Lily heard the familiar sound of Klara kicking off her heels in the hallway. 'Goodness, I thought you'd be back hours ago. You okay?'

'I'm fine, just tired. A bit wobbly, and I've got a lousy headache.' She tossed her coat onto the sofa.

'Wobbly again? You do overdo it, don't you. Never mind. I'll make fresh coffee. Hang on.'

'Thanks. Make it strong, will you, Lil.'

'Yeah, I know. Strong. Black. Your usual antidote.'

'Afraid so. God, I'm hungry.'

'Well, we got plenty eggs. I'll fix something for you. Over easy, okay? Give me a couple of minutes. Oh, and by the way, you had a visitor this morning.'

'A visitor? Who? Man or woman?'

'Old friend of yours. Anyways, that's what the guy told me. Never saw him before. Said his name was John Brown.'

'John Brown? You must be joking! What was he like?'

'Well, let's see. Tall. Thin. Slicked-back hair. A bit strange.'

'What d'you mean, strange?'

'Dunno. Sorta nervous. Never smiled. Smoked like a chimney. Come on, who is he?'

Klara was beginning to put two and two together. 'Black suit?'

'Yeah, spot on. How did you know?'

Now she knew who it was: that shifty-eyed guy who'd accompanied her in the art gallery's elevator that morning and told her to wait in the empty room. Can't have been anyone else. For sure, he was no elevator operator. None of those people were what they appeared to be. But why had he come to the Village? Obviously, not to see her, because he knew she was in the meeting.

'What did he want?'

'Said he just happened to be around here and wanted to say hello. I told him you were working and wouldn't be home 'til late. Er... I invited him in for a coffee. Well, actually, it was more like he invited himself in. Anyways, we had a nice talk.'

'You did? What about?'

'Everything, I suppose. How long I'd known you, our friends, my work for the fashion magazine. Lots of things. Nothing important, just chit-chat.'

'I see. Did he leave any message for me? A note?'

'No, nothing. I thought that was sorta weird. Said goodbye and left. Okay, eggs ready. Here ya go.'

So that's it, Klara thought. He'd come to the apartment when he knew she wasn't there, to check out her roommate, to find out if she was a liability of some sort. That would be exactly the sort of devious thing they'd do. A sensible precaution, no doubt, but they'd done it behind her back. She didn't like that. In any case, she wasn't planning to say anything to Lil or anybody else about her mission to find Schacht. She'd tell Lil she'd shortly be making a trip to South America to… to carry out research for an article about… say… cocaine production in Colombia. Something like that.

Lily was watching her. 'What's bothering you, Klara? You're not your normal chirpy self.'

'Really, it's nothing. A work problem. Don't you worry yourself about it. I'm fine. Mmm! This is delicious, Lil. Really hits the spot.'

'You're working too hard. You always do. Sounds to me like you need cheering up a bit. Why don't we go out somewhere tonight? Somewhere jolly, yeah? I think I know just the place.'

'Lil, I know the sort of places you like. To tell you the truth, I'm not sure I'm up to it.'

'Well, you better be!'

*

They were somewhere between Chelsea and the Meatpacking District, in a crowded, smoky basement. It was dark and the music was loud. They found it disorienting and the two of them shuffled about until someone guided them to a large black leather sofa. Almost immediately, a hostess with long legs and low neckline shimmied her way over to them. She had to bend low to make sure she could be heard over the din of the music.

'Hi, guys. I'm Mary Jo and I'll be looking after you tonight. Big celebration, huh? I guess it's champagne, right? Ya want domestic or French? I suggest—'

Lily cut her short. 'Bring me a Jack Daniel's on the rocks. What'll you have, Klara? Your usual, yeah?'

Klara nodded. 'Sure. That'll be fine. Lil, you know this isn't really my scene. I hope we get out of this place alive.'

'Alive and almost sober, I promise.'

'I'll drink to that.'

After her second vodka tonic, Klara was feeling more relaxed. She took a pack of cigarettes from her handbag, put one between her lips, and fished out her lighter. But before she could light up, a man appeared from out of nowhere, lighter at the ready, and without a word lit her cigarette for her. Klara thanked him politely. She wasn't particularly surprised when he sat down next to her on the sofa.

'That's cosy,' he said. 'You don't mind if I join you?'

Klara didn't reply. He was a tough-looking character with some sort of tattoo on the back of each hand.

Probably in his forties, but it wasn't easy to judge in the club's low light. He lit a cigarette. She could feel him inching closer. 'Hi!' he said. Then, she felt a heavy arm snaking its way around her waist. That did it. She wriggled free and glared at him.

'Hey, cut that out. What d'you take me for? Go find someone else to annoy.'

'Aw! Don't be like that, baby. I just wanna talk to you, that's all. And your friend. No harm in that, is there? Let me get you another… what're you drinking?'

Klara raised her voice. 'You deaf or something? My guy's on his way here. You better beat it if you know what's good for you. Scram!'

'Okay, okay, sister, if you gonna be like that. I get the message. Maybe some other time, okay?'

He got up and swaggered back to the dark corner he'd come from. He reminded Klara of a hungry rat which ventured out of its hole, sensed danger, and scurried back in.

Lily was impressed. 'Wow! I like the way you got rid of that creep. What a weirdo!'

Klara may have sounded tough, but her hands were shaking so much she almost spilled her drink. Her suspicions were racing ahead. Who the hell was he? What if he was a goddamn fanatic, sent by his handlers to do whatever was necessary to prevent her from pursuing Walther Schacht? Poison in her drink? Oh, come on! He wasn't the type. Approach too crude. Probably just some tiresome barfly with the customary agenda.

'That's the only way to handle guys like that, Lil. Come on, one more drink before we go, okay?'

THREE

The prospect of unearthing Walther Schacht was dominating Klara's thoughts day in, day out. She wondered how he'd react if he found out that those hunting him were closing in. When the hounds were at his heels, he'd be unlikely to surrender quietly, because he'd know that one way or another he'd face death if he was captured. He'd be desperate, dangerous, like a cornered beast. But that was way ahead. First, she'd have to find him, and that meant learning more about his habits and idiosyncrasies. The documents in the attaché case had nothing to say about that.

She'd often made good use of the New York Public Library's vast archive of press material, so it was the logical place to look for information about Schacht. She wasn't surprised to find his name occasionally cropping up in the more popular newspapers. There were stories about people who looked like him being spotted in São Paulo or Cape Town or Beirut, but these were just rumours. She turned to the German press: newspapers, magazines and additional material in microfiche. It involved a lot of hard digging.

And she dug up plenty. Walther Ludwig Schacht was born near Frankfurt in 1895. That meant he'd be sixty-eight now, so she couldn't expect him to look much like the man she'd seen in those photos taken two decades earlier, especially if he'd been living rough. What else? He'd enlisted in the German army just before the First World War ended, then joined the Freikorps, a military volunteer unit. She assumed that was fairly normal for a young man in those troubled times.

Then, she unearthed something which was far from normal. In 1923, Schacht and a few men from his Freikorps unit had murdered a rival, not by shooting or stabbing him but by bludgeoning him to death. She winced at the picture this conjured up in her mind. Schacht, along with the others, was arrested and served time in Landsberg Prison in Bavaria. Klara shook her head and sighed. What madness had engulfed Germany during her childhood there that would eventually lead Walther Schacht, a sadistic convicted murderer, to become one of the Nazi party's leaders? Then again, Adolf Hitler himself was a convicted criminal who'd been locked up for a few months in Landsberg in 1924. So why not? It was part of a pattern. They were *all* criminals.

Searching further, she managed to find eye-witness accounts from people who'd had regular contact with Schacht. They told of his heavy drinking and described his abominable behaviour towards the people around him. But that was only half the story. It was obvious that he wasn't just a simple thug. He was clever and ambitious, working hard to ensure his rise up the Nazi hierarchy, pandering to some while crushing others as best suited his purpose. And whatever he did, he carried it through with determination and unscrupulous force.

And this, Klara said to herself, *is the bastard I'm supposed to track down.* A real piece of work. What would she do, she wondered, if she ever met him face to face, the man responsible for the murder of her family? Was that likely? All she knew was that he was probably somewhere in South America. She felt sure that a man like Schacht would avoid the usual tourist spots like Rio, Buenos Aires, Lima, Caracas, and so on, because he'd attract too much attention. He was more likely to be holed up in some little-travelled backwater. That meant it was going to be tough.

She heard someone addressing her in German.

'You seem to be very interested in *Herr* Schacht, my dear.'

An old lady with a king's ransom in pearls round her neck was looking over her shoulder. She must have been in her eighties. It was someone she'd caught sight of before, sitting at a nearby desk.

Klara replied in German. 'Oh, hello. Yes, I'm writing an article about him for a magazine. How did you know I speak German?'

The old lady laughed. 'Why, look at all these German newspapers you've been reading. I myself come in here now and again to catch up with what the German papers are saying. I used to live in Munich in the good old days. It was a wonderful city then. I've often thought about going back to live there, but I suppose I've left it too late now.'

'It's never too late to follow your dreams, you know.'

'Perhaps not for you, my dear. It is for me. Anyway, it's all different now, isn't it. So much has changed. But what has your research told you about *Herr* Schacht? He's dead, isn't he?'

'Dead. Yes, you're probably right.'

'I expect you've heard the rumours that he's still alive and hiding in South America, in the jungle somewhere. I suppose that could be true, couldn't it?'

'Well, I guess nobody really knows.'

'No, I suppose not. I hope you realise that Walther Schacht was a very important person. You must write something respectful about him in your magazine. You know, my dear, those people weren't as bad as the newspapers keep trying to make out. And many of the things they did were very good for the Fatherland. They got us back on our feet again after that shameful Versailles agreement. That's what almost destroyed us. Thank God those people had the foresight to do something about it. Well, at least they tried.'

*

Klara was still seething at the old woman's remarks when she got back to Carmine Street. How could anyone be so blind to what "those people" had done? Okay, they'd managed to get Germany's economy back on the rails and had built a few *autobahns*. So what? That was irrelevant in comparison with the evils they'd cast on the world. Monsters, the lot of them. And what about her own father? Hadn't he been one of "those people"?

She was feeling tired, but her weariness evaporated when a distraught Lily thrust a copy of the *New York Times* at her as she walked into the apartment.

'Lil, what is it? What's happened?'

'Look!' She started to sob.

'Give me the paper.'

On one of the inside pages there was a photo of a man in a dark suit.

'It's that man… that friend of yours… the guy I told you about. The one who came looking for you when you were out. He's… dead.'

Klara's heart stopped. She recognised the person in the photo as the man who'd taken her to the empty room in the art gallery. The column above the picture was headed "Slaughter on Fifth Avenue" and described how Mr John Brown, a janitor working at a private gallery on 89th Street, had been the victim of a hit-and-run accident at the intersection of Fifth Avenue and 85th. The police had found the car, a stolen vehicle, abandoned on the other side of Central Park.

'My god, Lil. That's terrible.'

Lily was wiping her eyes on the sleeve of her sweater. 'It's awful. Do you think they'll find the… the person who did it? I mean, they must've been drunk or something.'

'Hard to say. So many of these hit-and-run cases. You're right. Probably a drunk driver.'

Klara spoke calmly, but her mind was reeling. Of course the driver wasn't drunk. This was no ordinary hit-and-run accident. It wasn't an accident at all. It was murder, premeditated murder. John Brown – probably not his real name – was no more a janitor than he was an elevator operator. He must have been an important cog in the machine put together to capture Schacht. His murder raised questions she couldn't answer. He'd visited Carmine Street, so did that mean Schacht's minders also knew about *her*? If they did, how come they hadn't dealt with her in the same way? Perhaps they were hoping she'd lead them to bigger fish.

Then it hit her. Fifth Avenue and 85th. Good god! The exact place where she herself was almost mowed down by that speeding car just after she'd left the gallery. Now she knew it wasn't as random as she'd assumed. Was it an attempt to kill her, or a warning to scare her off? It meant they must have known about her even back then. Maybe they'd listened in on that phone call. Or was one of the group she'd met at the gallery secretly working for the other side? Either way, it wasn't good. She'd have to be careful.

She was still brooding about this late into the night and didn't fall asleep until the small hours, a restless sleep blighted by troubling dreams.

FOUR

Some two thousand miles away, in the back row of the tourist-class cabin on a Sabena Airlines flight out of Brussels, Joszef Poganyi was also sleeping. Perhaps he too was dreaming. If so, it's certain his dream didn't feature Klara Brandt. Not then. He had no idea such a person existed.

The plane was about to start its descent into Mexico City's Aeropuerto Central.

Joszef had been a zoology student at Budapest's Corvinus University and was among the many thousands arrested by the Russians after the failed uprising in 1956. He'd managed to escape and had found his way to Paris. From there, he'd travelled to England and in due course became a naturalised British citizen. His mother and older brother were still in Hungary, but he rarely communicated with them. He had only the faintest recollection of his father, who'd been killed fighting against the Russians when they'd attacked Hungary in 1943.

Joszef was twenty-seven, and over six feet in height, but his pale, round face and jaunty way of moving sometimes made him seem younger. He'd spent the last two years teaching biology at a school in London. Now, he was taking a holiday. His plan was to spend two or three weeks exploring Mexico, then travel further south.

Despite feeling tired after his long journey, he was bubbling with excitement to have arrived in a world so different from the one he'd left. He'd spent most of his life trapped behind the Iron Curtain and until now he'd never set foot outside Europe. He wandered wide-eyed through Mexico City's streets, exploring bazaars crammed with brightly coloured clothes, painted pottery and silver jewellery. At every turn, he was accosted by little *muchachos* peddling cheap necklaces, straw hats and a hundred other things. In the *zocalo*, the main square, he marvelled at the cathedral's baroque façade, towering above him like a gigantic cliff of carved stone. He watched people enjoying themselves in the busy cafés, entertained by a never-ending succession of *mariachi* bands. The music reminded him of the gypsy bands he used to admire in Budapest's cafés in his student days.

He was hungry. He stopped at an outdoor café, shaded from the sun by the boughs of a giant tree. Before he sat down, he took a good look around him, as he always did whenever he was in a public place. It was an old routine, a ritual learnt during his time in Communist Hungary, where it was always prudent to check there were no secret police watching you or eavesdropping on your conversation.

The menu wasn't easy to decipher. Tortillas, enchiladas, fajitas… what were they? He started to flip over the pages of his pocket guidebook, but the waiter motioned him to put it away.

'Where you from, *señor*? America?'

'No. England.'

'Ah, England. Is very far away, no? You not know Mexican food? Okay, I bring you something you like. Is good?'

'Er… yes, good. And a beer, please. *Una cerveza por favor.* Er… *muy frío.*'

The waiter returned a few minutes later with a glass of chilled beer and several small dishes. Everything looked tasty and smelled good. Joszef sliced off a fragment of something and warily put it into his mouth. He blinked and surveyed the contents of his plate for a moment then beamed at the waiter. 'My goodness! Is excellent. Delicious.'

'You enjoy, yes? Enchilada. Is cornflour tortilla, maybe you say pancake, and inside some meat, some cheese, some bean, and on top is chilli pepper sauce. I tell cook no much chilli because I know you English no like too hot chilli.'

Chilli pepper! Joszef was ecstatic. He grinned at the waiter. 'Please, you bring me plenty more chilli pepper sauce, yes?'

*

Three weeks later, Joszef boarded a Pan Am flight and headed further south, to Costa Rica, the little Central American country "full of exotic wildlife", or so he'd read. The natural world had always fascinated him. That's why he'd studied zoology at university. As a boy in Hungary, he used to spend hours in the fields collecting butterflies, and his passion for them had never left him. Even now, the adrenaline surged whenever he caught a butterfly in his net and watched it struggle to escape its muslin prison. He felt a strange empathy with the little creatures, and often he'd feel compelled to let them go. He knew why. He too had been caught in a net, back in '56, and he understood that the urge to escape was an instinct powerful enough to overwhelm every other; it didn't matter whether you were a butterfly or a man.

He found an affordable room in a run-down place in an outer suburb of San José. In the evening, he joined a noisy crowd in the *pension*'s makeshift bar, where a single oil lamp cast its dim light through a haze of cigarette smoke. The locals watched him with a mixture of amusement and suspicion. The beer was served ice-cold and came with a plate of potato crisps, cheese and sausage. After that, all he wanted to do was sleep.

He cheered up in the morning. It was a lovely sunny day. He walked to a better part of town and managed to find a table on the crowded terrace of Café Moreno on Avenida Central. After a cursory inspection of the clientele, he sat down and asked for a coffee. He was thinking about ordering some breakfast when he heard someone addressing him.

'Excuse me… er… *perdóneme, señor.*'

He looked up to see a young woman, maybe in her early thirties. She was wearing a sun hat with an outsized brim, and her eyes were hidden behind a pair of white-framed sunglasses. Her loose dress was held in at the waist by a shiny leather belt. Good figure, he noted, and ran both hands over his curly hair in an attempt to smooth it down.

'Hello,' Joszef said. 'Yes?'

'I was wondering… this seems to be the only free… no one is using this chair? Would you mind terribly if I join you?'

Her request took him by surprise, but after a moment's hesitation, he said, 'No, not at all.'

'You sure? I don't want to disturb you. If you'd rather be alone…'

'No, you're not disturbing me.'

'Thanks. Gee, that's great. So crowded here today.' She sat down, removed her hat, and rested it on her lap. She pushed up her sunglasses so they perched on top of her head.

Joszef was dazzled. Her eyes were blue and her hair shone like gold in the sunlight.

She called the waiter over. '*Camarero, un café negro fuerte, por favor.*'

'Excuse me,' Joszef said. 'Pardon my asking, but you are an American, yes?'

'Yes, I am. I suppose it's pretty obvious, isn't it.'

'So how come you speak Spanish?'

'You can't live in New York for long without picking up a bit of Spanish. But my accent's lousy. How about you? I guess you're from Eastern Europe. Poland or Hungary or somewhere like that, right?'

'You can tell that from way I speak? Yes, originally, from Hungary, Budapest, but I live in London now. My own country is just terrible Russian satellite. You speak Hungarian?'

'Are you kidding? No way!' She took a pack of cigarettes from her handbag, lit one for herself, and offered one to Joszef.

'Thank you, no. I not smoke. Bad for health.'

'You're right, but it's hard to stop once you start. So, tell me, what are you doing here in Costa Rica, so far from home? Are you all on your own?'

Something about the way she asked that raised his suspicions. Was this really an accidental meeting, or had she targeted him for some reason? She didn't look like a hooker… hardly. But best play it safe. 'Is a bit complicated. What are *you* doing here? Oh, here comes your coffee.'

The waiter wanted to know if they needed anything else. She asked for a small vodka.

Joszef looked surprised. 'A bit early for that, no?'

'You think so? I find it kick-starts my day.'

'I see. I don't need that kind of kick. So, what you do in Costa Rica?'

'Me? Oh, nothing special. Just a tourist. I take a lot of photos.'

'What you take photos of?'

'Whatever takes my fancy. You, for instance.'

Joszef could feel himself blushing. What was she after? 'You don't look like a tourist. You look too… er… smart. Anyway, where is your camera? Your rucksack?'

'As it happens, I do have a camera, and a rucksack. They're back at my hotel.'

'I bet you stay at very grand hotel. I stay in terrible place. Is called Pensión Fernandez. Not proper hotel.' He paused to sip his coffee and couldn't help sneaking a quick look at her knees. 'So, how long you here?'

She laughed. 'All these questions! D'you think I'm a Russian spy or something? I see, it's because of the vodka, is it?'

'Sorry. For long time, I live in Hungary under the Russians. You end up suspecting everybody and trusting nobody. But don't worry. I don't think you are sent by secret police to spy on me.'

'No, but that would have been an interesting assignment, for sure,' she chuckled. 'So, tell me about you. I suppose you have a very Hungarian-sounding name?'

'I'm sorry. I should have introduced myself.' He got to his feet. 'I am Joszef Poganyi. How do you do, madam.' He sat down again.

'Very happy to meet you, Joszef Poganyi. Gee, for a moment, I thought you were going to bow and kiss the back of my hand. Isn't that what they do in Hungary?'

Joszef blushed again. 'In London, I am schoolteacher of biology. I came here to see the wildlife, and to collect tropical butterflies. I've never been to tropics before.'

'All this way to catch butterflies? No kidding? I know people come here to dig up old Mayan things, or to find rare orchids. But surely, not to chase butterflies?'

'You'd be surprised how exciting is to study butterflies, and Costa Rica is famous for them, especially shiny blue one, the blue morpho. I only see them preserved in museum in London, but I want see them fly in their natural place.' He could see she wasn't impressed. 'Also, I am hoping to find special big red butterfly. Very rare.'

'My goodness! A red butterfly! Sounds dangerous. Does it sting?'

He didn't like that remark. She was making fun of him. 'I also come to Costa Rica to climb volcano. You hear about it? Sleep for long time, but now is massive eruption.' He gestured with his arms: 'Boom! Not far from here.'

She nodded. 'Yes, I've heard about this volcano. Irazú, is it called? Anyway, something like that. But you're not really thinking of going there, are you? It's dangerous. Frightening photos in the newspapers last week. A lot of destruction, and many people killed.'

Joszef gave a nonchalant shrug. 'So what? Certainly I go there, danger or no danger. Right to top. Right to crater.'

'I see. So, Joszef, you like an exciting life, do you?'

'Of course. Why not? And it's a lot more exciting over here than in London.'

'I guess so. But I've heard that Budapest is an interesting city, isn't it? Why did you leave Hungary?'

'I didn't just *leave*. I have to escape from Russians. 1956, you know, the revolution. It was very risky. Dangerous times.'

'Sure, I remember what those goddamn Russians did. You must be a very brave man, Joszef.'

He seemed to swell visibly. 'I suppose so. I face many dangers in my time. I'm certainly not afraid of any volcano.'

She was stirring her coffee, slowly, gazing at the black liquid as it swirled around her cup. Then, she put her sunglasses back on.

'Quite fearless, aren't you, Joszef?'

'Thank you. Yes, I am. In revolution you have to be, or you are finished.' He looked up at the sky, trying his best to appear to be studying a passing cloud. 'Er... may I ask, please, how long you stay in San José?'

'Probably for quite a while, so perhaps we'll meet again. I feel sure we will. Wouldn't that be swell, Joszef? I'm staying at the Hotel Grano da Oro. Can you remember that? Oh, by the way, my name is Klara. Klara Brandt. I do hope you find your red butterfly.'

*

Joszef had had his dinner and was drinking his way through a bottle of third-rate red wine in the *pension*'s smoky bar. Those images of blue morpho butterflies which would normally be sailing through his mind had been displaced by visions of the attractive young woman called Klara he'd met that morning. He was musing on what he would say to her when they next met, and how she might respond. He felt pretty confident that they'd get on well together, even though she was quite a bit older than he was and, he readily admitted to himself, a lot more sophisticated. It was obvious she'd been around. And there was something else. He sensed that she wasn't telling him the whole story. It was hard to believe she was just a tourist; her light-hearted manner seemed to belie a more serious demeanour. Or was this just a figment of his own overly suspicious nature? But then, that scar on her forehead... the result of an accident? Or had she been involved in something she wouldn't want to talk about?

His reverie was broken by an unexpected greeting.

'Good evening, my young friend.'

He was surprised to see a short corpulent man with a Chaplinesque moustache smiling at him. Sweat was trickling down his face. He was carrying a crumpled white linen jacket over his arm. His nicotine-stained fingers were curled around a half-smoked cigar. He spoke slowly, with a strong middle-European accent.

'My good sir, I hope you do not object my coming over to chat you? A little conversation makes world go round, no?'

Joszef scrutinised him for a moment. 'Ah, I thought you looked familiar. Weren't you sitting on the terrace of that café this morning? What is it you want?'

'Quite true, my friend. You remember me? I am flattered. They do serve quite excellent coffee at Moreno's, no? That is what I wanted to talk to you about.'

'Coffee?'

'No, no, not coffee.' He sniggered. 'The blonde lady who joined you this morning. Very attractive, no? She is on her own?'

'Oh, her. I see. Really, I've got no idea. What you want with her?'

'As I said, she is very attractive lady. She told you her name, yes?'

Joszef pursed his lips and fidgeted with his wine glass. 'Afraid not. I really don't know anything about her. We only just met. Sorry.'

'But you know where she is staying, yes? Here in San José. Her hotel?'

'No. I have no idea. She didn't tell me.'

'Is that so? I see. My dear sir, let me order another bottle and I join you, yes?'

'Look, is getting late. I get myself off to bed now. Busy day tomorrow, but do help yourself to what's left of the wine if you want. They'll bring you a clean glass. So sorry I can't help you, sir. Goodnight.'

'But, please, my friend, just tell me her name.' He sounded desperate and was shuffling from one foot to the other. 'Surely she must have told you that?'

Joszef didn't answer. As he climbed the stairs, he tried to think of a reasonable explanation for what had just occurred. Who was this strange little man, and why was he asking all those questions about Klara? Was he a detective? Was she in some sort of trouble, perhaps with the police? On the other hand, it was quite possible the poor man simply found her attractive and was hoping to meet her again… but what an unlikely couple they'd make.

He was tired. Time for bed. He'd go round to her hotel in the morning and see what more he could discover about her.

*

Klara was perched at the bar in the Hotel Grano da Oro, smoking a cigarette and sipping a vodka tonic. It was late and most people had left, although a handful of men remained, sitting around a table in the corner, chatting over their beers. Now and again, one or other of them would cast an eye on Klara, but from a safe distance. They'd already witnessed how she quickly dispatched anyone who attempted to flirt with her.

Klara's thoughts were elsewhere. She wasn't making much progress in her search for Walther Schacht. The list of contacts she'd been provided with hadn't been of much help. One of the people she was supposed to talk to was Ramón Fuentes in Guatemala. He was a dealer in second-hand books, but she knew that was just a cover for his main business. He made his real money by trading in valuable pre-Columbian artefacts. Illegal but lucrative. His suppliers included scoundrels from every corner of the continent, men who kept their eyes and ears open. They brought him not only Mayan gold and Incan pottery but also colourful stories of illegal goings-on. They would occasionally tell him – for a price, of course – where this or that fugitive was thought to be hiding. Klara had arranged to meet Fuentes at his bookshop in Guatemala City, but when she got there she'd been met by the local police. They'd told her the shop had been broken into. There were signs of a struggle, but there was no trace of the bookseller.

She feared the worst, and now she was keeping her fingers crossed that the next contact on her list hadn't disappeared as well, a man who owned a coffee plantation not far from San José.

She stubbed out her cigarette and ordered another drink. It was lonely work. Wouldn't it be easier, she was thinking, if she had an accomplice? Somebody she could trust and confide in. Preferably someone... yes... who could serve as a cover for her real purpose. Why the hell hadn't she thought of that before? A proper secret agent would have arranged cover from the start, before leaving New York, right? Still, better late than never. She found herself picturing that innocent young man she'd met at Café Moreno that morning, that butterfly hunter. Joszef...

wasn't that his name? Yes, Joszef Poganyi. Pensión Fernandez. Nobody would suspect *him* of being involved in anything sinister. What he'd told her about escaping from Hungary in '56 meant he was probably older than he looked. It was worth thinking about. But would he go along with it? It was obvious he was attracted to her, and she knew plenty of ways of exploiting that. And he'd told her he craved excitement and boasted about his bravery. Was he on the level? She'd have to find out. If it turned out he was… well, then she'd do her best to persuade him. Maybe she could pretend to be collecting tropical butterflies as well. No. She knew nothing about butterflies. A wildlife photographer. Yes, working for an American magazine. It was all beginning to make sense.

FIVE

The moment Joszef woke, his thoughts turned to Klara. He lost no time in dressing then set out for the Hotel Grano da Oro. It was just as he'd been imagining it: smart, with a marble-floored lobby, polished brass chandeliers and tall vases of fresh flowers. It was a world away from his own shabby little *pension*.

The uniformed clerk at the desk was quick to welcome him. '*Buenas días, señor.* What can I do for you?'

'Er… please, I come to see my friend, *señorita* Brandt.'

'*Señorita* Brandt? Ah, yes, the American lady. But I am so sorry. I very much afraid Miss Brandt leave, *señor.*'

'She leave? She check out? I don't believe it. She leave any message?'

The desk clerk laughed. 'Oh no, no, *señor*. I am sorry. Not check out. I mean she leave the hotel. Ten minutes ago. You miss her. Is very unfortunate.'

Joszef breathed a sigh of relief. 'You know where she go?'

'Not exactly, *señor*. Perhaps just for walk. Sometime,

she go for breakfast. I know she like a little place on Avenida Central.'

'Café Moreno?'

'Ah, yes, I think that's it.'

Joszef's heart leapt when he reached the café, because there was Klara sitting on the terrace, drinking her coffee and smoking a cigarette. She didn't look surprised when she saw him approaching. It was almost as if she'd been expecting him. She smiled and waved him over.

'Hi! Come and join me. I was thinking of coming to see you at your *pension* after breakfast, but now you've saved me the trouble.'

'Good morning, Klara. Is very good I see you again.'

'I told you we'd meet again, didn't I.'

His eyes lit up. Not only had she remembered him but she was actually pleased he'd turned up. He noticed an empty vodka glass on the table but decided to say nothing. As he sat down, he scanned the other people sitting on the terrace. Out of the corner of his eye he saw a man in a white jacket, wearing a Panama hat, raising his coffee cup in salute and greeting him with an exaggerated smile. He recognised him as the sleazy character who'd been asking questions the previous evening. Joszef tapped Klara on the arm and nodded discreetly in the man's direction.

'Look. That man. Is it someone you know? He was here yesterday as well, sitting at the same table.'

Klara took a casual glance. 'So? Probably comes here every morning. Why so interested in him?'

Joszef leant over to her and quietly explained how the man had approached him the previous evening, enquiring after her.

For a moment, Klara looked alarmed. She'd been wearing her sunglasses on top of her head, but now she swung them down to cover her eyes. 'What did you tell him? Please, I must know.'

'Don't worry, I tell him nothing. Klara, maybe you in some sort of trouble? Maybe I help you?'

'Trouble? No, no, of course not. Nothing like that. I'm thinking maybe he's a lousy newspaper man trying to get a story. That's all.'

'A story? What about? You are famous or something?'

'No, but I'm quite well known in New York, and I can sure recognise a reporter when I see one. I'm a journalist myself. I didn't tell you that, did I?'

'So that's why you take photos.'

'Look, I'm on holiday here and I don't want to get involved with any newspaper people. Er… perhaps it's better if we finish our coffee inside. Let's go in and get some breakfast, shall we?'

Klara ate her breakfast slowly. She casually mentioned that she'd arranged to visit a friend who owned a coffee plantation. 'I'm going there tomorrow. A few miles from here. Coffee's big business in Costa Rica. Why not come with me and see how they grow it?'

'I thought you said you were a tourist. How come you have a friend who lives here?'

Klara chuckled. 'Still suspicious? His name is Peter Hoffman, and he's a friend of a friend. Apparently, he lives in an ancient hacienda, like in the old days. A beautiful place, I believe. It would be a pity not to see it while you're here. What d'you say?'

'I don't know. It would be interesting, but I was

planning to visit that volcano tomorrow. Irazú. I very much looking forward to it.'

Klara placed a soothing hand on his shoulder. 'Don't worry, that's no problem. The hacienda is on the way to Irazú. How about this? We'll go to the hacienda first, and after that… well… why don't I join you on your trip to the volcano? Let's see if I can be as brave as you are. Good idea? We'll meet in front of my hotel, say, at eight. You never know, you may find that red butterfly you're looking for… I mean at the plantation, not on top of the volcano.'

*

Klara was wearing a stylish green linen jacket and black slacks when she joined Joszef outside the Hotel Grano da Oro the following day. She looked flustered. 'Hi. Sorry. A bit late. That man you said was asking questions about me. Saw him again this morning, outside the hotel, talking to a couple of the locals.'

'Klara, I think something funny's going on. I wonder why he's taking so much interest in you. How did he find out where you're staying?'

'Search me. I couldn't hear what they were talking about, but I have to say they looked darned conspiratorial.'

'Come on, Klara. What you are up to? I can see you're upset about something.'

'Just a bit hot and bothered. I've been rushing.' She smiled and reached out to squeeze his hand. 'Right, off we go. We need a taxi.'

Several taxis were waiting in an orderly line in front of the hotel. Klara signalled to the car at the front of the queue. Immediately, one of the taxis further back screeched out of its place, drove to the front of the line, and pulled in at the kerb where they were standing.

The driver leant out of his window. '*Buenas días, señor, señorita*. Where you want go? I take you.' Some of the other drivers swore at him. He ignored them. 'I give you good price. These others, very expensive.'

Joszef looked at the driver then whispered to Klara. 'Unbelievable! See what he did? Shouldn't we take the one behind instead?'

Klara was shaking her head in amazement. 'What a cheek! If he tried that in New York, he'd be slaughtered on the spot.' She shot the driver a dubious glance and handed him a piece of paper. '*Señor*, we want to go to the Hacienda Hoffman. Okay? This will tell you the way.'

The driver glanced at the note then gave it back. '*Si, señorita*, the Hacienda Hoffman. I know. I take you. Not far. You get in now, please.'

'Really? You know the Hoffman estate? I'm surprised. I had no idea the place was on the tourist trail. Okay, swell, that's lucky for us… I had visions of our getting lost in the hills.'

'And after hacienda,' Joszef quickly added, 'we want go to Irazú. You wait for us at hacienda then take us there. To Irazú. Okay?'

'Irazú? You mean the volcano? Really, you want go there?'

'Yes, we do.'

'I see… okay. Wonderful. Great view from top. *Si, señor*. I wait. You no worry.'

They soon left the city behind and were travelling through lush green countryside. Joszef was elated. His dream was coming true. First, his ambition to visit Irazú was about to be fulfilled, and second, he was sitting excitingly close to his new friend, Klara. But one thing bothered him. He'd been expecting to see some sign of the volcano along the way, some smoke, but so far there was nothing. He turned to Klara.

'You sure we going right direction? Where is volcano?'

The driver must have been listening to their conversation, even though he'd been whistling to himself. 'You no worry, *señor*. Everything very good. We soon arrive at hacienda.'

'And then we go to Irazú, remember? By the way, Klara, this friend of yours at hacienda, Peter Hoffman. Sounds like German name.'

'Yes, it does sound German, doesn't it? We can ask him when we get there.'

'And your name, Klara Brandt. Isn't that a German name also? I thought you say you are an American.'

The driver's whistling came to an abrupt halt, then, after a few seconds, it started again.

'You're right,' Klara said. 'I was born in Germany and was brought to the US after the war. I *am* an American, a naturalised American.'

'Like me,' Joszef said with a grin. 'I'm a naturalised Englishman.'

After a while, they stopped. A sign by the side of a driveway read "*Bienvenido a Hacienda Hoffman*".

'See? We are here,' the driver announced. 'I drive you to house and wait for you.'

Peter Hoffman saw the taxi arrive and went outside to welcome his visitors. He was a tall, softly spoken man with a head of neatly combed silvery hair. His pale grey suit and lavender tie made him look as if he'd just returned from church, except it wasn't Sunday.

Klara fastened both buttons on her jacket and pulled the hem down over her hips. The driver got out of his car, lit a cigarette, and perched on the low stone wall surrounding the terrace.

Hoffman greeted Klara with a hint of a bow. 'Good morning, *Fräulein* Brandt. I trust you managed to get here without too many problems?' When he saw Joszef, he looked surprised. Klara made the introductions.

'Ah, you're from Hungary,' Hoffman said. 'A troubled country. You're fortunate to be living in England.'

'Yes, that's true. London is good… er… settled, compared to Budapest. You have beautiful house, *señor*. It looks very old.'

'It certainly is. About two hundred years. It was already an antique when my grandfather bought it. Ah, this is my wife.'

Frau Hoffman gave them a welcoming smile. 'So, you have come to see how we produce the world's best coffee, yes? Good. It will be a pleasure to show you around our plantation. I will take you myself.'

Klara spoke to her in German. She saw the look of surprise on Joszef's face and laughed. 'Of course I speak German. What did you expect? It's where I grew up. I've suggested to Frau Hoffman that we might have a cup of their home-grown coffee before we look around.'

As soon as the coffee arrived, Hoffman caught Klara's

eye. '*Fräulein* Brandt, what news of our mutual friend? Why don't you bring your coffee to my office, so we can get to know each another a bit better.'

'Of course.' She turned to Joszef. 'You don't mind, do you? Frau Hoffman will look after you. She'll tell you all the secrets of coffee-growing.'

Once they were in his office, Hoffman sat at his desk, pointedly leaving Klara standing. His demeanour had changed. He spoke rapidly in German.

'*Fräulein* Brandt. I hope you know what you're doing. Why did you bring this Hungarian person with you? This stranger. What do you know about him? This could put the whole operation at risk. How do you know he's just a tourist?'

'You're right to ask, but he's okay. I met him in a café in San José. Purely by chance. Anyway, he doesn't understand a word of German.'

'Are you sure about that? Listen to me. He may understand everything. He could be working for anybody.'

'I'm sure he's fine. Look, the point of bringing him along is because I want to encourage him to help me with what I've got to do. I know he's taken a liking to me… well, he's a bit infatuated. He's a sort of entomologist – catches butterflies – so he'd make a perfect cover. I've given it a lot of thought… Shh! Quiet!' She paused for a moment then whispered, 'Is there someone next door? I thought I heard something. Can they hear us from in there?'

'Don't worry. It's only a storeroom.'

'Oh, I see. Sorry about that. To tell you the truth, I've been feeling anxious ever since I failed to contact that bookseller in Guatemala.'

'What? Ramón Fuentes? You mean you couldn't find him?'

'Not a trace. They must've got to him.'

Hoffman gasped. 'That's not good. Not good at all. Poor Ramón. Bookselling was just a cover, of course.'

'Yes, I know that.'

'Fuentes was a rogue, but it's likely he would've been able to tell you something about Schacht's whereabouts. His disappearance is a bit of a disaster.'

'Especially for him,' Klara observed wryly. 'I've got this feeling someone's following *me* now, and it's no goddamn fun looking over my shoulder all the time. Well, it's just a feeling, but I know for a fact that a man in San José has been asking questions about me. That's worrying.'

'I agree. It is. These people are clever.' He frowned. 'Just a thought... look... is it possible they may be following you and deliberately letting you lead them to our people, so they can—'

'So they can liquidate them, one by one? My god! That's a horrible thought.'

'Yes, horrible. I agree. Let's hope I'm wrong. But that's the sort of game we're in. We'll have to be careful. Certainly, you will. Now, to business. They'll be back from their walk soon.'

'You have something for me, I think?'

'Yes, I have, but it's not quite as up to date as I'd hoped. My best link is with a man in Brazil. Wolfgang Müller, based in Manaus. You know that place? It's a city halfway up the River Amazon. It's hemmed in by jungle stretching hundreds of miles in every direction, which makes it a good jumping-off point for fugitives looking for somewhere to hide. Of all our contacts, Wolfgang Müller is the closest to where we think Walther Schacht may be lurking.'

'You mean Schacht may be hiding somewhere along the Amazon?'

'Correct. Somewhere around there anyway. I haven't heard from Müller for a long time, but in his last message he told me Schacht is probably being sheltered by missionaries somewhere up the River Negro.'

'My god! That's important. That narrows it down, doesn't it?'

'It does, but not by much, I'm afraid. There are plenty of missionary settlements up and down the Negro. When Müller contacted me, he was unable to be more precise. However, by now, he may've found out more. Unfortunately, I haven't been able to make any further contact with him.'

'What are you saying? You mean Müller's disappeared?'

'Hard to say. There could be many reasons. I suppose it's possible they got to Müller as well as Fuentes. That would be regrettable. Or perhaps they're waiting for you to lead them to him. Better bear that in mind. Be careful. In any case, I suppose you'll be going to Manaus? It's a long way to go, but that's our best hope – provided Müller is still… er… alive… and provided you can locate him. I'll give you the address I have for him.'

'I *have* to go there. It's the only decent lead I have.'

'Right. That's about it, then. I wish I could have given you more. Why don't we go back and see if they've returned from their walk.'

They were all together again, enjoying more coffee.

'So, Joszef, how do you like our plantation?' Hoffman asked. 'Tell me, did you notice a sprinkling of grey powder on the leaves?'

'Couldn't miss it,' Joszef answered. 'What is it? Insecticide? Fertiliser?'

'No, neither. I wish it were. It's ash from the volcano. Irazú. Have you heard about it? You can't see it from here, but it's shooting thousands of tons of this stuff into the air all the time. The wind blows it all over the place. It hasn't erupted like this for many years. We're in for real trouble if it gets any worse.'

'As a matter of fact, *Herr* Hoffman, we go there ourselves, today. We climb to top.'

'Really? You're going to the volcano? I hope you're joking. It's a bad idea, believe me. Very dangerous. In any case, I don't think you'll be able to get through. They've closed the roads and, anyway, the route to the top is probably blocked by ash.'

'That would be disappointing, but our driver didn't mention any problem, and he's agreed to take us there. That's him, you see, waiting on terrace.'

'That's not very wise of him. Irazú is causing havoc. Throwing rocks into the air. People have been killed.' He raised his voice. '*Fräulein* Brandt, do you know anything about this? You mustn't take any risks like that, you know. Listen to me. You should get your driver to take you straight back to town, not to the volcano.' He spoke sharply, as if he was ordering her not to go.

Klara had to choose her words carefully. 'A visit to Irazú is the main reason my brave companion here came to Costa Rica. Isn't that right, Joszef?' She threw Hoffman a sideways glance. 'Don't worry, we'll be careful. I know what I'm doing.'

'*Herr* Hoffman,' Joszef said, 'I'm sure we'll be all right. And, please, don't worry about Klara. She'll be fine. I take good care of her.'

Hoffman shut his eyes and shook his head in exasperation.

It was time for them to go. Hoffman walked with them to the taxi. 'Enjoy your stay in Costa Rica, you two. Remember, I've advised you most strongly not to go to Irazú. Very dangerous. *Fräulein* Brandt, you must be careful. Be always vigilant. I wish you good luck.'

SIX

They were driving through the hilly countryside near the little town of Cartago. Joszef practically bubbled over when he spotted a column of dark smoke rising into the sky from somewhere behind the mountains.

'Klara, Klara. Look, the volcano.'

'Yes, I can see it. You sure you want to go there? You heard what Mr Hoffman said… it's dangerous. Shouldn't we go back to town?'

'Hoffman was exaggerating. Surely you're not afraid of a bit of smoke, are you?' He called to the driver. 'You think you find a way up there?'

The driver nodded. 'Sure, you no worry.'

The entrance to the mountain road hadn't been cordoned off after all and they started on their way up. After a while, they noticed that much of the road, and the land on either side of it, was covered in black ash. As they climbed higher, the deposit of ash became deeper. Most of the trees wore a fuzzy coating of black too, as if they'd been caught in a blizzard of black snow. The driver slowed down to a crawl.

'Can't you go any faster than this?' Joszef asked. 'How much further is it?'

'Not far. You'll see.'

They drove on until they reached a point where the road was blocked by deep drifts of ash, eroded into intricate contours by the rain. Every tree had been smothered and scorched into a dead blackened stump. The driver stopped the car.

Joszef sat upright and glared at him. 'Why you stop? We want go all way to top, to crater. We told you.'

'Look,' the driver replied, 'is impossible drive further. Don't worry, crater not far. We walk. No problem.' He was already getting out of the car. Joszef and Klara followed.

The ash crunched under their feet as they walked. Klara appeared to stumble and Joszef hurried to help her. It was the oldest trick in the book. She thanked him, and then, to his surprise, linked arms with him, and they walked on together, arm in arm. Joszef glowed inwardly. Klara smiled to herself.

For a time, their view was obscured by the black slopes looming above them, but the volcano's grumbles and growls were getting louder all the time. Then, as they rounded a bend, they were greeted by an unforgettable sight. There before them, perhaps two hundred metres away, was the volcano's crater. From its throat came vast gushes of smoke and ash, now black, now grey, now black again, billowing upwards to a great height. The thunderous rumblings and explosions were alarming.

'Close enough for me,' Klara said. 'We don't want to get roasted alive. Let's go back. What's that awful smell?'

'Is burning sulphur,' the driver explained. 'No problem. No harm you.'

'I'm not convinced about that,' Klara said. 'It's hurting my throat, and my eyes are stinging. Let's get back to the car.'

'But we've come this far,' Joszef complained. 'Come on. Not much further to top.'

'Yes, not much further,' echoed the driver. 'You no worry. Last week, my friend he take tourist right to crater. He say very exciting. Fantastic view. I go with you. You follow me, yes?'

'Klara, come on.'

They tramped along a ridge and continued until they reached the rim of Irazú's crater. What a view! They were right on the edge, with the volcano's gigantic mouth gaping wide just a few metres below them, belching out black smoke and firing off a string of ear-splitting explosions. The danger was obvious. There was no way of telling what might happen from one moment to the next. The ground under their feet was shaking.

'Magnificent!' Joszef cried. 'The entrance to Hell!'

Suddenly the taxi driver was facing them, with a pistol in his hand. 'So, *señorita* Klara Brandt... or should I say *Fräulein* Weber... it really is you.' He was speaking in German. There was no trace of a Spanish accent. 'Just as we suspected. You gave the game away in the car. *Dummkopf!*'

He was holding them both at gunpoint. Klara felt her mouth go dry. Why hadn't she seen this coming? Her heart was beating violently, but she responded as calmly as she could, in English. 'What are you talking about, you silly man? Are you mad? Put that goddamn gun away.'

Joszef was stunned. 'What the hell's going on?' he bellowed. 'What he is saying? He's German, isn't he, not Costa Rican. Is this supposed to be some sort of fucking joke? Is not funny.'

The driver glared at him and continued in German. '*Fräulein*, believe me, there's no point in pretending. This is the end of the road for you. Get your hands up, both of you.' Klara raised her hands above her head. Joszef reluctantly followed her example. 'That's better. Why do you people want to mess with our great heroes? Why can't you leave them alone? They may be old now, but haven't they devoted the best years of their lives to the Fatherland? Don't they deserve our respect and our thanks? Haven't they earned the right to enjoy what's left of their lives in peace?'

Klara was frightened, and at the same time furious that she'd been taken in by this bogus taxi driver. His phoney accent should have made her suspicious.

'So, *Fräulein*, it seems that you didn't know we've been keeping a close watch on your coffee-growing friend, *Herr* Hoffman. We knew he'd make a false move if we waited long enough, and this morning he did, thanks to your interesting little chat with him. Yes, I heard it all. Very interesting about this man of yours in Brazil, *Herr* Wolfgang Müller. He's the critical link, isn't he? *Wunderbar*. We'll deal with him like we dealt with Fuentes. So now you and Hoffman are of no more use to us. I'm sure you know what that means.'

Joszef had lost his patience. 'This is fucking absurd. Ridiculous. I can't understand what the hell he's talking about. What's going on?'

Klara motioned him to keep his hands up and say nothing. She turned to the driver again.

'Look, this young man here. He knows nothing about this. He's got no part in it. Simply my companion, just a tourist I met in San José. Tell him to go away, to get back to town, then you and I can settle this between us.'

'You mean he doesn't know about you and your pathetic mission? Ah, I see… he doesn't understand German. Even so, he'll have to be eliminated along with you, and he won't even know why. So tragic. Look down there. What could be a better place for a disappearing act?' He pointed with his pistol at the crater's smoking furnace. 'There will be nothing left of either of you. Just a bit more ash, that's all, raining down all over Costa Rica. Are you ready, *Fräulein*? It's time to—'

He didn't finish. There was a deafening explosion, like nothing any of them had ever heard before. A massive barrage of gas and rocks burst from the crater and whooshed high into the air. The blast almost knocked them off their feet. A moment later, they were caught in a shower of red-hot cinders falling from the sky. Fiery hailstones, which landed on their heads and scorched their hair. The driver lowered his gun for a second. As quick as a flash, Joszef lunged forward and struck him hard on the side of the neck with the bony point of his elbow. The driver grunted and slumped to the ground. He lay there, not moving. Klara stared at Joszef in disbelief, and Joszef himself looked surprised. Then, they heard a deep-throated roar from somewhere down in the volcano's belly. For a split second they looked at each other, then ran for their lives.

When they were far enough away from the crater, they stopped and turned to look back. Irazú was venting its fury, hurling red-hot lava high into the sky. They watched the molten rock falling back to earth in great lumps, pulverising the place where moments before they'd been standing. Then, both of them collapsed to the ground, breathing hard, too shocked to speak.

Eventually, Klara raised herself to her knees and shook a flurry of ash out of her hair. 'My god, Joszef... you saved our lives. That awful man... that's the end of him, the bastard. Won't be bothering us anymore. But Joszef, how did you learn to use your elbow like that?'

'Klara! I think he was going to shoot you.'

'Not just me. He was going to shoot both of us... then dump our bodies in the volcano.'

'What? But why? Why on earth did he want to kill us? To steal our money?'

'No. Nothing like that. Something else. Something I haven't told you about.'

'Something else? What else?' Joszef got to his feet and looked at her with an expression she'd never seen before. 'Who *are* you, Klara Brandt? *Fräulein* Brandt... or is it *Fräulein* Weber? From the start, I know there is something you are not telling me. Now you almost get us killed. What kind of fucking game are you playing?'

'For crying out loud, Joszef, it's no game. What I'm doing is something important, not just for me but for the greater good.'

'I see. For the greater good. I wonder where I've heard those words before.'

'Look, you must believe me. I had no intention of

putting you in danger, and I'm terribly sorry I got you mixed up in this. It's entirely my fault, from beginning to end.'

'Mixed up in what? I am confused, Klara. What you are up to? You must explain.'

'Yes, I will. I promise. But not here, and not now. I've got to get back to the hacienda to tell *Herr* Hoffman what's happened. His life is in danger.'

Something else was stirring in her mind. She was having second thoughts about trying to recruit Joszef. She knew he had no idea about the real motive behind her friendliness towards him. She'd taken advantage of his youth, his innocence, his crush on her. She'd been thoroughly dishonest with him and now felt compelled to tell him everything. Then maybe she'd feel better about it.

They stayed there for a while, watching Irazú belching out its phlegm. Then, Klara began to walk down the slope, and Joszef followed. They trudged over the ash until they reached the car. Luckily, the driver had left the key in the ignition. Klara took the wheel and somehow managed to find her way back to the hacienda. It was getting dark when they arrived.

Hoffman was astonished to see them back again, especially when he saw that Klara was driving the taxi. He pulled open her door and she climbed out, slowly, grim-faced.

'*Fräulein* Brandt! What's happened? Where's your driver? Come inside, both of you.' They walked unsteadily into the house. Hoffman was wearing a black silk dressing gown over his suit. He called to his wife. 'Anke, please bring some coffee. They've come back.'

'Something stronger?' Klara pleaded as she collapsed into an armchair. 'You have vodka?'

Then, Hoffman noticed the ash on their clothes, and the smell of sulphur. 'You've been to that damned volcano! You idiots. You fools. And you, *Fräulein*… how stupid. I told you not to go there. I knew something like this was going to happen. I warned you to keep away. You're a pair of idiots!'

Klara faced him. 'Wait, *Herr* Hoffman. Listen to me. You're mistaken… don't blame the volcano.'

'I don't. I blame you.'

'You're wrong. That goddamn taxi driver… he was one of *them*. Heard us talking this morning. Took me completely by surprise.'

'*Gott im Himmel!* So that's it. A disaster. What happened? How did you get away from him? So now they must know everything.'

'Don't worry. Thanks to my friend Joszef here, he won't be able to tell anybody anything.'

'You're certain?'

'Yes, yes. Joszef finished him off like a professional, didn't you, Joszef?'

Joszef said nothing.

It took several minutes for Klara to tell Hoffman what had happened. He listened with his eyes closed, shaking his head all the while.

Joszef glared at them. 'Yes, that's what happened, but I want to know what's going on. What has this woman got me into?'

Hoffman spoke calmly. 'Miss Brandt and I will tell you everything. But you don't look well, either of you.

I'm not surprised. You should rest until you recover from what you've just been through. You'll both stay for dinner, yes?' He laughed. 'Don't worry about your appearance. We'll overlook it, just this once.' Then he spoke to Klara in German. 'How much does your Hungarian friend know about this business?'

'I haven't told him a darned thing. But I think now we're going to have to explain. I told you this morning about my plans for Joszef. Now I've seen for myself what kind of man he is, how brave he can be. He saved our lives on that volcano. I'm convinced he'd be a worthwhile asset, but I'm beginning to feel bad about taking advantage of him.'

'You may be right. But let's have our dinner first, then we'll tell him about it. He's just had a terrifying experience. Let him relax for a while. You too. Then we'll see how it goes.'

The meal, and the wine, revived them. They moved to the sitting room. Klara was smoking a cigarette and drinking straight vodka. Joszef and Hoffman were making short work of a bottle of schnapps, while Frau Hoffman was sipping black coffee from a tiny china cup.

Joszef turned to Klara. 'So now, *Fräulein* Brandt, you tell me everything.'

'Okay, then listen.'

By the time Klara had finished, Joszef looked dazed. 'So that's it. You're a gang of fucking spies or something. A bunch of troublemakers. Who cares about this Walther Schacht person? All that was ages ago. And you, Klara, you keep me in dark. You tell me you are tourist. You lie to me. I suspected there was something funny going on, but sure as hell nothing like this.'

Klara waited until he'd quietened down, then she said, 'Joszef, listen to me. First of all, we're not spies. And as for something funny going on, I can assure you there's nothing at all funny about it. Surely, you remember what the Nazis got up to in your country, or were you too young to understand?'

'Don't give me that. Yes, the Nazis. And the fucking Russians. I get into enough trouble with Russians, and with Hungarian secret police. Enough for lifetime.'

Hoffman asked his wife to bring more coffee, then he spoke to Joszef. 'You have every right to be angry, Joszef, as I would be in your place. But please think about it. These people we're talking about… monsters… barbarians… they did the most terrible things. Many of them are dead now, executed after the war, and others are serving long prison sentences. Don't you agree that any of them who are still alive and free, and still unpunished, ought to be brought to justice? Yes? I can see you agree. But who do you think is going to find them? You know the answer, don't you? People like us. People like Miss Brandt.'

Joszef paused to think before he replied. 'Okay, that may be so, but what have *I* got to do with it? I've been dragged into it by this *Fräulein* Brandt of yours. Probably not her real name, anyway… *Fräulein* Weber or whoever she is.'

'Look, I know how you must feel,' Klara said, 'and I'm truly sorry I've caused you so much distress. You were only a kid when those people did what they did, so I suppose it didn't affect you much at the time. But you must understand, I was right in the middle of it, in Germany. My life was made unbearable by what was going on around me. Not just my life. Millions of lives. Can you understand that?'

Joszef didn't say anything. He closed his eyes and remained motionless in his armchair. The others were watching him. Then, he sat up and looked at Klara, then at Hoffman. His eyes were shining.

'Now you listen to me, please. We Hungarians have always considered the Russians our oppressors. We think all the time about what they did. We remember 1956 fresh every day, how they crush us when we fight for our freedom. They were brutal. But we almost forget, before that, the Nazis invaded our country.' He stopped talking and stared at the floor for a while, then resumed, struggling to put into words something he could see in his head. 'I am remembering. I am only little boy, eight or nine maybe, but definitely I see German soldiers in grey uniform, some in black, in streets of Budapest, with big rifles. The Arrow Cross people as well… Hungarians. I didn't understand any of it. Only later I hear about the terrible atrocities. Awful things they did.' He covered his eyes with his hand.

Klara got up and walked over to him. She spoke gently. 'So, Joszef, you do remember some of it. Not all… you were lucky to have been so young. But maybe you can understand why we must find the man we're looking for.'

'This man you are looking for is big part of those horrors? In that case, I agree he must get what's coming to him. So maybe what you're trying to do is not so crazy.' He paused for a moment. 'Yes, is important you catch him. Anyway, I wish very good luck to you. But, please, leave me out of it. Enough is enough.'

It was late, and time to get back to town. They drove through the dark countryside back to the lights of San José. Klara dumped the taxi a few streets away from her hotel and they walked the rest of the way, agreeing to meet at Café Moreno in the morning.

As they neared the hotel, Klara stopped and grasped Joszef's arm. 'This is for saving my life,' she said, and surprised him with a kiss on his cheek and another on his lips. Then, leaving him rooted to the spot, she climbed the hotel's steps.

Before she went up to her room, she stopped at the hotel's desk and spoke to the clerk.

'Hi. Would it be possible to send a telegram to New York?'

'Of course, *señorita*. Is it urgent?'

'Yes, it's urgent.'

'If you dictate to me, I'll get it to the telegraph office at once.'

She dictated her message:

```
DEAR EDUARDO – STOP – ENJOYING COSTA
RICA VACATION – STOP – MET BUTTERFLY
COLLECTOR JOSZEF POGANYI FROM LONDON
HE COULD HELP ME – STOP – OUR COFFEE
FRIEND BELIEVES WE LIKELY FIND BIG RED
BUTTERFLY IN BRAZIL SO BLACK RIVER OUR
NEXT DESTINATION – STOP – IMPORTANT YOU
KNOW BUTTERFLY'S MINDERS ARE WATCHING
OUR COFFEE FRIEND – STOP – KLARA
```

The hotel clerk scratched his head as he read through what he'd written down. '*Señorita*, you are sure you want to send that? It doesn't make any... I mean, it doesn't seem very clear to me.'

'Yes, please send it, *exactly* as I've dictated it.'

Joszef was walking on air. The night was warm. Klara's perfume still lingered on him, and he was wondering if that faint cherry taste in his mouth came from her lips... well, from her lipstick. It had started to rain. He closed his eyes, raised his face to meet the warm raindrops as they fell, and smiled as he caught one on his tongue.

*

The sun was shining, and they were eating breakfast together at Café Moreno. Eduardo's reply had arrived during the night and confirmed that Klara's message had been received and understood. His contacts in London had cleared Joszef Poganyi for the role Klara had in mind for him.

Joszef stifled a yawn as he stirred his coffee. 'Sorry. Didn't get much sleep last night. Been thinking.'

'Oh? What about?'

'Everything. You. I don't know what to make of you, Klara. I like you... very much. But you can't be trusted, can you. You make a hell of a lot of trouble.'

'I know. I'm sorry. I like you too, Joszef.' She raised her cup to her lips and gave him an encouraging smile. 'So, what will you do now? I think you mentioned you were going to stay in Costa Rica for a while, catching your butterflies?'

'Yes, that's my plan.' He took a deep breath. 'A pity you go away, because I like… I – would – have – liked… to spend more time with you. Yes, is true, even with the trouble you give me.' He was wondering if she remembered last night's kiss.

'Well, it's really sweet of you to say that, Joszef.' It was now or never. 'Look, if you want to catch some interesting butterflies, how about coming with me on the next part of my journey? Where I'm going there will be gorgeous butterflies everywhere you look. And we'd get to know each other much better, wouldn't we?' She immediately regretted what she'd said. It wasn't on the level. It was downright dishonest. Why had she mentioned butterflies? That wasn't the point, was it? Too late now.

Joszef looked dumbfounded. 'What are you saying? Is joke, yes? You not serious I go with you.'

Was she serious about it? Klara had to decide, and *now*. 'As a matter of fact, Joszef, I'm deadly serious. Wouldn't it be a wonderful adventure for you? Just think about all the places we'd visit together. And you could be a great help to me.'

'I don't understand. How you think I help you? Not with that thing you have to do.'

'Listen, and I'll explain. You really can help me. You see, I have information that the man we want is somewhere in Brazil, somewhere around the River Amazon. So I *have* to go there. You do want me to find him, don't you? I know you do. Well, the closer I get to him, the more likely it is that he, or one of his minders – you know, like that phony taxi driver yesterday – might suspect I'm some sort of secret agent. That would make life difficult for me. And more dangerous. But with you being a butterfly collector... and I could pretend to be some sort of wildlife expert too... no one would suspect the real reason for our being there, would they?'

Joszef was staring at her. 'Unbelievable! You have it all planned out. You say you want me to help you find this terrible man. I'm beginning to think maybe you planning from start to get me with you. Yes? I am right?'

'Well... er... not quite. Well, yes, I suppose so. Sort of.'

'Yet you tell me nothing about it, until now. You are very devious woman.'

'Yes. Life is complicated, isn't it?'

'So now you come clean. But you remember what I say last night, yes? Leave me out of all the cloak-and-dagger stuff. I told you that.'

'I remember. But that was yesterday, and you said you'd been doing a lot of thinking.'

'Yes, a lot of thinking, most of night, but not about helping you catch criminal. This is something new. Anyway, I find hard to believe you really want me go with you.'

'But, Joszef, I *would* like you to come with me. Really. You know how important it is that I find this man. You'd make my job easier. We'd be together all the time. And I've seen how resourceful you can be when the going gets rough.'

'Oh, that.'

'Yes, that. You saved my life... both our lives. But don't worry, it's not as bad as it sounds. The good news is that my job isn't actually to *capture* Walther Schacht. I just have to find out where he is and tell some people in New York. Then, they'll send experts to do the capturing.'

'I know all that. You told me at Hoffman's. Well, I think about it. I don't know. Maybe I go with you, but maybe I stay here. I need more time. Very unexpected you ask me.'

'Of course. Let's think about it, then we'll talk more. It's up to you. You can either help me catch one of the most wanted criminals in the world, or you can stay here and catch a few more butterflies. Entirely your choice.'

'That's unfair. It's not that simple.'

'Yes, I know.'

They'd finished their breakfast and got up to leave Café Moreno. Joszef looked around him as he always did, then turned to Klara.

'Have you noticed? That little man who was asking all those questions about you. He isn't here today.'

'Yes, I did notice, and I'm not surprised. He's got quite a lot on his mind this morning, concerning a certain taxi driver. And, anyway, he didn't expect us to be here drinking coffee this morning – or any other morning for that matter.'

SEVEN

Joszef agonised for two days over Klara's proposal. He couldn't help thinking that unearthing Walther Schacht was likely to be more dangerous than she was willing to admit. Schacht was a murderous criminal, already condemned to death, so he wouldn't hesitate to kill again if he found out they were on his trail. And their experience with the bogus taxi driver meant that he probably had a network of dedicated minders who would do anything to protect him.

Despite this, Joszef's craving for adventure and the opportunity to see more of the world – and more of Klara – got the better of him, and he decided to go with her. In the back of his mind lurked the unchivalrous thought that if things got out of hand he could always pull out and return to London. He hoped it wouldn't come to that.

They'd taken a flight from San José to Belém, a city on Brazil's coast, where the River Amazon pours into the Atlantic. Now, they had to find a way of getting from there to Manaus to look for Wolfgang Müller.

The swarthy, moustachioed travel agent they consulted told them it wouldn't be easy. 'Never been there myself. Middle of the jungle. No road or rail links to anywhere. You know that? You'll have to fly or go by boat. How you like a boat trip? Cost a bit more than plane ticket, but you enjoy interesting voyage. I have good friend who'd be glad to fix you up.' He gave them an encouraging smile.

Joszef looked doubtful. 'Eight hundred miles up the River Amazon on a boat? How long would that take?'

The agent brushed the question aside with a wave of his hand. 'Probably not long, a few days. Who's in a hurry?'

'*Senhor*, forget the goddamn boat,' Klara said. 'We'll fly, and as soon as possible. See what you can find for us.'

'Okay. I could call Panair do Brasil, but they're expensive, and … you know… not always one hundred percent reliable. You could lose all your money. Your best bet is small airline I know. Is called VASP. I'll give them a ring, okay?'

Joszef smirked. 'I'll bet you have a good friend there, too.'

'Of course… my cousin.' He lit a cigarette and let it dangle from his lower lip while he dialled. After a long conversation in Portuguese, he put the phone down. 'Okay. All done. You're booked for tomorrow. You pay me now, American dollar, yes?'

Their flight sorted, they had time to take a look at Belém. They walked down a wide avenue, shaded from the sun by a row of ancient mango trees, and stopped to watch a gang of boys throwing sticks into the trees to knock down the ripe fruit. Eventually, they found themselves at the harbour. Boats set with triangular sails in brown and red were bobbing up and down in the muddy water. The air was hot and steamy. Men stripped to the waist were unloading bunches of bananas and melons the size of footballs, shouting and singing while they worked. The smells of fish, overripe fruit and a hundred other things came and went as they walked. The sight of a woman frying fish at a street stall reminded them that they hadn't eaten. They lunched on fishcakes topped with black olives. The food was tasty, and the coffee afterwards was excellent – black and strong.

They were feeling more relaxed and sat on the grass beneath a stand of tall trees. Klara lit a cigarette, then lay back and closed her eyes. Joszef gazed at her, thrilled to be in the company of someone so attractive, so experienced in the ways of the world. He began to wonder if he was falling in love, a thought more painful than joyous because he felt sure it was a one-way thing. He lay on his back next to her and looked up at the trees. Why would someone like Klara be interested in someone like him? He was startled by a flash of electric blue under the dark green canopy of leaves. It took him a few seconds to work out what it was – a morpho butterfly, as big as a bird, a Walt Disney cartoon butterfly, fluttering above him on wings of pure sapphire. He held his breath. It was as if a fragment of the shining blue sky itself had somehow fallen down and turned itself into this miraculous living thing, dancing in the air, trying to find its way back up to where it belonged. He patted Klara on the arm. She opened her eyes and they both watched the blue butterfly frolic around them. Then, with a few flaps of its wings, it lifted itself upwards and disappeared over the trees.

Klara was enthralled. 'What a beautiful creature!'

Joszef drew closer and looked into her blue eyes. 'Yes, a beautiful creature.'

She smiled and gently pushed him away.

*

The next day, they were on their way to Manaus on a DC3. Joszef was sitting next to the window, his gaze glued to the never-ending vastness of the rainforest. It struck him forcibly that a man could hide from the world down there for his whole life and never be found.

They reached Manaus in the evening and landed on a muddy airfield somewhere outside the city. In the terminal, a woman wearing a VASP uniform approached them and recommended a particular hotel in the downtown part of the city. It sounded like a suitable place from which to carry out their business, so they asked her to make a booking for a week's stay. The River Palace Hotel she'd called it, but when they got there, they discovered it wasn't all that its name implied. It was certainly large, but totally basic. A one-star place, Klara pronounced. Even so, they decided it would do, and besides, they were tired and hungry.

The hotel's dining room wasn't one of those places where you were expected to dress for dinner. Someone tramping straight out of the jungle would have blended in less conspicuously than they did. They strolled over to an empty table and did their best to ignore the stains on the tablecloth.

An unsmiling waiter, wearing a soiled apron, sauntered up to them. '*Olá*. American, yes? Okay, what you like eat?'

'*Boa noite, senhor*,' Joszef replied. 'You have a menu?'

'Sure. You want I get for you?'

'Yes, that would be helpful. *Obrigado*.' He glanced at Klara. 'What a place! I hope the food's all right.'

'Look, everyone else is eating it, so it can't be all that bad, can it? Incidentally, I'm impressed with your *boa noite*. When did you learn Portuguese?'

'Yesterday, but I'm afraid *boa noite, bom dia* and *obrigado* just about cover it.'

'Well, it's a start. I suppose if you're clever enough to speak Hungarian, any other language must be a cinch.'

The waiter returned with the menu. There wasn't much of a choice. They both ordered *sopa de seijao*, bean soup. Five minutes later, the waiter reappeared and placed before them two bowls, each full to the brim with a thick beige liquid.

'Looks lousy… but it smells okay,' Klara said. 'Why don't you try it first?'

Joszef confidently swallowed a spoonful. 'Not bad at all… quite good actually.'

Klara picked up her spoon then hesitated when she noticed the corpse of an insect floating in Joszef's second spoonful. Some sort of brown beetle the size of an almond. She put her spoon back down on the table. Joszef nonchalantly deposited his beetle on the tablecloth and carried on consuming his soup. A few chunks of bread and a glass of cheap vodka was all Klara had that evening.

*

The next morning, they set off to look for Wolfgang Müller at the address Peter Hoffman had given them. It was still early, yet the streets were already thronged with people. Men in fancy shirts and girls with shy smiles crowded around the kiosks, buying cigarettes and fizzy *guarana* and tiny cups of sugary *cafezinho*. It was hot. Music blasted from loudspeakers up in the *ficus* trees. Little rainbow-coloured buses growled their way through the streets, horns blaring. Hawkers were everywhere. One of them tried to sell Joszef a live armadillo; whether it was destined to become someone's pet or someone's roast dinner was anybody's guess.

They made their way down a maze of narrow lanes until they reached the main square, dominated by the Teatro Amazonas, its dome clad in coloured tiles. Klara recalled that the great Enrico Caruso had sung there seventy years earlier. It was easy to imagine what Manaus would have been like in those days. Ships from Europe would sail up the Amazon laden with coal for ballast and return home with a valuable cargo of smoked rubber latex.

The suburb where Müller lived was little more than a chaotic jumble of hovels, with roofs of thatch and rusting corrugated iron, and sometimes just a tarpaulin. Pigs and hens roamed freely in the streets, eating whatever they could find. Rows of black vultures were perched on the rooftops, drying their wings in the bright morning sun. Far out on the river, a paddle steamer was tugging a long chain of barges strung like beads across the shimmering surface of the water.

They found Müller's house, but no one was at home. A man dressed only in a pair of trousers, his tangled hair all over the place, was eyeing them suspiciously. He'd seen them hanging about outside his neighbour's house and approached them in the same way a well-trained Schnauzer might confront a trespasser.

'*Ei você.* You two. What you want, eh? You look for *senhor* Müller?'

'Yes, that's right,' Klara replied. 'He's a friend of ours. You know where he is?'

'No. Nobody know.'

'What d'you mean, nobody knows?'

'He could be anywhere, *senhorita*. Somewhere in jungle. Look for animal.'

'Animal? What animal? Why?'

'You not know he and friends collect animal for zoo and hunt jaguar for skin?'

'No.'

'*Senhor* Müller sell them to agent who come here. I thought maybe you agent.'

'Oh, I see. When d'you think they'll be back?'

'Impossible say when back. Sometime, go away many week.'

Joszef looked at Klara. 'This isn't what we expected, is it? What the hell do we do now?'

'Look, we've come a darned long way to see Müller. He's the only person who can tell us where Schacht's holed up… at least, where he thinks he is. We'll just have to wait, for as long as it takes. We have to be patient.'

'It could take forever.'

'No, I don't think so. They can't stay away for long, lumbered with a collection of live animals and a load of jaguar pelts.'

She turned to the neighbour again. 'Okay, we'll come back in a few days to see if *senhor* Müller has returned. If you see him, I wonder if you'd mind telling him to contact me. Tell him it's *senhorita* Brandt, staying at the River Palace Hotel. Tell him it's important.'

'Ah, the River Palace Hotel. Very nice. You staying there? Of course, *senhorita*, I watch for him. No problem.'

As they walked back to town, Klara said, 'When you think about it, Müller's being away, tramping around in the jungle, is good news in one sense.'

'Why? I can't see why it's anything to celebrate.'

'These long hunting expeditions. It could explain why Peter Hoffman found it hard to contact him. That's a hell of a lot better than discovering he's been got at by the other side.'

The sun was at its highest when they got back to the hotel. It was siesta time. Shopkeepers had put up their shutters and the crowds had evaporated, leaving the baking streets practically empty. The noisy street music had been mercifully silenced. Bliss. But barely two hours later, as if some film director had shouted 'Action!', the background music started up again, thousands of "extras" appeared from out of nowhere, and the city came back to life.

EIGHT

Several days later, the hotel's desk clerk handed Klara a folded scrap of paper. It was a message from Wolfgang Müller, explaining that if she wanted to see him she'd have to come to his warehouse at an address on the outskirts of the city.

The warehouse turned out to be a large barn located at the end of an overgrown track. The doors were open so they walked straight in. Inside, it was gloomy, and even warmer than it was outside.

Joszef wrinkled his nose. 'That smell!'

'Ugh! Like the Bronx zoo.'

They were startled by an ear-splitting squawk. It came from a scarlet macaw shuffling neurotically from one foot to the other on its perch, annoyed that two strangers had invaded its territory. A sleek ocelot, imprisoned in a miserably small cage, eyed them expectantly, while a large monkey, tethered to a wooden post, bared its teeth at them then started to howl. Joszef responded by making a face, which threw the animal into a fit of hysterical chattering. They briefly exchanged glances with a man in ragged overalls tinkering with a clattering air pump. Squatting on the floor next to him was a young boy, his skin the colour of copper. The moment he saw Klara he jumped up and shouted, '*Olá, senhorita. Olha isto!*' She could tell he was burning to show her something so she followed him. He lifted the heavy wooden cover off a pit and pointed excitedly to a boa constrictor coiled inside. It was sleeping peacefully but Klara pretended to be terrified. She threw her hands in the air and screamed, leaving the boy grinning from ear to ear.

They heard a door being opened at the back of the building and a shirtless grey-haired man appeared. He was wearing faded blue trousers and a straw hat. His body was lean and deeply tanned, his chest covered with a thin fuzz of white hair. He looked at the two visitors with a puzzled expression.

'*Sim? Como posso ajudá-lo?*'

Klara responded in English. 'Hello. Wolfgang Müller?'

'Ah, so you are the American lady from the hotel. Sure, I'm Müller. What can I do for you guys?' His accent was German, with a hint of American slang. 'You looking for skins? Ocelot, jaguar? I have best quality.'

Klara came right to the point. 'No. We're friends of *Herr* Peter Hoffman. You know, the coffee planter in Costa Rica. Sorry to come unannounced, but you know why we're here, don't you? I'm Klara Brandt, and this is Joszef Poganyi.'

Müller was visibly shaken. He stared at them in disbelief for a few moments then showed them into a back room. The pelts of various animals were scattered on the floor, and others were tied up in bundles.

'I'm sorry, *senhorita*,' he said. 'You took me by surprise. But this is excellent. I've been hoping to communicate with *Herr* Hoffman, but it wasn't possible from where I've been. So, he sent you guys to me, did he?' He looked hard at them.

'Correct. That's why we're here.'

'Good. A big welcome to you both. Okay, I make coffee, then we talk… but wait.' He took a bottle of something from a cupboard, obviously some sort of liquor. 'Maybe you rather have some of this?' They shook their heads.

They watched him take a fistful of coffee from a battered tin, drop it into an earthenware jug, and pour in boiling water. He managed to extract two enamel mugs from the jumble of things lying in the sink, gave them a cursory rinse under the tap, and filled them with a foamy brown liquid from the jug, straining it through a coffee-stained rag.

'Here you go. Coffee for you.'

'You're not having one?' Joszef asked.

He grinned. 'Something stronger for me.' He proceeded to drink whatever it was straight from the liquor bottle. 'Please, sit down and make yourselves comfortable.' There was only one chair, which he offered to Klara. With his foot, he shoved a wooden crate closer to Joszef. 'Hope that's okay?'

He told them he'd been lucky to get out of Germany in 1937. 'Didn't want to be drafted into Hitler's army. Hated the Nazis, those motherfuckers… what they stood for and what they were doing. All that bullshit. Eventually ended up here. After the war, some guys came to see me. I told them sure, I'd be glad to do anything I could to help them find any of those bastards. Now it's the turn of Walther Schacht, that fucking son of a bitch. He's still around.'

Klara nodded. 'Yes, I know. Still alive and kicking. He's the one we're after.' She couldn't quite make him out, this Wolfgang Müller. 'So, *Herr* Müller, what have you been doing all these years?'

'A bit of this and a bit of that. Worked for a logging company… timber… mahogany, you know. Spent a few years as a rubber tapper. Now, I go into the forest and trap animals and sell them… for zoos, as well as pelts for the fur trade, mainly jaguar. Good money in that. Sometimes, I live with one or other of the Indian tribes. Those guys can be very hospitable… and their womenfolk too, which makes life in the jungle a bit more bearable.' He explained how he used dogs when he went hunting. 'The dogs – big dogs – flush out a jaguar and chase it up tree. Then, I shoot it. If the dog gets it wrong, things can go the other way. I've had several dogs killed by jaguar.' He took another swig from the bottle.

'That's all very interesting, *Herr* Müller,' Joszef said, 'but we have a lot to discuss. Tell me, when did you and *Herr* Hoffman last meet?'

'Meet? You're joking. We never meet. We don't operate like that. We have our way of communicating, but even so we only make contact when it's absolutely necessary. We have to be careful. The guys trying to stop us… they have many ways of getting hold of information and passing it on. They keep their ears and eyes open, and you can be sure they keep in touch with that bastard you're looking for.'

'So what now?' Klara asked. 'You have some information for us?'

'*Senhorita*, you'd be surprised what you can learn over a beer with the guys who travel up and down the rivers. People off the trading boats, priests who move from one Catholic mission to another, guys off the planes that fly between the settlements. They aren't what you might call discreet, those guys, none of 'em. Wait. I make more coffee for you.'

Klara glanced at Joszef and quickly responded. 'Oh, please, no. That was delicious, but it was enough. Thank you.'

'No more? Okay. So, if you want to find Walther Schacht, it's almost certain you'll have to go up the Rio Negro. There's this German guy I heard about. Seems to fit Schacht's description pretty darned well… right age, and so on. A difficult character, they say, always arguing, possibly a bit mad. You'll have to go to Tapurucuara to check him out.'

'Where's that?' Joszef asked.

'Tapurucuara? It's a settlement up there, on the Negro. There's this mission, doing its best to convert the Indians to Christianity.'

'D'you think it's worth going to have a look?'

'It sounds like a good bet. He may be Schacht. Definitely worth a visit. Another guy I know, a boatman, told me he'd spent a couple of days at a different mission, a lot further up the river. Said he'd met someone there who spoke Portuguese but whose mother tongue was German. A man of about sixty-something, roughly the right age for Schacht. Think about it. Who else would be holed up way out there, far away from anywhere, except a fugitive of some sort? That's two guys I've heard about. I've had other reports, but mostly pretty vague. They've got missions all over the place up and down the river and along its tributaries. To be honest, Schacht could be hiding in any of them. Wait. Let me show you.'

He rummaged around in a drawer to find a sheet of paper and a pencil and began to sketch out a rough map. 'Look.' He drew a line from left to right and placed his finger at its midpoint. 'That's the Amazon, and this is where you are now, Manaus, where the Rio Negro joins the main river.' He drew a wiggly line going north-west from Manaus. 'See? This is the Negro.' He traced along it with his finger and made a pencil mark. 'This is Tapurucuara, and…' he made a second mark further along the wiggly line '… this is the other place I mentioned. It's called Constância.'

'Wow! That covers a lot of territory,' Klara said. 'Where d'you think we should start?'

'I think the best place would be Tapurucuara. You should go and see if you can find that German guy there. He may be our man. On the other hand, he may be totally innocent, a farmer or something.'

Joszef threw him a quizzical look. 'You haven't been to Tapuru… that place… to see for yourself?'

'No. An old German like me? If this guy *is* Schacht, he'd see through me in a flash. Bang! No more Wolfgang Müller.'

'I see. Then let's hope he doesn't see through *us*. But what if it turns out this guy isn't our man, what do we do then?'

'In that case, *senhor*, you should go and look at Constância, further up the river. You may be luckier there. If not, you may have to make your way up one or other of the tributaries. You'll have to be careful. It's dangerous. Some of those Indians don't like white men. I heard about two adventurers who paddled upriver near the border with Colombia, not too long ago. One of them raised his camera to photograph a group of Indians and...' Müller snapped his fingers '...that was that. Killed by an arrow. Anyway, that's the story the survivor told.'

'Not very encouraging,' Klara said, 'but never mind that. What we need to know now is what's the best way of getting to those places you mentioned?'

'Tapurucuara's no problem, *senhorita*. There's a weekly flight operated by Panair do Brasil, I think every Friday. They use those old American flying boats, Catalinas. Useful planes around here because they can land on the water as well as on the ground. But Constância... I'm afraid that's not so easy. I've never been that far up the river. There's no regular service as far as I know.'

'So, that would make it a good place for a fugitive to hide, right?'

'Right.'

'What about a boat?'

'To Constância? Well... I may be able to find you a boat, a trading boat doing business up and down the Negro, but you never know how far they go. It always depends on how good or bad the trading happens to be. And they're always slow, those old wrecks... and they aren't what you might call comfortable. From here to

Constância, maybe two or three weeks, probably more. Hundreds of miles up the river, and it's not a straight run.'

'So, it looks like we'd better take the easier option and go to Tapurucuara first. On Panair.'

'That's your best bet, *senhorita*, as I've already told you. Anyway, once you're in that part of the world, you can talk to the locals, and the missionaries. Those guys may be able to tell you about any other likely candidates.' He picked up the liquor bottle he'd been drinking from, discovered it was empty, and tossed it into the sink. 'Okay. I hope all this was helpful. But here's a dumb question for you. If you do find Schacht, what are you going to do with the son of a bitch? You can't be thinking of tackling him yourselves. Far too risky with a slippery guy like that.'

Klara nodded in agreement. 'You're right. Our job is just to find out where he's hiding and send the details to our… special friends. That's all. They'll come here to tackle him, not us. That's the plan.'

'So you say, but it won't be that easy, believe me. Let me tell you something. You may think you're closing in on him, sure, but that motherfucker is clever. If you get *too* close, he'll turn the tables on you. Then, you'd better watch out. It's happened before, at least once. Maybe you heard about it? It's like my dogs. If one of them gets too close to the jaguar and starts nipping at its legs – that's what they do, you know – that's when things get dangerous. Once the big pussycat gets cornered, it'll turn on the dog, and that always ends the same way: goodbye doggy! You guys better watch your step.'

They bade farewell to Wolfgang Müller. As they left his warehouse, the big monkey, now strangely quiet, followed them with soulful eyes, as if it knew something they didn't.

NINE

The River Palace Hotel was far from perfect, but it had become a sort of home from home. They were enjoying each other's company and beginning to understand each other's idiosyncrasies. Klara had been aware of Joszef's feelings for her from the start and had had few qualms about exploiting them for her own ends. To her, he was a comrade-in-arms, a friend, but by no means the sort of man who'd figure in her dreams. She knew what Joszef had in mind, what he was hoping for, but she herself had no such inclination. However, she'd gradually developed a platonic fondness for him, and that didn't surprise her. She was well aware that spending time with someone on a daily basis generally brings you closer together.

The hotel's desk clerk raised his eyebrows when they asked him about flights up the River Negro. 'Why you want to go that part of country? Is very dangerous. You starve to death, or eaten by hungry alligator. Or torn apart by jaguar.' He grinned. 'Or massacred by savages.'

Klara smiled. 'Yes, I see. Maybe all of those. But we have to go there. We want to photograph a rare butterfly.'

'Butterfly? Really? A strange job you two have. I think Manaus best place for you. Big city. Nice place... civilised... safe.'

Klara smiled to herself. She'd seen enough of Manaus to know it wasn't the safest place in the world. She'd already stumbled across the body of a murdered woman left lying in the street, ignored by everyone. And as for civilised, some of the things she'd seen had given her nightmares. That man at the market, singing to himself as he dismembered a river turtle with a few heavy blows from his machete – while it was still alive. And those monkeys, skinned from head to toe, hanging from iron hooks rammed into their skulls, roasted, blackened and burned, but still instantly recognisable as man's close relatives. They'd reminded her of something from her childhood back in Germany, something she'd seen in the German newspapers immediately after the war. She couldn't put her finger on it, but the image had frightened her.

'Well, relatively safe,' she conceded. 'Anyway, don't you worry about us. We know about the risks. Now, what can you tell us about transport?'

'You really want go up there? Okay, I've done my best to warn you.' He strolled over to a cupboard and returned with a timetable. 'See? Panair do Brasil. Rio Negro flight every Friday, stopping at Carvoeiro, Barcelos and Tapurucuara, then they fly back here. Good, yes?'

'That's great. Friday.'

'How about further up the river?' Joszef asked. 'Say, to Constância?'

The clerk scratched his head. 'Constância? Where's

that? No mention here. They fly only as far as mission at Tapurucuara. You want me get tickets for Friday flight there? Always plenty empty seats. *Dois?* Two?'

Joszef and Klara looked at each other, then Joszef turned to the clerk. 'We need to think about it. Give us a couple of minutes. Back soon.'

'You better be quick. Panair office soon close.'

Joszef took Klara's arm and led her to the garden square in front of the hotel. The sky had turned dark. A storm was brewing.

'Joszef, I know what you're going to say. And you're right. It's all a bit rushed if we've got to leave on Friday, but don't worry. I'm sure we can manage it.'

'No, it's not that. Something else. Listen. I've been thinking. When Müller told us about that man in Tapurucuara, he said he *may* be Walther Schacht, but he could be someone else, maybe an innocent farmer.'

'And?'

'Okay, let's just suppose we go there and discover he really *is* Schacht. You'll contact your New York people and our part of the job is done.'

'Wouldn't that be great! We could go all home. So what's the problem?'

'Yes, but supposing we find he isn't our man. Then, we'd have to go to that other mission Müller mentioned. You know, that place further up the river.'

'Constância. So what?'

'Yes, that's it, Constância. Let's say Schacht *is* holed up there. We've been warned that he communicates with a network of people protecting him. So, isn't it likely that while we're in Tapurucuara, his minder there would contact him and tell him that a couple of foreigners had arrived, asking a lot of questions?'

'I suppose so. But why this lecture?'

'Wait. If he's as clever as he's supposed to be, he'd assume we'd soon be trying our luck at other settlements, including Constância, asking questions there. What would he do? He wouldn't sit around waiting for us, would he? He'd probably flee into the jungle before we got there.'

'Hmm. I think you're right. Yes! I hadn't thought of that. The last thing we want to do is drive him away. Impossible to find him if he leaves the mission, either mission.'

'Exactly. So there's only one thing to do. We have to cover both missions at the same time. Right?'

'Come on, Joszef, get real. We can't be in two places at once, can we?'

'Of course we can. It's not magic.'

'Tell me.'

'We split up.'

'Ah, yes.' She chuckled. 'That's a thought. Well, maybe, but I don't like it much.'

'Why not? It makes sense. You go to Tapurucuara and I go to Constância – if I can find a way of getting there. And we each operate as invisibly as we can.'

'I see the logic in that. But, Joszef… how would you feel about being all by yourself in Constância, far away, in a totally unfamiliar place? You've heard how dangerous it can be.'

'It would be just as dangerous if we were together, wouldn't it?'

'What sort of logic is that? Really, Joszef!'

He saw the twinkle in her eyes. He wanted to kiss her. He wanted to say something affectionate. But he didn't. He said, 'Let's get back to the hotel.'

The storm finally broke and they hurried back through a heavy downpour. The hotel clerk tried to phone the Panair office.

'Too late,' he said. 'Closed for the night. I warned you.'

'Never mind,' Klara said. 'We'll deal with that tomorrow. But I'd like you to send a telegram to New York. I mean now, please. Can you do that for me?'

'Of course. What do you want to say?'

'I'll write it out for you.'

```
DEAR EDUARDO – STOP – LEAVING MANAUS
– STOP – WILL FLY NORTH-WEST ON BLACK
RIVER HOPE TO FIND RARE BUTTERFLY THERE
– STOP – ME TO TAPURUCUARA MISSION –
STOP –BUTTERFLY HUNTER TO CONSTÂNCIA
MISSION – STOP – KLARA
```

There was nothing else they could do that evening, so they found a table in the hotel's bar and Klara ordered a bottle of vodka. They were beginning to enjoy its effects when they heard shouting outside and went to the window. A tall palm tree in the garden square was being buffeted by the wind. As they watched, a strong gust bent the tree too far. There was a frightening crack and it fell to the ground with a loud crash. They looked at the fallen giant and realised they'd just witnessed the death of a tree which must have been growing in that spot for at least a hundred years. What timing! Neither of them was particularly superstitious, but they couldn't help wondering whether this was just a coincidence, or an omen of some sort.

*

In the morning, Joszef made his way to the Panair office.

He was greeted by a young man wearing a navy blazer several sizes too large for him. 'So, *senhor*, you want two seats on flight to Tapurucuara? Well, is possible there may be a flight up Rio Negro sometime next week.'

'Next week? But I was told there's a flight this Friday.'

'Maybe, but even if there is, is very hard to get tickets. How bad you need them?'

'Really? So why did the clerk at the River Palace tell me there are always plenty of empty seats?'

'He did? I see. Well, I could try if you like. Last week, this American wanted to fly to Salvador. I managed to get ticket for him and he gave me nice present.' He pulled a gold-plated fountain pen out of his breast pocket and waved it about.

Joszef could feel his anger rising. This was the sort of thing he'd thought he'd left behind on the other side of the Iron Curtain. He fixed the young man with a threatening stare.

'Listen. I don't want to play games. No more of this if you want to keep your job with Panair. You understand me? You do want to keep your job, don't you?'

'Okay, okay. Sorry. I look what is available for Tapurucuara.'

'The flight on Friday. Where does it stop? Does it go to Constância?'

'No. Our planes not go as far as that. Just as far as to Tapurucuara.' He saw Joszef's suspicious glare. 'Is the truth. They not have place for landing there. Is all jungle, and not land on river because all big rocks, dangerous rapids. Sometime, plane go bit further than Tapurucuara, but not as far as Constância. Flight like that only every four, five, six weeks. Only if passenger want go that far.'

'I don't believe you.'

'Is true.'

'Where does it go to? The one that goes further than Tapurucuara.'

The agent glanced at a chart taped to the wall. 'That flight go as far as place called Mercês.'

'Where's that?'

'Not sure where is.'

'Then we look at that map. Come on.'

The young man used his finger to follow the line of the River Negro. 'Look. Here is Mercês. Is just before Constância. I suppose plane land on river there because river very wide. See? But if Constância is where you want go, how you get there from Mercês? No road, just jungle. A problem, no? Anyhow, I tell you, plane only go that far not often. No demand. No one want go there, to that Mercês place.'

'*I* want go there. Look. Just find out when is next flight to Mercês. Come on. Do it now.'

The agent studied the chart for a few moments. 'Oh, *Dios mío!* You lucky, *senhor*. Flight to Tapurucuara on Friday is one of our specials. After Tapurucuara, will go further. Take three passenger to Mercês. Three nuns. They heading for mission at Constância.'

'Right. I want two tickets for that plane, one as far as Tapurucuara and the other all the way to Mercês.'

'Okay. I see what I can do for you.'

'No. Not good enough. Just get the tickets, for fuck's sake. And no more funny business about gold fountain pens. You understand me?'

'Okay, okay. No problem. I get for you.'

TEN

On Friday morning they got to the airport before dawn, sleepy but excited. A Catalina flying boat was standing on the tarmac. It was a strange beast: amphibious, a sort of mongrel, at home in the water as well as on the land and in the sky. The front part of the fuselage had a hull like an oversized speedboat, while the rear section curved gracefully upwards. It was an old American plane, almost certainly a relic of WW2. Boarding it involved climbing up a ladder and then stepping down through a hatch. Joszef surveyed their fellow passengers. Some of them looked as if they'd come directly from working in the fields or the nearby oil refinery. They'd simply dumped their belongings on the floor: battered suitcases, tin buckets and various parcels tied up with string. One woman was carrying a basket holding two squealing piglets. In stark contrast, three young nuns in meticulously laundered white habits appeared to have no luggage at all.

The pilot and co-pilot were sitting in the cockpit, which was simply the front section of the cabin. A pair of legs dangling from the roof belonged to the flight engineer, perched in his cubicle above the main compartment. The pilot turned round and shouted '*Bom dia*' to his passengers, then they took off. The two engines made a thunderous din and eventually dragged the old Catalina off the ground and into the air. There were two loud thumps as the wheels were retracted into the fuselage.

It was hardly less noisy once they'd reached cruising height. Klara had closed her eyes and was trying to catch up on some sleep, resting her head on Joszef's shoulder. He could smell her hair and feel its softness against his cheek. How young she looked, almost like a child. He looked at the scar above her eyebrow, with its two rows of tiny puncture marks where the stitches had been. He wanted to touch it, but didn't. Through the porthole he watched Manaus recede into the distance, a small man-made scar on an otherwise infinite expanse of green forest. The River Negro was directly below them, twisting its way through the jungle like a giant black snake.

Their first stop was Carvoeiro. As the pilot made his descent, the amorphous dark green carpet they'd been flying over gradually showed itself to be what it really was – a magnificent forest of densely packed trees, many ablaze with yellow and purple blossoms. The crew prepared for a landing on the river, yelling instructions to one another. The flight engineer strained at the red-painted handle which lowered the wing-tip floats. They flew low and Joszef held his breath. There was a bump as they hit the water and the plane scooted over the surface. Just before they came to a halt, the pilot swung it round and taxied closer to the village. Then, he switched off the engines and dropped anchor, as if it was a boat.

Carvoeiro appeared to consist of little more than a few dozen houses, many of them just shacks, clustered around a small chapel on the riverbank. Two young boys in a canoe paddled up to the plane. They held on to a wing strut while they collected the few passengers who wanted to disembark there. The hatch was closed again and they were ready to go. The engines coughed a couple of times before they came to life. The pilot taxied to the middle of the river and pulled out the throttle. The engines roared and the plane sped across the surface, throwing sheets of water into the air. Some of it streamed into the cabin through chinks in the hull. The entire contraption shuddered alarmingly. Joszef noticed that some of the passengers were making the sign of the cross. A frightening screech from somewhere below sounded as if the plane's sheet metal bottom was being ripped off. Then, they broke free of the river and climbed into the air.

The landing on the river at Barcelos went smoothly, but when the pilot was taking off again something went wrong. He revved the engines and the plane gathered speed. Joszef felt a sudden bump. The roaring of the engines stopped and the Catalina drifted to a halt. There were frantic shouts among the crew. Joszef's thoughts were racing. What was happening? Was the old Catalina going to sink? Would they have time to get out before it did? One of the crew rushed to open the hatch, shouted something to whoever was out there, and hurled out a couple of lifebelts.

Klara had managed to sleep through all this. Joszef gave her a shake. She rubbed her eyes. 'What's going on, Joszef? What's all that goddamn shouting?'

'Christ! Look at that. People in the water. See? That man... his face... covered in blood. Can you see him?'

She leant across and peered out of the porthole. 'Oh my god! Look, he's holding a little girl... not moving. Is anybody doing anything to help?'

'Look over there! Clinging on to something. See? Two women... and the children. Hell! We must've smashed into their boat.'

The people in the water were screaming for help. It was obvious that the lifebelts the Catalina's crew had thrown to them weren't going to be of much use.

'*Do* something,' Klara yelled.

The flight engineer leant down from his cubicle. 'No need to be alarmed, *senhorita*. The captain had to abort our take-off because those stupid idiots didn't see us coming. Steered their canoe right in front of us. Unfortunately, we hit them. Their boat was damaged, but don't worry, no one is badly hurt. People like that... they shouldn't be allowed on the river at all.'

Joszef and Klara stared at each other in disbelief.

'What utter rubbish!' Klara yelled back. 'Those people need to be rescued and looked after. Those little children. They'll drown, for Chrissakes.'

She was ignored. The hatch was closed and a minute later they were up in the air, on their way to Tapurucuara, as if nothing had happened.

'Unbelievable!' Joszef said. 'All in a day's work for these people, I suppose.'

'Bastards, the lot of them. A human life doesn't seem to count for much around here.'

When they landed at Tapurucuara, the Catalina was hitched to a wooden raft. It was the end of the journey for most of the passengers. Those who were leaving walked along the gangway that linked the raft to the riverbank and wandered towards the village, carrying their belongings.

The pilot called to his remaining passengers. 'Gotta refuel her before we take off for Mercés. She's a greedy son of a bitch. It'll take us about an hour to fill her up. You'd better get out and wait on the raft.'

Klara, Joszef and the three young nuns disembarked. The nuns, all in their early twenties, were talking excitedly in Italian. Klara introduced herself and asked them where they were heading. One of them responded in English while the other two listened.

'We go to the mission at Constância. We are so excited, as you can see. This is our first time away from Italy. I am Sister Rosalia, and I am looking after these two.'

'And how long will you stay there, at Constância?'

'We plan three years. More if goes well. We have a lot of work to do. Many of the people there are still wild and have not heard God's word. They are not yet baptised Catholic and their souls are in jeopardy. Miss Klara, won't you introduce your friend?'

'Of course. This is Mr Joszef Poganyi.'

Joszef greeted the three young women with a warm smile. 'Hello. I also go to Constância, like you.'

Sister Rosalia looked puzzled. 'But you are not a

priest, Mr Joszef, so why you go there?' She glanced at her two companions and said something in Italian.

Joszef laughed. 'No, I'm certainly not a priest. I'm going there to catch butterflies.'

'Why you catch butterflies?'

'I collect them.'

'You collect butterflies? But you don't kill them, do you?'

'Well, sometimes.'

'But you mustn't. They are God's creatures. He is offended if you kill them. You know? And besides, it's cruel.'

'True, but life is often cruel, sometimes very cruel, isn't it? Look what happened when we took off at Barcelos. Perhaps God looks away when bad things happen.'

Sister Rosalia's face turned red. She backed away and got into a huddle with her two companions. They babbled among themselves, occasionally eyeing Joszef as if he was a murderer.

Klara glared at him. 'You certainly know how to make friends, don't you? You've upset them. More to the point, you never know what they may say to the mission people. They could make things difficult for you.'

'How? I don't think so.'

'Okay, never mind. Enough. Let's get down to business. I think it's pretty straightforward, what I have to do. I'll introduce myself to the mission's director. *Hello. I'm a wildlife photographer working for an American magazine. Would you please put me up for a few days?*'

'Good, but don't tell him your name. Or anyone else. Remember what happened in Costa Rica.'

'How could I forget! I'll just tell him I'm Klara. I'll keep my eyes skinned for that argumentative German guy. If he's really Schacht, I'll telegraph New York so they can get on with their part of the job. Have I forgotten anything?'

'No, sounds good, but you'll let me know straight away if you find him here, won't you. If I see him at Constância, I'll telegraph you.'

'Sounds too easy.'

'Yes, I agree.'

They watched the Catalina's crew complete the refuelling operation, which entailed hand-pumping the fuel from steel drums lined up on the riverbank. The pilot shouted to his remaining passengers that it was time to leave. The three nuns were in high spirits. But not Klara and Joszef. They were about to go their separate ways.

Klara took hold of both Joszef's hands. 'Look, are you absolutely sure about going to Constância on your own? It's not too late to change our plans, you know, if you're having second thoughts.'

'But I'm not. We've been through all that.'

'Okay. You'll be careful, won't you. What you and I are doing is important, but don't do anything too risky. You must look after yourself.'

'You too.' He hesitated then added, 'I'll miss you.'

'I'll miss you too, but it's okay. We'll be together again soon.'

'Klara, before I go… you know… I like you… very much. You understand what I say?'

She nodded. She could tell he'd struggled to get those words out. 'Yes, of course I understand. I'll be thinking of you.'

He broke free of her grip. 'Well, I better get going or they fly without me.' He turned to walk to the plane, but she grasped his arm to keep him there and kissed him lightly on the cheek, then let him go. He hadn't expected that. He looked puzzled.

She watched him climb through the plane's hatch. Before he disappeared below, she saw him wave to her. The hatch was closed. The two engines coughed as they always did, then revved into action. She watched the Catalina skim across the water, a giant silver bird with young Joszef in its belly. She tried to suppress a sneaking thought that she may never see him again.

ELEVEN

The long take-off run made Joszef nervous. The roar of the engines was deafening and everything shook and rattled, yet, despite the plane's speed, its hull was still ploughing through the water. It occurred to him that if they didn't get airborne – and high – very soon, they'd crash into the trees at the next bend in the river. He could see the pilot straining at the controls, but the ancient plane seemed reluctant to cooperate. He gripped the back of the seat in front of him so tightly that his fingers turned white. The three nuns had closed their eyes and were clasping their hands together in prayer. Joszef found himself desperately hoping that their pleas to the Almighty would succeed. Evidently they did, because seconds later, with the engines screaming at full power, the plane pulled clear of the water and climbed sufficiently steeply to avoid the treetops – by what seemed like a very narrow margin.

They continued to follow the black river. Joszef tried to sleep but only managed to doze. When, later, he looked out of the porthole, he saw an isolated group of jungle-clad peaks in the distance, rising abruptly out of the flat terrain.

The pilot shouted in English over his shoulder. 'Look, on your left. See those mountains? The Serra Curicuriari. That means we'll soon be landing at Mercês. If you're going to the mission at Constância, there should be some sort of boat to take you there. Unfortunately, it isn't possible for me to land any closer to the mission because of the rapids.'

Joszef stretched and yawned heavily. This was good news. He'd had enough flying for one day and was looking forward to getting back down to *terra firma*. He'd take a walk around Mercês and get something to eat there before continuing to Constância.

The river was wide, its surface was smooth, and the pilot made a perfect landing. A large canoe – a hollowed-out tree trunk fitted with an outboard motor – was coming towards them, steered by a brown-skinned man with thinning grey hair. As the canoe reached the plane, he stood up, grabbed hold of something on the fuselage, and manoeuvred his boat so it rested against the hull right below the hatch. The three nuns were ecstatic. One after the other they climbed out and, with a certain grace, lowered themselves into the canoe as if it was something they'd done a hundred times before. Joszef ignored the hostile glare from Sister Rosalia. The old boatman looked puzzled. He'd been expecting the three young women, but he didn't know what to make of the tall young man with the heavy rucksack.

The Catalina's pilot appeared in the hatch and scowled at Joszef. 'You. Where are you heading?'

'Anywhere where I can get some food. I'm starving.'

'The only place around here is Constância. Surely you know that, don't you? There's nowhere else. You better go with them.' He nodded in the direction of the nuns. 'When you get there, speak to the padre in charge of the mission.'

'But what about Mercês? I was thinking of going there first. They must have some places to eat there.'

'Mercês? That's Mercês over there.' He pointed to two white-painted shacks on the riverbank.

Joszef screwed up his eyes. 'You mean that's Mercês? Just that?'

'You've got no fucking clue, have you. That's it. I don't know what you were expecting. Another Brasilia, I suppose. Maybe I should take you straight back to Manaus. You'll live longer there. Listen to me. Go to the mission with them. I tell you, it's the only place.'

'How far is it from here?'

'In that dugout? Maybe five or six hours. It's upstream, so you'll be going against the current. Just wait 'til you see those rapids! I wish I could fly you there. We'd be there in a few minutes, but I can't. Here, take this if you're hungry.' He fished a bread roll out of his pocket and handed it over. 'Good luck. You'll need it.' Then he slammed the hatch shut.

Joszef lowered himself into the canoe and the boatman paddled his four passengers to a rudimentary pier below the two shacks. As they alighted, he heard the by-now familiar coughing of the Catalina's engines as they started up. He turned to watch the plane speed across the surface of the black river, leaving a trail of white spume in its wake. It strained noisily into the air and slowly climbed out of sight and beyond hearing. His last link with the world he knew had gone.

A middle-aged woman wearing a grey smock emerged from one of the shacks and beckoned him inside. She handed him a mug of coffee. Evidently, her little hovel served as the Mercês air terminal. Sister Rosalia and her two companions were already inside. They were talking in Italian to an older nun, perhaps in her fifties. When Joszef entered, their conversation stopped abruptly. The older woman fidgeted with a shiny crucifix hanging from a chain around her neck, then smiled and addressed him in English.

'So, you're the young man they've been telling me about. Your name is Joszef, yes? Welcome. I am Sister Vittoria. You'll be joining us on the voyage to our mission? I'm sure Padre Mazzanti will be happy to see you… the mission's director. We get few visitors from the outside, so this is quite an occasion.'

She told Joszef she'd been stationed at the Constância mission for many years. She'd come from there that morning with the boatman to welcome the three new arrivals. Joszef was expecting her to ask him why he'd come to this remote part of Brazil, but she didn't. He suspected the young ones had already informed her he was a murderer of butterflies. That was perfectly satisfactory, because he certainly didn't want anyone to know his real reason for being there.

The boatman was sitting on the pier with his feet trailing in the water, waiting for them. Slowly and respectfully, he helped Sister Vittoria into the canoe, then the three young nuns. They were bubbling with excitement. Joszef climbed aboard with his rucksack and managed to squeeze into the prow. The boatman crouched in the stern, next to the outboard. He tugged on the pull-rope a couple of times and the engine burst into life.

The first hour of the journey was pleasant. The river was wide, the water was calm, and with its powerful motor the canoe had no problem cutting through the modest current flowing against them. Because of the noise from the outboard, there was little conversation. Nor was there much to see apart from the black surface of the river and, far away, an unbroken wall of jungle on each bank.

Then, without warning, the engine cut out. The boatman swore and made some sort of apology to Sister Vittoria. The canoe slowed down, stopped for a moment, and then began to drift backwards with the current. One of the young women screamed. Sister Vittoria said something to calm her down. The boatman removed the metal cover from the engine and swore again.

Sister Vittoria lifted a finger to her lips. 'Shh! *Ascoltate*. Listen.'

Joszef was astonished. Apart from the soft rippling of the river against the sides of the boat, there was silence. Whichever way he turned, he could neither see nor hear the slightest sign of human activity. Just the untouched forest and the wide black river. This, he mused, was like the world used to be before monkeys learnt to walk on two legs.

The steamy heat on the river was overpowering, something which hadn't been apparent when the boat was travelling fast. The three young nuns hooted with relief when the boatman restarted the motor.

They enjoyed another half-hour of gentle travel on the placid water. Then, everything changed. The wide river had broken into several channels, and the current working against them became stronger. A few minutes later, they hit the rapids. The canoe was being pushed around like a toy. Joszef turned round to see if his fellow passengers were as alarmed as he was. The women were no longer smiling. Their faces were contorted with fear and they were gripping the sides of the boat with all the strength they could muster, as if half expecting to be tossed overboard at any moment. The older nun had lifted up her face to the sky and was chanting something in Latin. Then, it got worse. There were huge boulders everywhere. The boatman had to work hard at the tiller, his face creased with concentration as he steered the boat's prow into the great torrents of water surging between the rocks. The world seemed to be moving dizzily around them. The women screamed every time the canoe lurched forward or swung sideways or dipped downwards. It was heavily loaded and lay low in the water, and each time the river tossed it about, it seemed to be on the verge of capsizing. Joszef gripped his rucksack tightly between his knees. He was picturing what would happen if the engine cut out again, now. That would be the end of all of them. It fascinated him to think that his life – all their lives – was in the hands of this elderly man straining at the tiller.

The rapids further upstream were less alarming. At last, after voyaging for several hours, Joszef caught a glimpse of a white spire in the distance, by the side of the river, rising above the trees. There was a cry from the nuns. 'Constância. *Bellissima! Bellissima!*'

Sister Vittoria crossed herself and, with a hint of triumph in her voice, said, 'See? Our mission. That's our little chapel. God has preserved us. We're home.'

A few minutes later, the boatman switched off the engine and used the paddle until the canoe's bottom crunched onto a sandy beach. They were immediately surrounded by a gang of noisy children who took hold of the boat at either end and pushed and pulled it further up the slope. They swarmed around the new arrivals like wasps on an overripe pear and followed them as far as the mission's main entrance. Someone was waiting there: a tall, balding man, bespectacled, wearing a white cassock which hung down to his sandals. When he saw the children, he growled and made as if to chase them. They ran off giggling and screaming.

Sister Vittoria spoke in Italian. 'Padre Mazzanti, I see you are in good spirits today. Director, I would like to present to you our three new sisters.' She gestured towards them, and each in turn modestly lowered her eyes, clasped her hands together and bowed her head.

Padre Mazzanti welcomed them with a warm smile. 'How did you like your journey in our little boat? An exciting voyage, I think.' He threw them a mischievous glance. 'It would have been very sad if we'd lost any of you overboard before you reached our mission, wouldn't it. You were fortunate to have Sister Vittoria to look after you.' Then, he turned to Joszef. 'And who might this young man be?'

Sister Vittoria gave him a long explanation, which Joszef couldn't understand.

Mazzanti addressed him in English. 'Mr Joszef, you too are most welcome. I understand you are... er... a biologist of some kind, a subject which interests me greatly.'

'Yes. I studied zoology at university in Hungary. I'm especially interested in insects.'

'Ah! So, you are Hungarian. That is exciting. I don't think we've had a Magyar here before. You and I must get together so you can tell me what's going on these days in your country. Some of the news I've been hearing isn't so good.'

'That's true. I'd be happy to talk to you about it. But I no longer live in Hungary. I live in England, in London.'

Sister Vittoria had been listening patiently, but she was tired and was looking forward to getting some rest. 'Excuse me, Padre,' she said. 'Our three young sisters here have had a long journey today, by aeroplane and boat, and they are tired – and no doubt hungry. So, with your permission...'

As they took their leave, Sister Rosalia threw Joszef a caustic glance, which he returned with a smile.

He was alone with Mazzanti. 'Padre, I'm grateful to you for allowing me to stay here. Naturally, I'll be happy to pay you whatever is required. I've got American dollars as well as *cruzeiros*.'

'Joszef, we can talk about such things another time, but we have little money, and a contribution from you would allow us to buy things we cannot grow or make ourselves. In the meantime, we'll provide you with a room, and also with your meals. Food is something we're never short of here. We grow our own vegetables, we keep hens, and the river, through God's good grace, provides plenty of fish and turtles. And, for sure, you will never want for a banana.'

'Thank you, Padre. But I think now I ought to tell you more specifically why I've come to Constância… in case you have any objection. It's true I'm a zoologist, but I've come to—'

'Joszef, you don't need to tell me why you came here. Your secret is out. I already know what you're planning to do.'

Joszef stiffened. He'd said nothing to anybody about his real reason for coming. Had there been a leak? That would mean danger. He wasn't sure how to handle this. 'You… already know?'

'Yes. Sister Vittoria heard about it from one of our newcomers. She's not at all happy, but there's no need for you to feel guilty. But please be as discreet as you can. I used to collect butterflies myself when I first came here. I'm sure the sisters would be appalled if they knew that. But it was a long time ago, when I was young. I gave it up years ago.'

Joszef breathed again. 'Butterflies. Ah, I see. Yes, that's what I wanted to tell you. In case you objected.' He waited for his head to clear. 'So, you used to collect butterflies? You don't anymore?'

'No, I stopped. Killing God's beautiful creatures used to upset people. I don't myself regard catching butterflies as a sin, but I'm sure you'll agree that it's undesirable to offend others gratuitously. So, Joszef, catch them if you must – and I know you've travelled a long way to get here.'

'Thank you. Padre, there's something I'd like to ask you. You told me you eat fish and turtles. That means someone has to catch them and kill them – God's beautiful creatures. So why aren't people offended by that?'

'Indeed, some people are. Some of us are vegetarian. But it's almost unavoidable to eat at least some meat and fish, especially in these parts – for the protein, you see. Just as it's unavoidable for the jaguar to eat the wild pig. God provides for all. And, speaking of eating, I think you're ready for your supper, yes? Then, you will sleep.'

Joszef picked up his rucksack. The director led him down a whitewashed corridor where several ceiling fans were doing their best to cool the air. Apart from a few framed pictures of saints and a row of low wooden benches lined up against the wall, there was little else.

'Is no one here, Padre? It's quiet.' He was wondering if there was any chance of catching sight of the man Wolfgang Müller had mentioned.

The director laughed. 'Yes, it's quiet. Most of our children are in bed – or they ought to be. Wait until morning. Then you'll find out how noisy they can be.'

He stopped in front of a brown-painted door and knocked gently. It was opened by a stout figure draped in a full-length brown cassock. He was obviously pleased to see Mazzanti and greeted him with a cheerful smile.

'Good evening, Padre.'

'Angelo,' said the director, 'I'd like you to meet Joszef. Joszef, this is *Clerico* Angelo.'

Angelo bowed slightly then shook Joszef's hand. He tried his best to speak in English. 'Good evening, Joszef. Welcome to our mission. You will be staying with us?'

The director answered for him. 'Joszef will be staying with us for some time, I think. Would you please be good enough to show him to our little guest room and arrange for him to have a meal. He's been travelling since early this morning.' Then he turned to Joszef. '*Clerico* Angelo has been with us for five years – nearly six now, isn't it, Angelo? He knows everything there is to know about this place, so he'll look after you. I'll say goodnight now. *Buon appetito* and sleep well.'

Joszef followed Angelo into a wide quadrangle. At the far end there was a collection of wooden shacks and on each side a low white-painted building. He pointed to one of them.

'That's where our boys sleep.' A few children were kicking a ball around in front of the building. Angelo waved his hands in the air and called out to them sharply. 'They are all supposed to be inside now, getting ready for bed. Some of the older ones can be difficult. This building on your left… that's where they have their lessons, and over there is the *cantina* where they eat their meals.'

'Are they all the children of local people? Indians? I mean… indigenous.'

'Most of our children are from the Tukano tribe, but we also have many who are of part-European ancestry, some more, some less. Mixed, you know.' The hem of his long cassock trailed on the ground as he walked, raising little clouds of dust. 'So, what do you think of our mission?' He spread out his arms and turned half a circle.

'It's bigger than you thought when you first saw it from the river, yes? Now, here's your room. I hope you'll be comfortable. I'll go arrange for your meal. Half an hour, okay? We'll meet again in the morning.'

The room was small. Next to the wall there was a narrow wooden bed with a mosquito net suspended on a string above it. Joszef pummelled the mattress with his fist. It felt hard and he could tell from the smell that it was stuffed with straw. On the mattress, neatly folded, were a thin cotton sheet and a small towel. There was also a pillow, without a pillowcase. A chair was tucked underneath a wooden table. A naked light bulb dangled on a wire from the ceiling, which made him wonder why they'd left him an oil lamp and a box of matches. He soon discovered the reason – the mission's generator was shut off each evening at eight o'clock.

It was getting dark by the time a small boy arrived and led him to the *cantina*. He pointed to a long wooden table where some food had been laid out, and looked at Joszef with a serious expression. '*Bom apetite, senhor,*' he said, then added, '*Boa noite, senhor.*'

As he left, Joszef called after him, '*Obrigado. Boa noite,*' then he sat down and surveyed his supper: a bowl of warm soup, cold meat of some kind, fried strips of manioc, two hunks of white bread, and bananas. He was hungry and savoured every mouthful. After he'd finished eating, he was overcome with weariness. He found his way back to his little room, undressed, lowered the mosquito net, and tucked himself under the sheet. Even the noise of the river didn't stop him from quickly dropping off.

*

He was woken in the morning by a gentle tapping on the door. He rubbed his eyes and yawned. Bright sunlight rebounded off the whitewashed walls and made him blink. It was unbearably hot and he was covered in sweat. The smell of damp straw drifted from his mattress. He realised he'd slept far longer than he'd intended. There was more tapping on the door.

'Come in,' Joszef called from his bed. He was only half awake.

The door opened a few inches and a boy's face appeared. '*Bom dia*,' the boy said. '*Café, senhor.*'

Joszef recognised him as the boy who'd shown him to his supper the previous evening. '*Bom dia* to you, too,' he replied. 'You please wait while I put on some clothes. *Obrigado.*'

He was surprised to discover that his shirt and trousers were as stiff as if they'd been starched. Yesterday's sweat had dried overnight, leaving his clothes encrusted with salt, a phenomenon he realised he'd have to get used to.

He followed the boy to a trestle table set up in the shade. The bitter black coffee was just what he needed, and there were bananas and bread.

Later, he walked down to the stretch of river just below the mission. A dozen women were wading in the shallows, doing their laundry and gossiping loudly. When they saw Joszef, they stopped what they were doing and stared. It occurred to him that they'd seldom, if ever, seen a young white man, at least not one whose body wasn't concealed by an ankle-length cassock. He wanted to show them what a friendly, good-natured fellow he was and gave them a cheery wave. This provoked a burst of laughter. After that, they ignored him and carried on with their washing.

He strolled along the riverbank until he found a more secluded spot, then took off his clothes. He washed them in the brownish water and left them to dry on a sun-warmed rock. He gazed at the smooth, slowly moving river then plunged in, naked. The water was deep and cool. He swam for a while, keeping close to the bank. He'd never been a good swimmer and knew the current would be stronger further out. Afterwards, he felt completely refreshed. His things were already dry. The sensation of dressing in clean clothes made him whoop with delight. It didn't cross his mind that they'd soon be saturated with his sweat again.

TWELVE

The director of the mission at Tapurucuara had been delighted to welcome the charming young American lady, the wildlife photographer who'd arrived on Friday's Catalina. He'd arranged for her to be put up in the sisters' quarters. Once installed, Klara had quickly made a point of befriending one particular individual, Sister Giovanna, a young woman of about her own age, originally from a village in the south of Italy. She seemed well informed about the people living in Tapurucuara, and Klara planned to take advantage of that in her search for the man Wolfgang Müller had mentioned. The one he'd described as "always arguing and possibly a bit mad".

The two of them were sitting on a bench just outside the mission's walls.

'Miss Klara, I think you must have taken some nice pictures with your camera, yes? Birds and animals?'

'A few fairly decent ones, but it's not easy. Animals don't pose for the camera like people do. You know, it would be great if I could get some photos of the children, and some of the older villagers as well. D'you think they'd mind?'

'Is okay with the children, but the older people are more... how you say... traditional. They believe camera steal their soul... you point camera at them, they cover face with hands, for protection.'

'Really? That would make it difficult, wouldn't it. Even trying to *talk* to the villagers is a problem because my Portuguese is so lousy. Do any of them speak English?'

She laughed. 'Some, yes, but even worse than me. We never get English people here. Oh! I'm sorry. Except you, of course... Oh! Sorry again. You are American, not English.' She tried to conceal her embarrassment with a giggle.

'And I suppose the same goes for French and German, and so on. Not very useful languages around here.'

'You speak French? I know one family from France here, but I think they speak mainly Portuguese now. German is different. Plenty people from Germany in village.'

Klara shut her eyes for a moment. She was doing her best to suppress her excitement, but even so, her heart rate must have risen by several points. 'That's interesting. I wonder how people from the outside, from all these different places, manage to fit in with the style of life here. It must be difficult. I'll bet I could write an article about that... maybe sell it to an American magazine. What d'you think?'

'I think is a wonderful idea. If you're interested, I can introduce you to young German I know. His name is Ernst. I don't know his family name. We don't get many visitors here, so he'd be glad to meet... how you say... a new face. If you're free tomorrow, maybe we go then, after chapel.'

*

Ernst's house was down by the river. The door was opened by a man of about forty, with strikingly dark eyes and long black hair tied in a ponytail. He scratched his head when he saw the two strangers. Sister Giovanna introduced herself.

'Of course!' he said, with a broad smile. 'Now I remember you. But all you sisters look alike in your uniforms. Hard to tell one from another.'

She eyed him sweetly. 'Is not a uniform. Is called a habit.'

'Excuse me. I meant to say your habit. And you, *senhorita*? Who are you? Certainly, you are not dressed like one of sisters. By the way, I am Ernst.'

'And I'm Klara. Hi. I'm from New York, USA,' she replied with a broad smile, stressing her American accent and hoping that neither Ernst nor anyone else in Tapurucuara would detect any trace of her German origins.

'Tell me, please, what do you two ladies want with me?'

'I'm a photographer,' Klara said. 'Wildlife. Birds and animals. That sort of thing. I flew in from Manaus a few days ago.'

'I see. You want to take pictures of the wildlife inside my house?' He grinned. 'Cockroaches mainly. Where you stay? At the mission?'

'They've put me up there. I'll be staying for a few more days.'

'Good. But nature photography is not the reason you came to see me, I hope.'

'How did you guess! No, I happened to mention to Sister Giovanna that I'm interested to learn how people coming from other parts of the world manage to settle down here in this isolated place. I'm thinking of writing an article about it. You know the sort of thing: a small community, how new arrivals fit in, the tropical climate, and so on.'

'Ah, I see. And you have chosen me for your article? I am honoured. Well, you better come inside.'

Klara was surprised to find herself in a comfortably furnished room. She took off her sunglasses. There were colourful rugs on the floor and rows of books on the window ledges.

'What a nice house, Ernst. By the way, you speak very good English. A lot better than my Portuguese, which is hopeless.'

'Thank you. I speak it okay. Ah, I get you both something to drink, yes? Beer? Something stronger perhaps? Schnapps?'

'Schnapps sounds good to me,' Klara said. 'I'm afraid they all seem to be teetotal at the mission.'

Sister Giovanna shook her head. 'Do you have a glass of water?'

Ernst was dressed only in a T-shirt and a pair of shorts and was padding around the room in bare feet. She found him interesting. He seemed to be a sociable character and she felt sure that if anyone would know about the other Germans living nearby, he would.

'That rifle I see in the corner there, is it your old German army gun?'

'No, not an army gun. A shotgun, for the jaguar. They prowl around at night looking for easy prey. Hens and pigs. Sometime, they eat our dogs as well. One or two gunshots scares them away. If I kill one, fine, because I get money for the skin.'

'Goodness! I hope I don't meet any of your jaguars. Ernst, your house is so neat and tidy. It makes me think you are not a family man.'

'Quite true. I live on my own.'

'Gee, that's a shame. You don't mind if I ask you why, do you? I mean… why you haven't married.'

'It would be nice, but I have not met anybody. The right woman, I suppose. Difficult here.'

'Perhaps one day then. Next question! I presume you were born in Germany?'

'Yes, I was. But you don't want to know about that, Miss Klara, do you? Not interesting.'

'But it's very interesting. Background stuff. Go on, tell me about it.'

'All right. Well, I live with parents in Leipzig, but then came the war, and after the war, life was difficult, especially under the Russians… Communists. I leave Leipzig and manage to get a job in Berlin – East Berlin, of course. Didn't suit me. I was lucky to cross border to the West. That was before they built the Wall.' He caught Klara's eye. 'But you don't take notes? You remember it, everything I tell you? You must have fantastic memory. Okay, then. I could stay in West Germany, but I have no money, and anyhow, I have enough of Europe. All my life was trouble there… and you never know what the Russians do next. Look what they did in Hungary in '56. Anywhere could be next. Czechoslovakia. Even West Berlin is not safe.'

'What? You really think so?'

'No one knows what the Russkies are planning, but nothing would surprise me. Anyhow, I work passage to Suriname on a Dutch cargo boat. I get into a bit of trouble in Paramaribo... but you don't want to know about that. I go down coast to Belém. Later, I take Amazon steamer to Manaus. Is okay so far? You can remember?'

She gave him an encouraging smile. 'Ah, Belém. I've been there. Big city. Didn't you like it?'

'No. Belém didn't suit me. Stuck it for a couple of years. Was enough.'

Sister Giovanna tried to stifle a yawn. 'I am sorry to interrupt. Is time for my nap and I must go back. Miss Klara, will you come with me, or will you stay here a bit longer?'

'I'm sorry you have to go, but I'd like to hear the rest of Ernst's story. Would you mind if I stayed?'

'No, not at all.' As they walked to the door, she whispered, 'Miss Klara, that was most interesting. You are good interviewer. Like a professional. I didn't know all that about him. We really know so little about our neighbours, don't we.'

For some reason, Klara felt more comfortable once Sister Giovanna had left. 'Gee, that's an amazing story, Ernst. What did you think of Manaus? Er... d'you think maybe we could have another schnapps before we go on?'

'Why not? Coming up!' He refilled their glasses. 'Did I like Manaus? Crowded, noisy place. I work in bakery there, save a few *cruzeiros*. Then I move here, five years ago. I like it here. I buy this house for peanuts. It was totally... what's the word... derelict, and here by the river is not best part of town. River people come and go. You never ask who is your neighbour, or what they are up to.'

'You've made it into a comfortable home.'

'Thank you. I'm good with hands. I earn money mending equipment, machinery… anything. Enough money to improve house like you see.'

'Ernst, do you miss Germany at all – the culture, the food?'

'You have been to Germany?'

Klara sidestepped the question. 'We had to learn a bit of German at school, in Brooklyn. I remember a few words. *Gute nacht… danke…prost…* and so on.'

'*Sehr gut, meine Fräulein*! I think there are many Germans living in New York, yes?'

'There sure are, and plenty of delicatessens serving German food.'

'So, you like German food?'

'Yes, I do. Well, most of it. Maybe not sauerkraut so much.'

'Not sauerkraut? That is pity. I make wonderful sauerkraut. You want try some? You change your mind if you taste.' She laughed and shook her head. He looked at the floor for a moment then turned to face her. 'Miss Klara, I hope you will not think me too much bold, but I have been thinking. There is birthday party soon.'

'Yours?'

'No, not mine. Friend of mine, Hermann. It has become a tradition. When one of us has a birthday, it's celebrated with all German families here. Is a lot of fun. Plenty good German food, all home-made.' He hesitated.

'Er, Miss Klara, how you feel about me taking you to party? I hope you will forgive me asking.'

Now, she thought, *at last I'm getting somewhere.* 'Sounds like a good party. German beer?'

'Sorry, no, but they ship in some good Brazilian stuff from brewery in Manaus.'

'Okay, why not. I'd love to go with you. But won't the others mind if you turn up with a complete stranger?'

Ernst's face lit up. 'No, not at all. They all will be delighted. Most of them speak at least a bit of English.'

'When is it, this party?'

'Let me think. Yes, Friday, in evening.'

'Friday? But that's so soon. And I've got nothing to wear. I'm living out of my rucksack.'

'Oh, Miss Klara! This is not New York. You wear anything. Some people come in their work clothes. Anyway, if you do not mind me saying so, you will look wonderful whatever you wear.'

She gave a little curtsey. 'Why, *danke schön, mein herr!*'

He laughed. 'Very good, Klara, very good indeed. And your pronunciation is excellent. You must have had good teacher in Brooklyn.'

*

By the time Friday evening arrived, Klara had everything worked out. Whatever might happen at the birthday party, no matter who may be there, she was ready. Ernst called for her at the mission and showered her with compliments about her appearance. She smiled to herself.

All she'd done was put on a pair of black slacks and a white cotton top, and touch of lipstick. As for Ernst, he'd obviously made a big effort, but on such a warm evening he must have been uncomfortable in his grey double-breasted suit. It looked like something he'd brought with him from East Germany.

The moon was half hidden behind dark clouds, and it looked as if a storm was brewing. The hut where the birthday party was being held was already crowded when they got there, with men, women and children jostling each other and making a terrific din. The space was poorly lit by oil lamps, and there was a strong smell of beer. Many of the guests seemed to be still in their work clothes. Ernst grabbed two large glasses of beer from the table and handed one to Klara. They laughed when both of them shouted '*Prost*' at the same time. With a mischievous wink, he sneaked a little bottle of something out of his pocket and poured a generous amount of it into their beers. Klara nodded her approval. As they pushed through the crowd, Ernst introduced her to some of his friends. One of them was Hermann, a big man wearing a plaid lumberjack shirt and baggy trousers. Klara raised her glass and wished him a happy birthday. Hermann thanked her politely, in English. Then, he climbed onto a chair and greeted his guests in German.

'*Guten Abend, meine Freunde!* Thank you for coming to my party. It's not the first time I've met you lot, is it.'

There were shouts of 'No. It bloody well isn't,' and everyone laughed loudly.

Ernst assumed that Klara could understand little of what was being said, so he diligently translated everything into English for her. He explained that their birthday celebrations always started like this, and all that shouting was a long-standing tradition.

Hermann continued. 'Okay. Let's get on with the party then, shall we. You've all got a beer? Okay!' He swung his glass high. '*Eins, zwei, drei, Prost!*' The room was filled with the clinking of glasses and a chorus of *Prosts*. '*Blutige hölle!*' he bellowed. 'I think you've guzzled most of the beer already and we've only just started. What will the neighbours think when they see you staggering back home dead drunk?' This provoked more laughter. 'And there's all this food for you. I don't want to see any of it left behind, uneaten. So, are we all here now?'

Someone shouted, 'No, old Ludwig hasn't got here yet.'

Ludwig! Klara shivered. Ludwig was Walther Schacht's middle name.

Hermann groaned theatrically and clasped his hand to his brow. 'Oh, I forgot about old Ludwig. He's always late for everything. He'll come in his own good time. Let's eat. It's his own fault if he's two beers and a sausage behind everybody else.' They all laughed again.

Klara turned to Ernst. 'Did I hear him mention someone called old Ludwig? What's so special about him?'

'Ah, Ludwig. Hasn't arrived yet. Strange old man. To tell you the truth, no one knows much about him. Doesn't get on well with rest of us.'

'Why?'

'They say he had some bad experiences during war. A bit of a mystery man. I don't think he's quite all there, if you know what I mean. Always picking arguments, for no reason at all. I don't think he has any real friends here.'

She gulped down most of her beer and took a deep breath. 'Ah, I see. Likes arguing, does he? That's so typical of old men, in my experience. Just how old *is* this old Ludwig?'

'I don't know… but is good question. I think maybe in his sixties, late sixties maybe, but I'm guessing.'

Late sixties! Walther Schacht was born in 1895. That would make him sixty-eight now. Her heart was pounding and her brain kept repeating *Schacht… Schacht… it's him*. For a second, she felt weak at the knees.

Ernst caught her by the shoulders to steady her. 'Hey! I think maybe you've had enough. Let's get some food. That's what you need.'

They heard a loud chuckle from Hermann. 'Well, here you are at last, Ludwig. Come on in then. Better late than never, eh?'

Ernst punctually explained in English that Ludwig had arrived.

Klara forced herself to remain calm. 'Oh, he finally came to join us, did he?' She sounded almost nonchalant. 'So, where is this old Ludwig?'

'I have not yet seen him. So many people. Wait a minute. This is Ludwig over there, sitting on his own. See what I mean? Not exactly everyone's favourite companion.'

Klara's heart beat faster. *So that's old Ludwig*, she was thinking. *There he is, sitting hunched on a chair by the wall, drinking his beer and looking on with disdain at the goings-on around him. He's chosen a dark corner for himself. Yes, he really could be the man in those photographs: SS-Gruppenführer Walther Ludwig Schacht. Now twenty years older, of course. Less hair than in his pictures, but the essential features look right – the shape of his head, his eyes, his ears.* She could feel the adrenaline pumping through her veins. That, combined with the schnapps-fortified beer, was affecting her in a way she didn't like. That old wobbly feeling came over her. She was aware that her thoughts were drifting backwards and forwards and round in circles, but she couldn't do anything about it. *Don't panic, don't panic.*

Ernst sensed that something was wrong. 'Klara, you don't look very well. Too much schnapps! You would like go outside for the fresh air? A little walk?'

'No. Please, Ernst. I'm fine. Really. But poor old Ludwig, sitting there all on his own. I feel sorry for him. What's the matter with him? He looks upset about something.'

'Please, don't worry about old Ludwig. I don't think anybody cares much about him. He's always like that. We all know how unpleasant he can be. Ha! How you like to interview *him* for your magazine?'

'Hmm... yes, why not? It might be interesting. Shall we?'

'Oh, come on, Klara. I only joke.'

'No, I'm serious. His story would make a good contrast to the others.'

She looked at Ludwig again. At last, here he was, the bastard responsible for the murder of her family. The monster who'd once wielded immense power as one of Hitler's top henchmen, now a lonely, mixed-up old man, spending his remaining miserable years here, in the middle of nowhere.

The light wasn't good and she needed to get a better look at him. She took a firm hold of Ernst's hand. He tried to resist, but she pulled him over to where Ludwig was sitting.

'Introduce me,' she whispered.

'No!'

'Yes!'

'No!'

'Yes, go on!'

Ernst gritted his teeth and spoke to Ludwig in German. 'Ah, Ludwig. Good evening. It's nice to see you again. Enjoying the party?'

Ludwig scowled. 'Who is it? Oh, it's you. What do you want? Leave me alone, can't you. I just want to drink my beer.'

Klara was surprised at his grouchy response, but Ernst wasn't deterred. 'Ludwig, I want to introduce you to my new friend, Miss Klara here. She's an American. She's a wildlife photographer. Takes pictures of animals.'

'An American? What the hell is she doing here at Hermann's birthday party? What the fuck does she want with us? Tell her there are no wild beasts to photograph in here.' He turned away and continued to drink his beer.

'She's with me. I brought her. I invited her. She's staying at the mission.'

'Then take her back to the fucking mission.'

Ernst's English translation for Klara was a bit more diplomatic. 'I'm afraid he's not feeling very well, but he says welcome. Okay? Enough. Now we go. We get another beer, yes?'

Klara forced herself to smile. 'Ernst, it's nice of him to be so welcoming.' Then she addressed Ludwig directly, in English. 'I'm very glad to meet you, Ludwig. Aren't you feeling well?'

Ernst grudgingly translated this into German.

Ludwig's face turned red. 'You tell her it's none of her fucking business. What the hell does she care how I'm feeling? Get rid of the woman. Tell her to get the fuck out of here.'

Klara was incensed. She struggled to stop herself from yelling back at him in German. Ernst couldn't hide his embarrassment as he gave Klara a fake translation: 'Ludwig said thank you for your kind consideration. Something like that. Anyway, that's as good as I can translate what he said.' He grasped Klara's hand. 'Can we go now? I have more than enough of old Ludwig.'

'No. I think something's troubling him. Let's sit down and talk to him for a bit.'

'Klara, please, no.'

She peered into Ludwig's eyes and sat down. She was about to say something when, in a sudden movement, he swung round to face her and yelled at her in English. 'Why in God's name can't you leave me alone, you bitch. Just leave me alone. Go back to your fucking America!'

For a moment, she thought he was going to throw his beer over her. Everyone turned to look. Ludwig spluttered, stamped his feet on the floor, and stood up. Klara jumped up too and stared after him as he hobbled through the crowd to the other side of the room, still clasping his beer. The last thing she heard him say was, 'I don't know why I came to this fucking party. To hell with the lot of you.'

She was shaking and breathing rapidly. She leant on the wall for support. Ernst grasped both her shoulders and looked into her eyes. 'Klara, are you all right? That was horrible.'

'Well, that was really something, wasn't it. But I'm okay. Don't worry, I'll be fine. Give me that little bottle of yours.'

He took the bottle from his pocket and handed it to her. 'Here, you better finish this. I did my best to warn you about old Ludwig. I'm sorry. You should have listened to me.'

'He was so rude, your Ludwig, shouting at me like that. Gave me quite a shock.'

But that wasn't it at all. In one split second, it had become as clear as daylight that old Ludwig wasn't Walther Schacht. He couldn't possibly be. It was when Klara saw him on his feet. He'd towered above her when he'd stood up. He was well over six feet. She remembered that Schacht's height was five feet eight inches, about the same as hers. Some men shrink a bit as they age, but no one ever gets taller.

By the time she and Ernst left the party, the storm had broken. They walked by the river in the rain. The air was warm and smelled of damp earth, and she found the raindrops too were warm when they landed on her skin.

THIRTEEN

'*Senhor*, what sort fish you catch with net like that?'

Joszef had been strolling by the river with his butterfly net, ruminating about the futility of looking for Walther Schacht. He hadn't come across anybody with a German background at Constância, either at the mission or in the village, and was thinking of contacting Klara to tell her there was no point in his staying there any longer.

The man who'd asked him the question introduced himself as Félix, the village's telegraphist. The buttons on his khaki shirt had been left undone, and he seemed happy to parade about with his prominent beer belly exposed for all to see. He scratched his head and laughed loudly when Joszef explained what his net was for. 'Really? You joke, no? What you do with butterfly? Why anyone want catch butterfly?'

'Many reasons. For one thing, they are beautiful.'

'You think? Well, maybe. For me, it's tropical fish. I breed them. Now *they* are beautiful. You interested in fish as well as butterfly?'

'Sure. I'm interested in many things.'

'Really? Then you come look at my beautiful fish, yes?' He gestured towards the opposite bank of the river. 'Over there, my little farm. I go there just now.' He pointed to a canoe tied to a post driven into the mud. 'How about you come with me if you want? I show. Okay, you sit in front of me in canoe.'

It turned out to be hardly a farm. Just a fenced-off field where the bush had been cleared, inhabited by a few pigs, a couple of goats and a gang of hyperactive hens who followed Félix around, pecking at his boots. He jangled a bunch of keys, chose one to unlock the door of a wooden shed, and ushered Joszef inside. A large glass tank supported by four empty beer crates contained an army of tiny fish. Dense swarms of them created swirls of iridescent blue every time the shoal changed direction.

'See what I mean?' Félix grinned. 'Very nice, yes? Beautiful, yes? *Tetrazes-neon*. You look. Make yourself at home. But now you please excuse me. I have to do something. Not long.'

The fishes' manoeuvres held Joszef's attention for a few minutes, then his gaze fell on a pile of books lying on a table. He picked one up at random, an old dog-eared paperback. The text was in Portuguese. It appeared to be some sort of thriller or detective story. He picked up another, in a similar genre. He was about to return to the fish tank when he noticed a book lying on the floor. He didn't know whether he'd accidentally knocked it off the table or whether it had been there all the time. He bent down to get it. On the book's cover was a picture of a familiar-looking character wearing a tweed cape and a peaked cap, whom he instantly recognised as Sherlock

Holmes, one of his boyhood heroes. He glanced at the book again and caught his breath when he saw the title: *Der Hund von Baskerville*. A quick flip through the pages confirmed it was a German translation of the famous story.

Félix, who'd been busy shovelling grain into a sack, looked at him for a second and stopped what he was doing. '*Senhor*, we go back now. All done here.'

Joszef put the book down. 'Okay.' He sneaked a glance at some of the other books. Sure enough, several of them were in German. He wondered what that meant. Possibly nothing. Possibly something.

Félix became insistent. '*Senhor, senhor*. I said we must go.'

'All right, I'm ready.'

As they walked down to the river, Joszef said, 'What a nice little farm, and I'm impressed with your amazing fish. Thanks for showing me, Félix. You come here a lot?'

'Yes, of course I come here a lot.' He seemed agitated. 'You think the animals look after themselves?'

'No, no. You are right… your collection of fish… beautiful. And your collection of detective novels. It's a pity they're all in Portuguese because I would have liked to borrow a few.'

'Yes, I don't suppose you read Portuguese very well, do you?'

'I'd have enjoyed that Sherlock Holmes one, but it was in German and I can't read German. Can you?'

That stopped Félix in his tracks. 'One of the books in German? Really? You are sure? I suppose is possible. No idea where those old books come from. I think books there when I buy farm.'

'Oh, I see.' Joszef felt certain Félix was hiding something. Could it be that someone in Constância, someone who could read German, was in the habit of visiting the little farm from time to time, relaxing there with a collection of detective stories? Walther Schacht, for instance? It would be an ideal place for him to hide whenever an outsider was visiting the mission. But that was just a supposition.

*

Twice a day, the padres paraded around the compound together chanting in Latin. That afternoon, Joszef made a point of watching the procession. When the parade was over, he made sure he caught the director's eye. He was wondering whether Mazzanti would be able to throw some light on the telegraphist and his German detective stories.

Mazzanti greeted him with a warm smile. 'Good afternoon, Joszef. How are you getting on? What luck with the butterfly hunting?'

'Thank you for asking, Padre. Plenty of interesting butterflies, but I still haven't caught the sort I really want – those big blue morphos.'

'Ah, morphos, those flying jewels, the most beautiful butterflies in the world. Not the easiest to catch. So, you must tell me what you've been up to. Why don't we go to my study and we'll have a cup of coffee.'

Joszef wasn't surprised to find the director's office a modest affair. There was a desk, a brown-painted cupboard, a few chairs, a couple of shelves loaded with books, and various items of religious paraphernalia.

'Tell me, Padre, when you collected butterflies, did you ever catch a morpho?'

'Yes, of course I did. Several different species.'

'That must have been satisfying. What about the wonderful red one? The sunset morpho. Did you ever catch one of those?'

'Ah, that one! The colours of God's glorious sunset. *Morpho hecuba*, if I remember correctly. I'm afraid not. I don't think they live in this part of the forest.'

'You know, I think hunting butterflies, chasing them, catching them in your net, is the most exciting thing about collecting them. Once they're dead and pinned in a glass case, they lose a lot of their interest.'

'I have to agree with you. I remember visiting a famous museum in Milan. They had a wonderful collection of everything. All God's creatures, great and small – skinned, stuffed, dried and pickled. It was very interesting, but it told me nothing about how these creatures live and what they do to enjoy this wonderful world.' He opened the door and muttered something to someone in the corridor, then closed the door again. 'Our coffee will be here in a few minutes.'

'Thank you. A cup of coffee would be nice.'

'You know, Joszef, you must be careful when you go butterfly hunting in the jungle. You have to watch out. Wild pigs – you're in serious trouble if a group of those attacks you. They can do a lot of damage. And poisonous snakes.'

'But I thought there weren't any dangerous snakes around here.'

Mazzanti laughed. 'Who told you that? There are plenty. Let me tell you something. Last year, one of our

Indians was bitten on the foot. They brought him to me, hoping that by some miracle my prayers to God would cure him. But it was too late. The poor man's leg had decayed to the bone and had to be amputated. We still see him now and again. He gets around quite well, hobbling on his wooden leg.'

'That's a bit scary. I'll be careful. But on a different subject, I love reading and I've been wondering if you've got any books here written in English. All the ones I've found so far are in Portuguese or German. I can't read either.'

A boy brought in a tray with coffee and a few bread rolls. Mazzanti thought for a moment. 'You know, I don't think I've seen any English books here, but leave it with me and I'll see what I can find. You say you've come across some books written in German? That's interesting. And surprising. I've never thought of Otto as someone who would spend much time with a book.'

Joszef could feel his heart beating. Otto! With some difficulty, he managed to remain calm. 'I don't think I've met Otto.' He was watching Mazzanti closely as he poured the coffee. The director seemed less confident than he'd been a moment before, possibly a bit nervous.

'He's generally here for most of the time,' Mazzanti explained, 'but he's away at present, visiting one of his friends. He has a canoe. Sometimes, he stays away for two or three weeks.'

'I see. Sounds like an interesting character.'

'No, not really. Otto's just our handyman. German. Er... could be Austrian, I suppose. Came to us several years ago, looking for work.'

'Do you know what he did before he came here?'

'Told us he'd been a rubber tapper. We always call him Otto. He's never told us what his real name is, and he seems quite happy for us to use his nickname.' He quickly drank the last dregs of coffee from his cup.

It wasn't easy for Joszef to keep up the pretence of being only vaguely interested, but somehow he managed it.

Mazzanti continued. 'We're lucky to have Otto with us here. He's strong and does all sorts of jobs around the mission. Not the most charming character, but he works well and keeps our children in line.' He laughed. 'He orders them about like a *sergente maggiore*. Er... a sergeant major. You've finished your coffee, have you?'

'Yes, Padre, I have.' He wondered why the director had found it necessary to give him this lengthy justification for employing Otto. 'Maybe I'll meet your handyman when he returns.'

Mazzanti stood up and smiled. 'You're sure to. But I don't think you'll find him very interesting, or all that pleasant, to be honest.'

Joszef also stood up. He thought otherwise. Otto might turn out to be extremely interesting. It was now a matter of sitting tight and awaiting his return. 'Thank you for the coffee, Padre. I enjoyed our chat.'

Mazzanti was no longer smiling. 'Joszef, please remember what I said when we were talking about hunting butterflies. There are many dangers around here, so please be careful.'

'Thank you for the warning, Padre. Don't worry, I'll be careful.'

FOURTEEN

The verbena bushes growing on the hillside behind the mission were attracting a continuous succession of visitors: hummingbirds. They hovered in the air on almost invisible wings as they sucked nectar from the blossoms. Joszef made several attempts to catch one in his net and eventually succeeded. His captive was so tiny that it might have been mistaken for a large moth. Its wings were paper-thin and its body was clad in miniature feathers of iridescent ruby and emerald, arranged like the overlapping scales on a goldfish. Joszef felt sure the children at the mission would be interested and hurried back down the hill with the hummingbird still trapped in his net. He spotted a group of boys at the far end of the mission compound and started to walk over to them. Then, he saw one of the padres coming towards him, an old man, walking slowly with the aid of a stick.

The man called out to him. 'You. Yes, you, boy. Wait.' He shuffled closer, wheezing, and pointed with his stick at Joszef's net. 'What have you got in there? Is it a butterfly? I know you've been catching butterflies and killing them.'

Joszef was taken aback by the padre's tone. 'No, not a butterfly.'

'Don't lie to me, boy. Of course it is. Butterflies may be small and helpless but they were created by God and fulfil an important purpose in His plan. It is wicked of you to kill them. They feel the pain, and so does God. Don't you know that? You are a very wicked boy and one day you will be punished for what you are doing.'

Joszef glared at him. 'God created everything, didn't he, Padre? Even the tiny stinging ants you stamp into the ground every time you walk. It's not just the pretty things like butterflies. Mosquitoes. Your God created those too, didn't he? Doesn't he care when they bite innocent children and give them malaria? What about fleas... germs... viruses like polio. Perhaps those were his mistakes?'

The padre's face had turned purple. He was shaking. 'How dare you say such things. It is downright blasphemy. You will surely go to Hell. Who are you to question the Almighty's plan? And you talk of innocent children. Children are *not* innocent. Every one of them is born tainted by Original Sin. How ignorant you are of God's ways. You are wicked and arrogant. You have the Devil inside you and you are doing his work.'

Joszef said nothing more. What would be the point? The old man turned around and ambled back the way he'd come, mumbling under his breath. Joszef felt a pang of remorse for the way he'd handled things. He shouldn't have behaved like that. After all, the padre was only saying what he truly believed, however misguided. Why had he behaved so badly? He knew why. He disliked being referred to as a boy. Immature. Not a grown man. That's what had upset him. It always did.

He remembered the hummingbird in his net and hurried towards the crowd of children. He'd assumed they were on their own, but now he could see they were gathered around an elderly man sitting on an upturned metal bucket. A white man, but not one of the padres. He was wearing a ragged grey shirt and a pair of faded brown trousers, and black leather boots. Boots, in this heat! He had half of a huge jackfruit balanced on his lap. Joszef could smell its sickly sweetness from several metres away. Flies swarmed around it. The man was feeding the boys with chunks of its sticky flesh, which he gouged out with a knife. The children were unusually noisy. Joszef couldn't understand what they were saying. Then, one of them stretched out his hand and shouted, '*Mais, por favour. Otto! Otto! Mais pra mim.*'

Joszef caught his breath. He dropped his net and the hummingbird darted to freedom. So, this was Otto, the mission's handyman. He'd returned.

They were so busy with the jackfruit that neither the children nor Otto had noticed Joszef. Then, something made Otto look up and their eyes met. Joszef panicked. He wasn't ready for any direct contact so he picked up his net, turned round, and walked away. He was beside himself with excitement. Could this scruffy worker actually be Walther Schacht, the elusive monster sought by secret agents for the past twenty years? His appearance had a lot in common with Klara's old photographs – at least, as far as he could remember them. True, he looked older. His hair was grey and his cheeks were covered in at least a week's growth of stubble, and he had a prominent belly. But wasn't all that to be expected of someone who'd aged twenty years?

He wasn't sure what he ought to do and wandered back to his room. Lying on his bed, staring at the light bulb hanging on its wire, he began to wonder if he could be mistaken in his assumption about Otto's identity. He admitted to himself that he *wanted* this man they called Otto to be Walther Schacht. What a fantastic discovery that would be! But that didn't mean he *was*. He seemed like a miserable, pathetic character, not someone who could have had any influence on such a headstrong madman as Adolf Hitler, or take pleasure in organising the atrocities Schacht was credited with. How could this wreck of a human being, with such a menial job, wearing clothes which were virtually rags, be that same arrogant official who'd once stood in his smart uniform at Hitler's side? Maybe he was just someone who'd fallen on hard times and had been fortunate enough to find work and friendship at the mission. On the other hand, wouldn't Walther Schacht, who knew he'd face the hangman's noose if he were discovered, be prepared to put up with *anything* to remain hidden? There was only one thing to do. He'd have to get closer to Otto and find out what sort of a person he really was. But how could he do that without arousing his suspicion?

Another thing worried him. If Otto was a meek lost soul, there would be no problem, but what if he was a dangerous psychopath, ready to lash out if he was cornered? These thoughts bothered him for the rest of the day and kept him awake for most of the night.

The next day, Joszef did his best to keep out of Otto's way. He watched from a safe distance as the handyman shepherded the mission children into the *cantina* at mealtimes and into the schoolroom when it was time for their lessons. The children seemed to like him and looked entirely happy to be guided by him, and by all appearances he liked them. He wondered again if this man could really be the notorious Walther Schacht. And there was something else. Even if he *was* Schacht, was it possible that over the years he'd reformed and somehow managed to put his past behind him and was now doing whatever he could to redeem himself? Perhaps during his self-exile he'd undergone some sort of transformation… a spiritual metamorphosis. This possibility worried Joszef. It raised ethical and practical issues he couldn't get his head around. If Schacht was indeed a penitent, intent on doing good deeds, wouldn't it be unjust to punish him for the crimes he'd committed when, to all intents and purposes, he was a different person? He couldn't figure that one out.

*

Joszef observed that when Otto had finished his work, he'd usually return to his shack at the far end of the compound. He'd spend hours sitting on a chair outside, sometimes sleeping but more often gazing into the distance, mumbling to himself, apparently daydreaming. It was at such a time that Joszef decided to approach him.

Otto must have sensed his arrival, because he instantly snapped out of his dreamlike state and fixed him with a stare. '*Quem é você? O que você quer?*' he asked. The lack of any response told him that the young man didn't understand Portuguese. He continued in English. 'So, it's you, is it? I've seen you watching me. What do you want?'

Joszef managed to force a smile. 'I wanted to say hello, *senhor*, because we haven't met before. I believe it's the polite thing to do. My name is Joszef.'

The handyman grunted, stretched, yawned, and grunted again. 'I see. Well, hello, Joszef. It's nice to see a fresh face. Tell me, what you are doing here in Constância? You are training to be a priest?'

'No, nothing like that. I've come here to collect butterflies.'

'Butterflies? Oh yes. You had a net with you when I first saw you, didn't you.'

'That's true. I often take it with me. You never know when something worth catching may turn up.'

'Very wise. You're having some good luck, I hope? I must agree with you that some of the butterflies around here are beautiful. You are professional with butterflies? You sell them? Your business?'

'No. Just a hobby.'

'An unusual hobby. Have you managed to catch anything special? You know, to make your expedition a success? You must have come a long way to get here. From the United States, yes?'

'Actually, all the way from England.'

'Then I hope you find what you came for. Look, let me get you a beer. I don't often get to meet people from other places. We have a drink and a nice talk, yes?'

'Beer? Where can you get a beer around here? I thought alcohol wasn't allowed in the mission.'

'Don't worry, I have plenty bottles inside. Wait, I get. Then you tell me all about yourself. You can call me Otto.'

A strange feeling came over Joszef. He was finding it hard to coordinate his thoughts with his actions. He felt as if he was on autopilot. Had he really just agreed to have a casual drink with a mass murderer? Oh, come on! Who said Otto was Walther Schacht? It was just a hunch. This guy seemed perfectly okay. Anyway, it was a good opportunity to find out more.

Otto emerged from his shack with a bottle of beer in each hand and gave one to Joszef. 'Let's sit in the shade over there,' he said.

He started off by enquiring about Joszef's background and wanted to know what life was like in London, and in Europe more broadly. Soon, he began to ask questions about how the Russians were behaving in those parts of Europe they now occupied. Inevitably, the conversation turned to the matter of a divided Germany. For a few seconds, he listened quietly to what Joszef was telling him, then, without warning, he leapt to his feet and screamed, '*Scheiskommunisten!* Fuck them, fuck them all!' and hurled his half-empty beer bottle with all his force against the trunk of a nearby tree. He stared at the tree as if he couldn't understand why the blow hadn't knocked it down, then shrugged his shoulders and sat down again, looking embarrassed.

'Sorry, Joszef. I don't know what came over me. I'm getting tired. You let me rest, okay? We speak again tomorrow if you like.' His eyelids were beginning to droop. He was slipping back into dreamland.

Joszef didn't know what to think. On the face of it, Otto seemed like a normal, friendly character. Polite. Civilised… apart from that single outburst. But what did that say about his true identity? Nothing. No progress on that score. Otto had said little about his own background, other than what Mazzanti had already told him. There was only one thing to do. Catch him off guard. Provoke him into saying more than he intended. That could be risky, but it was worth trying

'*Senhor* Otto,' Joszef called out. There was no reaction. He raised his voice a couple of notches. '*Senhor!*'

'What is it? Oh, you again. Can't you see I'm trying to rest? I'm tired. The padres make me work very hard. Me, an old man of sixty-eight. They don't care a fuck about me. Please, you leave me now. Go and have your supper. We talk again tomorrow.'

Joszef flinched. Jesus! Didn't Klara once tell him that Schacht would be sixty-eight now? 'Goodness, Otto! Sixty-eight. You should be enjoying your retirement, not working.'

'Ha, enjoying my retirement! You make a good joke.'

'Maybe we can have another beer, yes? I like talking to you.'

'Not now, I need to rest. You go away now. I see you tomorrow.'

'But, Otto, I just want to be sociable.'

'Sociable? Why you want to be sociable with me? Go and be sociable with the fucking padres. I'm just the *heimwerker* around here, the handyman, the dogsbody.

And I'm tired. *Hau ab!* Go away!' He growled something unintelligible then closed his eyes again.

Joszef didn't go away. He took a good look at Otto. His hands were big and rough, like a labourer's, and his neck was short and thick. The mat of grey stubble that covered his unshaven face had trapped little globules of sweat; they glinted in the late-afternoon sun like the scales on a dead fish.

Otto's eyes flicked open. Black eyes, like a shark's.

'You still here? I told you go away. Leave me alone. Are you a fucking idiot or something? Didn't you hear me, you fucking Engländer?'

Joszef was shocked by Otto's sudden change of tone, but he stood his ground.

'What's the matter with you, Otto? Why you are talking like that? Are you ill, or have you gone crazy?'

That was too much. Otto bellowed something incomprehensible, got up from his chair again, and pushed his huge bristly face close to Joszef's.

'No, I'm not crazy. You want to know what's the matter with me, do you, Engländer? I tell you.' He was breathing hard and looked unsteady, as if he was about to fall over. He started to say something but stopped. His eyes flickered upwards and, for a moment, only the bloodshot whites were visible, like the eyes of a prize fighter struck on the chin by a knockout blow. He started to mumble something and for a while seemed to be sliding into a different world. Then, his eyes fixed on Joszef, he delivered a ranting monologue, blustering on for ages in German, occasionally punctuating his diatribe with a malicious laugh. At one point, he grabbed

Joszef by the shoulder, perhaps just to steady himself, but Joszef instinctively wriggled free and took a couple of steps backwards. He was able to understand little of what Otto was going on about, but he recognised a few words, like *Reich* and *Führer*, both of which he heard over and over again, but he could only guess at the context. His provocation had evidently ignited some sort of violent political tirade which must have been smouldering in Otto's head for a long time.

The rant came to an abrupt end. Otto appeared to have exhausted himself and was now sitting in his chair, apparently asleep, with his head slumped forward, his bristly chin resting on a sweaty collarbone. Joszef was shaking, but he'd succeeded in getting the mission's handyman to show his true colours. He walked slowly back to his room.

It took quite a time for Joszef to regain his mental balance. Two things were clear. First, Otto was some sort of Nazi. No doubt about that. Second, there was no reason to believe, at least at this stage, that Otto *wasn't* Walther Schacht. But still, it would be a mistake to get Klara's contacts in New York to start the ball rolling without being certain. What he needed to do was to get Klara to come to Constância to check out the handyman for herself. She understood German and would be able to pry more out of him than he could.

He decided to send a telegram to her at the Tapurucuara mission. He'd already made the acquaintance of the local telegraphist, Félix. He didn't fully trust him – those German-language books he'd spotted at his farm across the river hinted that he may be a friend of Otto's –

but there was no other way of contacting Klara. He'd have to take a chance. He'd word the telegram so it looked like an innocent message between friends. He knew she'd be able to fathom its real meaning.

*

Félix was surprised when Joszef walked into his ramshackle office in the village. 'Ah, it's you, the butterfly catcher. *Bom dia*. How I can help you? And how is your butterfly hunting?'

'*Bom dia*, Félix. That's what I wanted to talk to you about. Butterflies.'

'Me? Really? You joke, no? I know nothing about butterfly. *Nada*. You manage to catch big blue one you look for?'

'Afraid not, but I'll keep trying. Now I have a new challenge. I think yesterday I saw a very rare butterfly, a red one. A big one. I only saw it from a distance. I wonder whether you've noticed any butterflies like that around here. Maybe when you're visiting your farm?'

'No. I've got plenty else to do at my farm. But I can look if is important for you.'

'I'd really appreciate that, Félix. I'm dying to tell my friend about it. She's a wildlife photographer, and she specialises in photos of butterflies. She's staying at the mission in Tapurucuara at the moment. Supposed to be joining me here, but she's been sick with malaria.'

The telegraphist raised his eyebrows. 'Malaria. Sorry to hear that. Is plenty malaria here, all along river. Is bad. Some die. But for sure the sisters at Tapurucuara have good treatment for your friend. Quinine, something like that. Make her better.'

'I hope so. I don't suppose you can contact Tapurucuara by telegraph from here, can you, Félix? Too far away?'

Félix laughed. 'Too far away! That is funny. You joke, no? Yes, of course I can. I can telegraph most places along river. And much, much further. Anywhere in the world. I easily send telegram to your lady friend if you want.'

'Really? That would be nice.'

'No problem. Easy. Very quick. You tell me what you want to say.'

'Okay. Shall I tell you now? Let me see. *To Klara at Tapurucuara mission.* Er... *I miss you.* Er... *I hope your malaria is getting better.* Hang on a second. Let me think. *Exciting butterflies here at Constância... I think big red butterfly we look for but need you to identify species.* Er... wait, there's more. *Please join me here as soon as you are well enough to travel.* How does that sound, Félix? Is it okay? Please, sign it Joszef.'

'As good as done. Telegraphist at Tapurucuara is good friend. He make sure is delivered to your Klara very quick.'

'That's good. How much do I owe you?'

'Don't worry. Is on the house. Come back if you expect answer. And good luck with red butterfly.'

FIFTEEN

Klara had no difficulty in interpreting Joszef's telegram. She was excited by the news and was finding it hard to think about anything else. At last, some real progress – unless it was another false alarm like her encounter with old Ludwig.

She asked the telegraphist at Tapurucuara to send a reply:

TO JOSZEF POGANYI – STOP – MALARIA GETTING BETTER – STOP – FINISHED MY PHOTOGRAPHY HERE – STOP – WILL COME TO CONSTÂNCIA AS SOON AS POSSIBLE – STOP – NO PLANE UPRIVER FOR 3-4 WEEKS SO WILL TAKE RIVERBOAT – STOP – LOOK AFTER YOURSELF – STOP – KLARA

She decided it was important to keep Eduardo up to date about Joszef's news, in case he needed to make some early preparations, even though at this stage nothing was certain. What Eduardo decided to do with the information – if anything – would be his decision, not hers. She recalled the warning she'd received at that meeting in New York about the possibility that Schacht's minders had ways of intercepting Eduardo's communications. That was just conjecture, but even so… She screwed up her eyes to help her think. Lily! That's it! They wouldn't be watching her roommate. She'd send a telegram to her at the Carmine Street apartment. No, two telegrams. The first, addressed to Miss Lily Wang, would explain that she'd shortly be receiving a second telegram, addressed to Miss Lily Ed Wang. She must immediately take the second one, unopened, to a man called Eduardo at the art gallery on 89th Street.

Klara worded the second telegram cautiously:

DEAR EDUARDO – STOP – BUTTERFLY HUNTER THINKS FOUND BIG RED BUTTERFLY AT CONSTÂNCIA ON RIVER NEGRO – STOP – SOUNDS PROMISING BUT I NEED TO CHECK EXACT SPECIES – STOP – I LEAVE TAPURUCUARA ASAP TO JOIN HIM AT CONSTÂNCIA – STOP – KLARA

*

Joszef was relieved when he collected Klara's reply from Félix. Until then, he'd half suspected that his message may not reach her. Now, he was full of smiles. It would be wonderful to see her again. Together, they'd act quickly and come to a definitive conclusion about Otto's identity. They'd inform New York, then their role in all this would be finished and they'd go back to civilisation. But wait. What if Klara concluded that he wasn't Walther Schacht after all? They'd be committed to looking further afield. He wasn't too happy about that. But that was in the future. As far as the present was concerned, he'd have to be careful not to arouse Otto's suspicions while awaiting Klara's arrival.

*

Félix was worried. He'd been thinking about Joszef's message to Klara, and what she'd said in her reply. Something didn't look right. All this fuss about butterflies. Did it make any sense? Joszef's lady friend, still recovering from malaria, was coming all the way from Tapurucuara on a slow riverboat just to photograph butterflies. He knew those old riverboats. You wouldn't want to travel on one even if you were in the best of health. It didn't ring true. And why had Joszef been so interested in those German-language books when he'd visited the farm? Otto! Could all this be connected with Otto? If so, the repercussions could be grave.

He sent one of the village boys running to Otto's shack to ask him to come over as soon as he could. Otto lost no time in getting there, and it took him no more than a few seconds to interpret Joszef's telegraphed message, and Klara's reply.

'*Dummkopf! Kompletter vollidiot!* You imbecile! Even a fool with the brain of a cockroach would know what this means. He stamped his heavy boots on the wooden floor and cursed like a madman. 'Do you know who is the big red butterfly? It's *me*! Those two *Schweinhunde* want to catch *me*. You fucking idiot. They're hunting *me*, not butterflies.' He gave Félix a heavy thump on the back with his clenched fist.

Félix was shaking. 'Otto... I am very sorry. I make big mistake. But how was I to know? The Britisher tricked me. Otto, forgive me, I beg you.' He bowed his head and clasped his hands together.

'That fucking Engländer! I knew he was up to no good. I'll deal with the bastard myself. But this woman friend of his, this Klara bitch. You find out more about her, yes? You make enquiries. You know who to contact. She may have already told her people everything. They'll come for me, from wherever they are, and the game's up. Listen carefully, Félix. No more mistakes. You must warn our telegraphist friend at Tapurucuara and tell him he must not under any circumstances send any more of that fucking bitch's telegrams to anybody, anywhere. None. You understand? And tell him that whatever he's already transmitted for her, he must send a copy of every message to you, *immediately*, so I can read them.'

'But, Otto—'

'You understand me? Do it now. *Schnell!*' He paused. His mouth curved into a twisted smile and he rubbed his hands together. 'So, *mein* Klara, you're coming to Constância, are you? Don't worry. I'll be waiting for you.' His eyes narrowed as he turned back to Félix. 'As for you, you are in great trouble. You should pray that your mistakes can be rectified. You may yet redeem yourself. If not... we shall see. You're becoming something of a liability, my friend.'

SIXTEEN

Lily Wang was roused out of her dreams by the ringing of the doorbell. She swore under her breath as she wriggled herself into her dressing gown. 'Okay, okay, I'm coming.'

A young man in Western Union uniform was at the door. 'Good morning, ma'am. Telegram for Miss Lily Wang.'

'So darned early in the morning?'

'It may be urgent, ma'am. I sure hope it ain't bad news.'

She thanked him and ambled back to her room. She sat on the edge of the bed then sliced open the envelope with her fingernail. A happy smile crossed her face when she saw the telegram was from Klara in South America. But the smile didn't last long. There was no cheerful greeting or news about her travels, just a puzzling request… actually, an instruction. It told her to wait for a second telegram to arrive, addressed to Miss Lily Ed Wang, then to drop everything and rush with it, unopened, to someone called Eduardo at a gallery just off Fifth Avenue, on 89th Street. What was that all about? It didn't make any sense. The message was headed "important and urgent", so she'd have to do it.

She dressed quickly, downed a mug of coffee, and waited. She leafed through a few magazines and waited some more.

The telephone rang. It was a man's voice. 'Good morning. I'm calling from Greenwich Village Western Union office. We got a telegram for a Miss Edwang. Is that you?'

'Who?'

'Sorry, my mistake. Miss Lily Ed Wang. Carmine Street.'

'Oh… er… yeah, that's me.'

'Sorry, I got no one here to deliver. Can ya come and collect? Sorry, ma'am.'

'You serious? No one to deliver? Jesus Christ! Okay, I suppose I can collect. Give me the address, will you.'

It was raining heavily. Fortunately, the telegraph office wasn't far from Carmine Street. When she got there, she had to squeeze past several people sheltering in the doorway. One of them, in a crumpled raincoat, took a half-smoked cigarette out of his mouth and tossed it into the street. Lily threw him a look of disgust, mumbled something about the Village going to the dogs, then hurried inside. The woman at the counter asked for her ID, examined it, then handed her the telegram. She slipped it into her handbag.

Back in the street, she hailed a passing Yellow Cab. 'Fifth and 89th, please.'

By the time she reached 89th Street it was after nine.

She paid the driver and began to navigate her way through the noisy crush of people hurrying to wherever they were heading. She'd almost reached the entrance to the gallery when someone collided with her. She could feel herself reeling backwards, then she lost her balance altogether. She was on the ground, looking up at a circle of shocked bystanders.

A man got down beside her and apologised for his clumsiness. 'So sorry, lady. Real sorry. I guess I wasn't looking where I was going. Are you all right?'

Someone said, 'You oughta be more careful, buddy!'

Lily tried to say something, but all she could do was groan in pain.

The man crouching next to her spoke sympathetically. 'Here, let me help you up, lady.'

But he didn't. She could feel his knee pressing hard on her right arm and his hand pushing down on her left shoulder. She couldn't believe it. What the hell was he up to? She was too shocked to shout and had no chance of throwing him off. Then, in a flash, the man released her, stood up, and shouted, 'There's a lady on the ground here. Can someone please get help? I think she's hurt.' And he was gone.

Two men helped her to her feet. She was dizzy, and her bruises were hurting. It was then she realised her handbag was missing. 'Oh my god! My purse! He stole my purse, the bastard!'

She was staggering about, desperately hoping to spot the thief. The people around her seemed as shocked as she was. Then, a woman rushed up to her and pushed something at her. It was her handbag. She gave Lily a pat on the arm. 'You poor thing. I saw everything. He snatched it while you were on the ground. You okay?'

Lily breathed a sigh of relief. 'My god! I don't believe it! How did you get it off him?'

'I didn't. No way. He tossed it into a doorway. Didn't want the cops to catch him with it, I suppose. Lucky for you.'

Lily snapped open the bag and quickly checked its contents. 'Gee, thanks a million. I was beginning to panic. I'm real grateful.'

She was still shaking when she entered the art gallery. A man wearing a black three-piece suit approached her. She explained that she had a message for someone called Eduardo. The man looked her up and down then led her to a private office. Another man, also in a black suit, was sitting behind a desk. He gazed at her quizzically then welcomed her with a smile. 'Hi. What can I do for you?'

'You're Eduardo, are you?'

'That's right. Say, are you all right? You're as white as a sheet. Here, you'd better sit down. And you're all wet.'

'Yeah. It's still raining. Some clumsy oaf bumped into me and knocked me over. Stole my purse. I'm still a bit wobbly.'

'Oh… I'm real sorry to hear that, ma'am. No wonder you're upset. Would you like me to ring the police?'

'No. No need. Somebody found it. I need to rest for a minute.'

'Well, that's something. Not your usual scenario. You're very lucky, aren't you. Can I get you anything? Coffee?'

'No, thank you, but I have something for you. A telegram. She said to bring it to you as soon as it arrived. It's from your friend Klara.'

Eduardo's jaw dropped but he quickly recovered. 'Ah, now I understand. From Klara Brandt. You must be her roommate, right?'

'Yeah, I'm Lily. Lily Wang. But how on earth did you know? I don't get it.'

'The telegram. Let me have it, please.'

'Sure. Wait a sec. It's in my purse.'

Eduardo jumped up. 'In your purse?' He yanked the bag out of her hand.

'Hey! What the hell do you think you're doing?'

He shook the bag's contents onto his desk.

'Watch it! That's my stuff.'

'Never mind that. Take a look at all this.'

'What for? It's all here. I've already checked. He didn't take anything. Look. My keys. Cash. Even my gold bracelet. All my other stuff. Nothing's missing.'

'But where's that telegram? Was there really a telegram? You sure it isn't in your coat pocket?'

'I told you. I put it in my purse. But it's gone. I don't believe it! Why would anyone want to steal a telegram and leave all the rest? Anyway, it must have been about Klara's newspaper stuff. You can ask her to send it again.'

'Lily, do me a favour. Check your pockets, will you?'

'Why? Okay… if you want… See? No telegram.'

'Listen. What did he look like, this man who pushed you over? This is serious.'

'It was serious enough for me. I could've been badly hurt. He pushed me real hard.'

'Miss Wang, I asked you what he looked like.'

'Yeah, I know you did. You seem more interested in him than me. What's so important about that telegram?'

'Lily, please answer me. Can you describe the man who attacked you?'

'Dunno. Maybe I can if you'd give me a chance to think, okay? I don't remember anything about him. I was confused, okay? I was scared out of my wits.'

'I can understand that. But, Lily, please. Think. Come on, let's start with his clothes. Was he wearing a coat?'

'Coat? Yeah, of course he was wearing a coat. It's raining, isn't it? A sort of beige raincoat. One of those trench coats, I think. You know? Wait… just a minute.' She closed her eyes and clenched her fists to force her brain to remember something. 'Funny. I saw a man in a coat like that in the Western Union office when I collected Klara's telegram. Do you think there's some sort of connection? It's unlikely, isn't it?'

'My god! This is a disaster.'

'A disaster? What are you talking about? He only took the telegram, nothing else. Not the valuable stuff.'

'Believe me, you've got no idea what's going on. That man who knocked you over was no amateur bag-snatcher. He was a highly trained agent. The telegram. That's all he wanted, and he got it. If it's gotten into the wrong hands, as I'm sure it has, it could ruin everything. Years of work down the drain. And it means your friend Klara's life is in danger, and the butterfly hunter's as well. I have to warn them.'

'What? Have you completely lost your mind? What do you mean, butterfly hunter, and why on earth would

Klara be in danger? She's miles away, in South America somewhere. Didn't you know that?'

'Miss Wang. Lily. Please, go home, and stay out of sight for a day or two. We don't want any more trouble. I mean it, for your own safety. Just go home.'

'Don't be ridiculous.'

'You heard what I said. Take a cab back home right now and stay in your apartment for a few days. If anything out of the ordinary happens, let me know. Phone the gallery straight away. Go home, Lily.'

'Well, it's obvious you don't want me around.' She scooped her things off his desk, tossed them back into her handbag, and strode to the door. 'Okay, I'm outta here.'

Once she'd gone, Eduardo paced around the room, spouting a whole catalogue of curses. Then, he sat at his desk with his eyes closed, his head propped in his hands, trying to evaluate the position. One thing was obvious. They'd found out about Klara. Cover blown. But *how*? Could one of the telegraphists be in the pay of Schacht and his friends? Maybe *all* of them, up and down the river. A network like that would make it easy for Schacht to communicate with his people anywhere in the world. Almost instantly. But what had Klara said in her telegram that made it so significant? They must've seen through her attempt to conceal the real meaning of her message, whatever it was, but presumably only after the telegraphist had transmitted it to Lily Wang. But if they already knew what the telegram said, why did they go to the trouble of getting one of their agents in New York to snatch it? He thumped his fist down on the desk.

Of course! They were desperate to stop *him* from reading it. That meant there must have been something critical in that message. Had Klara found out where Schacht was hiding? That could explain why she'd sent it through Lily, as a precaution.

He picked up the phone, intending to dictate a telegram to Klara to warn her that her cover had been blown. The receiver hovered in his hand for a moment, then he slammed it down. Fuck! No more telegrams. But somehow she had to be told. The last telegram he'd received from her, sent from Manaus, said she was heading to a Catholic mission at a place called Tapurucuara on the River Negro. It was vital that he contact her there. But how, if not by telegram? How about short-wave radio? Technically feasible, but who would know how to get through to some obscure mission in such a remote part of the world? He went to the open window and gazed at the baying herd of Yellow Cabs on 89th Street. Then it came to him. The owner of the gallery was on friendly terms with some of the most influential people in New York. He'd be able to arrange it if anyone could.

SEVENTEEN

Klara had seen several trading boats come and go while she'd been in Tapurucuara. They'd all looked dilapidated, and the one now anchored in the shallows with its name, *João*, stencilled on its hull was no exception. It was a small vessel, no more than fifteen metres from bow to stern. Whoever owned it hadn't bothered to give it a paint job since the dawn of time. Some of its timbers appeared to have rotted away. Still, it was due to sail upriver as far as Constância, and that's where she wanted to go.

She'd spoken to its skipper, a man with a weatherbeaten face and a mop of untidy greying hair. At first, he'd declined to offer her a passage, explaining that *João* was a cargo boat and they had no facilities for passengers. However, he changed his mind when she offered him 5,000 *cruzeiros* on the spot and another 5,000 when they got to Constância. He warned her that they'd never covered that stretch of the river in less than four or five days. He'd make no concessions for her… she'd have to put up with the same conditions as the crew.

Now, she was waiting on the beach below the mission, watching the crew trudging back and forth along a narrow gangplank as they loaded cargo.

The skipper ambled up to her. '*Senhorita, bom dia.* Sorry, a bit of a delay. You ready to go? That's all you have, just that rucksack?'

'Yes, *senhor*, that's all. Ready to go.'

He helped her along the gangplank and when they reached the deck suggested she find something to sit on. Instead, she leant on the handrail and gazed at the mission's white-painted chapel, musing about the people she was leaving behind.

The old hulk's timbers creaked as they slowly got under way. She could hear the dull throbbing of *João*'s engine. Everything began to shake, including a huge quantity of empty beer bottles stacked on the deck in their crates. The skipper was right when he'd told her this would be no luxury cruise. She'd have to put up with the bottles' incessant clinking for the duration of the voyage. She'd also have to live with the smell of overripe bananas and the putrid stench of rotting flesh, which she traced to a stack of maggot-infested alligator skins.

She watched Tapurucuara slowly slide out of sight. Then, there was only the black river, with an unending wall of green jungle on either side. They were travelling against the current, but that wasn't a problem for a boat of *João*'s size. She'd assumed they'd continue like this for the rest of the day and was surprised when, after an hour, they steered towards the right bank and dropped anchor close to two vessels moored next to each other. The skipper was shouting instructions to his crew and she walked over to watch. The boats turned out to be engineless barges, which the men lashed to *João*, one on each side of her. Then, they resumed their voyage upstream, sailing at a crawling pace because of the added bulk.

She discovered that the barge on the starboard side was a floating shop, stocked with everyday items the river dwellers were keen to bargain for. Plastic hair combs, rolls of fabric, packets of biscuits, guns, cartridges – many of the things you might expect to find in a local corner shop. A separate part of the barge was used for housing livestock. Two fat pigs, a cage packed with hens, a resplendent rooster and fresh meat in the form of live river turtles, their sharp jaws safely bound with twine. The barge on the port side was used for storing cargo, but it also served as the dining saloon. The galley, with a wood-burning stove, was in its stern. Klara found the food quite vile: heavily salted pirarucu fish stewed with rice and beans. But hunger had to be satisfied, and she forced herself to eat everything, washing down each mouthful with a gulp of water.

In late afternoon, they steered towards an isolated shack on the left bank. The gangplank was set and some of the crew went ashore to bring on board several massive balls of smoked rubber latex. The skipper was leaning on the handrail, counting the goods as they were loaded. He turned to Klara, who'd also been watching, and nodded towards his crew.

'I hope you're keeping away from those guys. You may think they look okay, but don't be fooled. They can get pretty wild. That's why I've ordered them to leave you alone.'

'I gathered as much. But I think it would be interesting to talk to them. They must have some great stories to tell.'

'Not a good idea, believe me. Keep as far away from them as possible. Look at them now. See what I mean?'

They'd finished loading the cargo and were splashing about in the river, shouting profanities and pushing each other around like a horde of unruly kids. But the moment they heard the sound of *João*'s diesel starting up, they scrambled back on board. No one wanted to be left behind in the middle of nowhere. Several of them continued to joke around on the deck. Klara heard a pair of them chatting in Spanish and, after a moment's hesitation, went over to join them.

'*Hola. Buenas tardes.*' She could see their eyes light up. 'My name's Klara. I'm from the USA. Where do you two come from? Originally, I mean. From Colombia?'

One of them answered. '*Hola.* You speak good Spanish for an American. No, I'm from Venezuela. From Ciudad Bolivar. He is *colombiano*. Can't you tell from the funny way he talks?'

'Ah, I see. How did you get this far from home?'

'You know Ciudad Bolivar? On the Rio Orinoco. I was working on the riverboats there. I don't like it much here, but it's difficult for me to get back home. Maybe you can help me?'

His request took her by surprise and she rapidly turned to the Colombian. 'And you, *señor*. What about you?'

The Colombian chuckled. 'You mean why did I come here? Ha! I didn't have much choice. I was wanted by the police for... well, something I'd done. I managed to cross over into Brazil and ended up in Manaus. It's terrible working on these boats. They pay you peanuts. But I can't go back to Bogotá.'

Several other crew members had gathered around them, including a tough-looking character wearing an orange T-shirt. He was older than the rest, broad-shouldered and muscular, with both arms covered in tattoos.

'Well, *senhorita*,' he said, 'are you going to help Guido get back to Venezuela? You heard he wants to go back there. Won't cost you much. How much money you have? How much you earn? A lot in United States, I think.' They were all eager to hear her reply.

Klara hadn't expected such directness. 'Money is a problem for me. I take photographs of birds and animals and try to sell them to magazines back in America. Not much money.'

'I see, but you have some money you can spare, no? We saw your camera. Looks expensive. How much you could get for a camera like that?'

'I'm afraid I don't know. It's not mine. It was loaned to me by one of the magazine people.'

'How much your watch cost?'

'Not much. It's a cheap watch.'

She was no longer enjoying the conversation and could feel the tension mounting. She pulled her sunglasses down over her eyes. 'You must excuse me now. I have something to do. See you again soon.' She broke away from the group to a chorus of mocking remarks.

The skipper was shaking his head. He'd been watching her. 'Don't say I didn't warn you. You have to watch your step with those guys. Especially Carlos.'

'You were right. Which one is Carlos?'

'The big guy in the orange top, the one who asked you about money. That's Carlos. My engineer. Maybe you'll know better in future.'

In the evening, while they were sailing at a snail's pace, Klara watched a canoe coming towards them, paddled by an almost naked man. When he reached *João*, he tied his little boat to one of the barges. The skipper leant over the handrail to talk to him. The man handed him a bundle of capybara pelts, the skin of an ocelot, a feather-decorated bow and half a dozen arrows, then he climbed aboard the barge to do his shopping. Another canoe arrived, and further customers came and went throughout the evening.

It was getting dark. Klara found the skipper again. 'It's been an interesting day, *senhor*, but I think it's time I went to bed.'

'Up to you, *senhorita*. I find you a hammock. You hang it where you like.'

The hammock was damp, but that didn't worry her. She was tired, and sleep was the only thing on her mind. She noticed that *João* was no longer moving. They'd stopped for the night, close to the riverbank. Some of the crew were busy with ropes, lashing the vessel to a tree. Then, in ones and twos, the men waded through the shallow water and headed into the forest. She watched them sling their hammocks from tree to tree. In the moonlight, they looked like a cluster of giant white cocoons. She wondered whether she should do the same. That is, until Carlos walked past, wearing his hammock like a bullfighter wears his cape around his shoulders.

'Come on, *senhorita*,' he called to her. 'It's quieter among the trees. You'll sleep a lot better there than on this old tub. Come with me and I show you a good place where we won't be disturbed.'

That was enough for Klara. She didn't trust him, or any of them. It was more than likely that at least some of the crew were downright rogues, cutthroats who wouldn't hesitate to take what they wanted. They were miles away from anywhere. There were no police or anyone else to keep law and order. Her imagination raced ahead with a sequence of horrifying scenarios. She decided it would be safer to stay on board than to sleep with the others. If she got off the boat, she might wake up in the morning to find that *João* had already sailed, leaving her stranded in the endless jungle. She slung her hammock on the deck, between a wooden post and the handrail, and climbed in.

She didn't get much sleep. Carlos had been right. A bilge pump was clattering noisily all through the night, and the smell from the alligator skins didn't help. At five in the morning, it was still cold and dark, and the crowing of the ship's rooster made further sleep impossible. A little later, the crew tumbled out of their cocoons and yawned their way back on board. *João*'s engine chugged into life and they continued slowly upstream, with the river ahead of them dimly lit by the faint morning moon.

She was feeling miserable. She was tired, her clothes were damp, and the air was chilly. However, a mug of hot coffee and a few biscuits revived her surprisingly quickly. She leant on the handrail and watched the dawning of the new day. It started with an orange glow where the dark line of forest separated the river from the sky, and not long afterwards the sun came up and she felt as if it was warming the whole world.

EIGHTEEN

Joszef wasn't sleeping well. The night was hot and humid. He'd gone to bed naked to try to keep cool, but despite that, he'd woken up sweating and restless. He knew he wouldn't be able to get back to sleep and decided to go for a stroll by the river, where the air was likely to be cooler. He put on his trousers and pulled his shirt over his head. It was dark as he made his way through the trees. The frogs had quit their singing, and all he could hear was the sound of the river rushing over the rocks. The water level was higher than it had been because of heavy rains further upstream and the current was strong. He sat on the bank with his feet dangling in the cool water and watched the moon playing hide-and-seek among the clouds. He heard a splash. Two river dolphins were cavorting in the moonlight. They were pink and, every now and again, made a loud snort.

Then, he heard something else: the sound of dry leaves crackling under someone's feet. He turned round. A man was standing behind him, a black silhouette against the sky. For a few seconds, a glimmer of moonlight lit up the man's face. It was Otto. Before Joszef could move, he felt Otto's boot against his back and a heavy push sent him tumbling into the river. The sudden chill of the water jolted through him like an electric shock. He panicked, splashing about frantically, spluttering, trying to get back to the bank, but he could feel the current dragging him downstream. He heard Otto shout, '*Auf Wiedersehen*, you fucking Engländer! No more butterfly hunting for you!'

He was flailing around in the water but getting nowhere. The river was pulling him along, taking him closer to the rapids. He knew that if he was dragged that far, it would be the end of him. Instinctively, he shouted for help, in Hungarian: '*Segitsen! Segitsen!*', then in English, even though he knew it was pointless. He made a desperate effort to swim against the flow, but all that did was sap his strength. *Swim, swim*, his brain was telling him, but his body was unable to respond. He sank beneath the surface and began to swallow water, and more water. His arms and legs had gone limp. They no longer felt a part of him; they were just lifeless appendages trailing through the water.

Until then, he'd been barely conscious of what he was doing. It was all instinct. But now, for some reason, the panic and confusion cleared and he was thinking lucidly, aware of everything happening to his body, aware of every tug of the river as the torrent swirled around him. Now he knew beyond doubt that he was going to drown. Strangely, he accepted it. The rapids were just ahead of him. He let himself drift, knowing what that would mean. Klara's face flashed before him, and he could hear her voice, clear, like a bell. He could see his mother in her kitchen in Budapest. Other thoughts rushed into his mind. What would happen afterwards? The missionaries would eventually realise he'd disappeared. They'd find his address in his rucksack. Weeks or probably months later, the news would come through that he'd gone missing, presumably drowned in the River Negro. They wouldn't find his body. The alligators.

What happened next took him by surprise. He felt his knees bump against the riverbed, a glancing contact with the solid world he thought he'd left forever. A moment later, he found he was kneeling on the sandy bottom, with the river at that point shallow enough for him to keep his head above the water. The current was still tugging at him, but he summoned enough strength to struggle against it and managed to crawl to the bank. He rested his head on the earth and coughed up a lot of water.

Even though he was beyond exhaustion, something made him turn to look back at the river. His eyes settled on a huge rock, shining wet in the moonlight, some ten metres from the bank. The rock was diverting the main torrent out of its headlong rush, setting up a crosscurrent which, miraculously, had washed him into the shallows. He knew he owed his life to that rock. Too weak to move anymore, he could feel the river still trying to drag him back into deeper water. He felt dizzy and his vision was blurring. He could tell he was about to pass out.

*

It was cold and dark when Klara woke up after her fourth night aboard *João*. By now, it was routine for her to start the day with a mug of strong coffee and a biscuit or two. At eight-thirty, the boat pulled in at Constância. She gave the skipper the second 5,000 *cruzeiros* she'd promised him, swung her rucksack onto her back, and made her way to the mission. The little chapel was gleaming white in the morning sunshine. She asked one of the children to take her to the mission's director.

Padre Mazzanti couldn't have been more surprised when Klara appeared in his office and introduced herself. He welcomed her with a look of incredulity. 'So, my dear lady, you've come all the way from Tapurucuara on that old boat? It's a miracle you ever got here. How was the voyage?'

'Long. Four days, Padre, but far from boring.'

'I suppose not. You're a wildlife photographer, you say? I'm sure you'll find plenty of creatures to photograph around here. Naturally, you're welcome to stay at our mission if you wish.'

'Gee, that really is kind of you. Thanks.'

'I'll ask one of the sisters to find a room for you. Her name is Sister Vittoria. As it happens, we have another young visitor staying with us. He came here to collect butterflies.'

'Yes, I know. That's Joszef, a friend of mine. We often work together.'

'Ah, you know Joszef?'

'I'd like to see him. He's expecting me. You know where he is?'

'That's a good question. To tell you the truth, Miss Klara, I've been worrying about your friend. I haven't seen him for several days. That wouldn't particularly alarm me as I spend much of my time either in my office or in the chapel. However, the others haven't seen him either, and they tell me he hasn't appeared for his meals. That's most unusual.'

Klara felt a dull, throbbing pain deep inside her chest. Mazzanti must have noticed her discomfort because he patted her on the back and sent one of the boys to fetch her a glass of water.

'Padre, that doesn't sound good. Very worrying. D'you think he may have left Constância for some reason?'

'But where would he go? And why? I thought he may be resting in his room, perhaps not feeling well, so I went to have a look. His rucksack was there, but there was no sign of him. Come, I'll show you where his room is. Perhaps he's come back by now. I hope your friend is all right.'

Joszef wasn't in his room. Klara sat on the edge of the bed. 'Padre, could he have gone somewhere to catch butterflies?'

'No, no. He wouldn't be chasing butterflies all this time without coming back here. No. He knows it's dangerous to stay in the jungle once it gets dark. And look over there. His net.'

'But where else could he be? Somewhere in the village?'

'It's possible. He's a sociable young man. I believe he's made friends with some of the villagers.'

'Thank you, Padre. I'll go and have a look around. I ought to go straight away, in case there's some sort of problem. Please excuse me.'

'Good luck, *senhorita*. I'm sure you'll find him. Then, you must both come back here. We'll have a hot meal ready for you. You must be hungry.'

There was no sign of Joszef in the village. Klara was becoming increasingly concerned. Someone suggested she look for him by the river, where people went to do their laundry. She found *João* still moored there and cheered up a bit when she saw the familiar faces of the crew. She half expected to see Joszef waiting for her near the boat, but he wasn't. She approached a group of women doing their washing. Every one of them gawped at her, but none of them had seen the young white man from the mission.

As she walked further, following the course of the river downstream, she came across fewer people and eventually found herself on her own. She continued, not quite knowing what she expected to find. With every step, she grew more fearful that something dreadful had happened to Joszef. She stopped and gazed at the river. Upstream, it had been wide and full, its surface smooth and black, and there was something almost serene about it. But here it was turbulent, powerful, forcing itself through a maze of rocks, turning it into dozens of leaping white torrents. She found it unsettling, because she knew those fierce rapids would go on forever without caring about anything or anybody. She was overcome by a feeling of emptiness, of longing, something she hadn't felt for a long time. She was tired, and it occurred to her that she hadn't had a good night's sleep since she'd left Tapurucuara. She sat on the ground and closed her eyes, her head swirling with confused, fragmented memories.

*

That bizarre state of mind somewhere between dreaming and reality... that's where Joszef was. He thought he could hear a voice. A man's voice. Faint at first, and then louder: '*Senhor! Acorde por favor.*'

He could see someone leaning over him. Bare-chested, dark eyes, brown skin, shiny black hair. One of the Tukano. More of them... an old woman, children. All watching him. He suddenly realised he was lying on the ground, on the bare earth. Above him, not a proper ceiling but a roof of thatched palm leaves. His nostrils caught the whiff of woodsmoke. A young woman was squatting on the floor, cooking something over a fire in a clay pot.

The dark-eyed man who'd woken him was struggling to speak in Portuguese. '*Bom dia, senhor*. You sleep much. Day, night, day, night. Is very good you sleep. Now you much better.'

Joszef was in a daze. He had a splitting headache, and every joint in his body was sore.

'Asleep for two days? That long? What... happened? Where am I?'

'We find you in river. You bad, but you okay now.' The man shouted a few words in a strange language to the young woman. She approached, carrying a steaming bowl of something which looked like porridge. Joszef had eaten that stuff before. Tasteless. Made from manioc. 'You eat, *senhor*. Is good, make you strong.'

He managed to swallow a couple of spoonfuls. Then he stopped and put the bowl down on the ground.

Something the Indian had said... something about the river. Of course! Now he remembered. Otto! Everything snapped into focus. The dirty bastard had tried to kill him. Tried to drown him like an unwanted puppy. He'd have gotten away with it, too. He must've discovered what he was really up to. But how? Ironic that just a few days ago he'd had moral scruples about bringing the son of a bitch to the hangman's noose. No more! So what now? Back to the mission, have some decent food. That would get him back on his feet. No! The mission was the last place he should go. Otto thought he'd succeeded in drowning him, and he'd continue to think so if he stayed out of sight. This was the perfect hiding place. This Indian's hut. Klara! He'd forgotten about her. She'd be looking for him when she arrived off the boat. He'd talk to the Indian. Maybe he'd agree to watch out for her.

*

Klara was lying on the riverbank where she'd dozed off. The sound of shouting woke her up. It sounded like "*Kla-ara. Kla-ara*". She felt disoriented and had no idea how long she'd been asleep. It may have been minutes; it may have been hours. Then, she saw a man walking towards her. She stood up to get a better look at him. An Indian. A young girl was clinging to his arm.

The man's eyes flickered nervously as he approached. '*Você... você é Kla-ara?*'

'Yes, yes! I am Klara. Please, you know where my friend is? White man? I want to see him. Can you take me to him?'

He motioned her to follow him and led her along a narrow path through the trees. His hut was in a small clearing. As she entered, acrid smoke from the wood fire made her nose tingle and her eyes sting. The light wasn't good, but she recognised the man lying on the ground.

'Joszef! Joszef! I've been looking everywhere.'

When he saw her, he jumped up with such abandon that he almost fell over again and had to grasp her arm to remain upright. He managed to utter one word. 'Klara!'

'Joszef! Thank God you're all right!' With a sudden impulse, she threw her arms around him. They were both surprised by the sensation of warmth and comfort which engulfed them. Neither of them spoke. There was too much to say.

Eventually, Klara said, 'Don't you dare disappear like that again. You scared me to death. What's going on? Why aren't you at the mission?' She peered at him more closely. 'What's happened to you? You've really let yourself go since you left me. You look lousy. Just look at you! Have you been ill?'

'My god, Klara! You don't know what happened. It was terrible. Unbelievable. That pig. He tried to kill me.'

Klara turned white. 'What? Who did?'

'The bastard we're looking for. Tried to drown me. Pushed me in the river. Thinks I'm dead. That's why I'm hiding.'

'Jesus! What are you saying?' Her eyes flashed with anger. 'He tried to *kill* you? You mean Schacht? Joszef... Joszef. I can't believe it. No wonder you look so terrible. But you're okay, aren't you?'

'I suppose so. I was lucky. My Indian friends here. If they hadn't found me, I'd be dead. Drowned. It's only because of them I'm still alive.'

'Thank God! Oh, Joszef. You've no idea how glad I am about that.' She bowed to the Indian. '*Obrigada. Muito, muito obrigada, senhor.*' Then she turned to Joszef. 'So that's why you're staying here. Now I understand. Lying low. That's good. You mustn't let anybody see you. Word gets around quickly. There's no telling what he'd do if he knew.'

'Yes, I know all that. But what I don't understand is how he found out about me. How could he know I'd come here to find him?'

'We'll work that one out later. The main thing is, you're alive.' She took hold of his arm and steered him out of the smoke-filled hut. Outside, they sat on the ground side by side. 'Joszef, you don't look well. What've you been eating?'

'Mainly manioc. Not very exciting, but I suppose it's nutritious. Klara, it's so good to have you back with me again. I feel better already. Tell me what happened at Tapurucuara.'

'I will, later. I'll tell you everything, I promise. But we've got more important things to talk about right now. Him. D'you think it's really him? Walther Schacht?'

'Otto? Yes, I do.'

'Otto? Who's Otto?'

'Him. Schacht. That's what the missionaries call him. Otto. No one knows his real name. Works as a handyman at the mission. Looks after the children. Does odd jobs.'

'Good grief! The missionaries' handyman.' She smiled ruefully. 'Quite a demotion for someone who was once *Herr* Hitler's handyman.'

'That's a thought.'

'But is it *him*?'

'Well, he's a fucking maniac, and if he was so ready to murder me, he must've murdered others. Funny, I'd been wondering whether someone who'd been a vicious thug could reform and turn himself into a decent human being. Well, now I know the answer.'

'Yes, but what does that prove?'

'Klara, everything about him shows he's a ruthless Nazi. It's obvious from the things he said and what he did. He even told me his age. Sixty-eight.'

'Sixty-eight! Well, it's got to be him, hasn't it?'

'Looks like it, but we have to be sure. You have to go and look for yourself. He spouted a lot of hate stuff at me. In German, so I couldn't understand much of it. But you… you're bound to get a lot more out of him than I did.'

'I hope so. I guess he doesn't know anything about me, does he?'

'No. Nothing at all. You'll surprise him. You should be fine. He doesn't even know you exist. Even so, you'd better be careful. He's obviously a dangerous freak.'

'You're right about that. But, dangerous or not, I have to go and see him. And the sooner the better. How do I find this Otto?'

'When he isn't working, he likes to sit outside his shack… it's at the far end of the mission compound. But listen. Don't go anywhere near him unless there are other people around. Promise me. You never know what he'll do. He went berserk with me. Another thing. Whatever you do, don't let him know you speak German or he'll suspect you immediately.'

'Obviously. D'you think I'll recognise him?'

'No problem about that – he looks like the Schacht in those photographs.'

'Well, that's encouraging, isn't it.' She was silent for a moment then looked at him almost pleadingly. 'Joszef, you've no idea how sorry I am for what you've been through. This wasn't supposed to happen. New York told me it was all watertight, but something's gone wrong. I don't know what. It seems as if your goddamn Otto knows too much.'

'You can say that again. By the way, have you thought about where you're going to stay? At the mission?'

'Yes. I've already met the director. He's worried about you.'

'Ah, that's perfect. Let's keep them in the dark. It's safer. So, tomorrow, you'll go and see Otto?'

'Tomorrow? No. Why wait? Why not now?'

'I'm not sure that's such a good idea. You feel up to it? You look exhausted and you'll need to have your wits about you. I tell you, he really freaked me out.'

'Don't worry. I'll be able to handle him.'

'I'm not so sure about that. You don't know him like I do. Just watch out.'

'Honestly, Joszef, believe me, I know what I'm doing.' She squeezed his hand. 'Okay, I'd better get going.'

'What? You mean you're going right now? You've only just got here.'

'Right now.'

'I don't like it. Klara, please, just be careful.'

'Where will I find you? Afterwards, I mean.'

'I'll stay here, with my Indian friends.'

'That makes sense.'

'I'll be thinking of you. I'd even pray for you if I believed in that sort of thing. *Sok szerencsét!*'

'Shuck what?'

'*Sok szerencsét*. It means good luck. You'll really have to brush up your Hungarian. Give me your rucksack. Better leave it here. We don't want our Otto to find out what's in it, do we.'

NINETEEN

Klara could feel her heart pumping. After twenty years, she was about to meet the man who'd ordered the brutal massacre of her family, the man who'd turned her into a lonely, anxious child living on her wits. It just had to be him.

She stopped to catch her breath. Two young mission boys approached her, curious about this woman who was neither one of the sisters nor someone from the village. One of them asked her bluntly, 'Who are you, *senhorita*?'

She responded with a cheerful '*Olá*,' hoping that a few moments of casual conversation would calm her down. They were intrigued when she told them she'd come to Constância to make pictures of wild animals. 'But now I have to go and find someone,' she said. 'A man called Otto. Do you know Otto? Do you know where he is?'

They laughed and one of them said, 'Can't you see him? He's with them, over there.' He pointed to a group of boys at the far end of the mission compound. 'He's funny. Is he your father?' They laughed again.

Klara didn't laugh. 'No, he isn't my father. So, he's over there, is he? *Obrigada*.'

When she got closer, she saw him, standing in the middle of a noisy crowd of boys. She'd promised herself a hundred times that if she ever came face to face with this monster, she'd remain calm and rational, no matter what might or might not happen. But now the moment had arrived, her breathing was rapid and shallow and her pulse was racing. She felt half paralysed by waves of numbness rolling through her body. There he was, SS-Gruppenführer Walther Ludwig Schacht, no longer a character from the history books but a living, breathing person, just a few metres away from her. A beast with the blood of untold numbers of men, women and children on his hands.

These mission children were more fortunate. He was handing out bananas, smiling grimly, like a reluctant Father Christmas dispensing presents. He looked unsteady and she could see why. Every so often, he'd take a hefty swig of something from a bottle. She moved forward, slowly, until she too was standing among the boys. She saw him take a quick look at her. It was just a glance but it raised a prickle of goosebumps on the back of her neck. *Keep calm*, she kept repeating to herself… *don't worry… he has no idea who you are… just get him to talk*.

She returned his glance with a broad smile. 'Hi there! Gee whiz, that's a helluva lot of bananas. Those kids must be real hungry.' She was hoping the exaggerated American accent would conceal any hint of her German background.

Otto's reaction astonished her. It went far beyond anything she'd anticipated. He glowered at her with unconcealed hate. Without taking his eyes off her, he lifted up the heavy bunch of bananas until it was level with his shoulders. 'You want one?' he growled. Then, he wrenched a banana off the bunch, using the same sharp twisting action you'd use for wringing a chicken's neck, and squeezed it in his fist until the flesh burst out of its skin. He tossed the mess to his feet and ground it into the dirt with his boot. The children laughed aloud at his antics. Klara recoiled. This wasn't the sort of reception she'd been expecting.

She did her best to pull herself together. 'Sorry if I surprised you. I don't think we've met before, have we?' She pointed to the camera hanging over her shoulder. 'I've come to take photographs of the wildlife here. It's all so exciting.'

Otto scowled. 'Oh, so you're a photographer, are you? You take pretty pictures of birds and bees, yes? What else?'

'Well, something like that. Gee, what a nice lot of kids you've got here. D'you like looking after them?'

He took another swig from the bottle. 'You want to know? Of course I like looking after these... these little angels. These dear little darlings. I'd like to look after you as well.'

She didn't like the sound of that, although the children seemed to find it entertaining. 'You look tired,' she said. 'You poor old man. You're working too hard. Why don't you go and have a rest?'

'So, you think I'm a decrepit old man, do you? I'll show you just how decrepit I am. If you know what's good for you, you'll mind your own fucking business. Whatever that is.'

'Just listen to yourself! You're disgustingly drunk. It's obvious you're a man who can't hold his liquor. Why don't you ask these kids to teach you some manners.'

Otto's face turned red and he shook a fist in the air. 'Enough, *Fräulein*! You dare talk to me like that? To *me*? Don't you know who I am? Of course you do. That Engländer… he found out, didn't he. But he was careless. Too bad for him. Butterfly hunter! I drowned him like the disgusting rat he was. And you, Klara, you bitch, I'll deal with you later.' He seemed unaware that spittle was leaking from his mouth, dribbling down his chin. His eyes widened and his body began to shake. Klara was frightened, but she could see that the volcano was about to erupt and was anxious to discover what it would spew out. He let fly with a violent tirade of abuse, in German, not knowing – and probably not caring – whether or not she understood. She understood everything. It all came out. His vitriolic hatred of Americans, of the British, of Jews, of Russians and Communists. He poured scorn on everyone who'd colluded in thwarting the Führer's efforts to extend the Fatherland's glory to the whole world. His state of agitation swelled as his ranting continued. He was no longer looking at Klara but was raving to himself. The children seemed to be enjoying the spectacle.

She'd seen and heard enough. It was time to go. He was still ranting as she hurried away. She pointed her camera at him and took a photo. He didn't seem to notice, so she quickly took another. It was only then she realised she was trembling.

*

She was still shaking when she got back to the Indian's hut. Joszef leapt forward to greet her.

'My god, Klara! What happened? Are you all right? Did you find him? I told you he was dangerous.'

'Dangerous?' She paused to catch her breath. 'He's a goddamn maniac.'

'I know what you mean. I've seen him like that. You took a big risk.'

'I guess I'm okay. He yelled a whole bellyful of rubbish at me. I've never seen anyone so full of venom. Must've been festering inside that head of his for years. He hurled it all right at me.'

'Bastard! But do you think it's him, Schacht? Do you?'

She closed her eyes, took a deep breath, and exhaled slowly while she thought about it. 'You know, it's impossible to be certain. He sure looks like Schacht and from everything he said, he's certainly a goddamn Nazi, up to his eyes in hate and vengeance. Let's have a look at those old photos again. By the way, I managed to take a couple of him.'

'You what? Jesus, Klara, you shouldn't have risked that. What if he'd seen you?'

'I don't think he saw me. At least, I hope not. I don't know if they'll be any good. I was running away when I snapped them. D'you think they'll be able to develop the film at the mission?'

'Unlikely. Anyway, I wouldn't risk it. Wait until we get back to civilisation.'

Klara reached into her rucksack and took out a plastic envelope containing Schacht's 1943 photos. Although twenty years had elapsed since they were taken, there was an undeniable resemblance between that proud Nazi with his swastika armband and the old man who at that very moment was alive and kicking just a couple of kilometres away.

'Joszef, look. It's him, isn't it? He's the bastard. This Otto is Walther Schacht, I'm sure of it. He even boasted about it. He said, "Don't you know who I am?" Yes, that's exactly what he said.'

'That doesn't mean he's Schacht.'

'No, but what else could he mean? I'm certain he's Schacht... well, ninety-nine percent certain.'

'If you think that... well, great! Fantastic! So what do we do now?'

'Good question. Wouldn't it be best to telegraph New York straight away, tell them what we think, and why, and let them get on with their part of the job? They may have agents already in Brazil somewhere for all we know, ready and waiting.'

'I agree. Then we'll get out of here. I mean, as soon as we can, before Otto gets another opportunity to go on the offensive.'

'He's a madman. He was gloating about drowning you in the river. Thinks you're dead. Threatened to take care of me, too. Made it obvious he'd like to get rid of me. We'll have to keep well out of his way until we leave. Wait... wait a minute... he mentioned my name. Yes, I'm sure he did. He said, "Klara, you bitch." Yes... that's what he said. Oh, Jesus! Where did he get that from?'

'He said that? He knew your name? You sure you didn't tell him?'

'I'm sure I didn't. I'm not that stupid.'

'Hell! Could be Félix.'

'Félix? Who's Félix?'

'The telegraphist here. That scumbag! I suspected he may be a friend of Otto's.'

'My god! That could explain everything. That's how Otto knew about you, and why he tried to kill you. Félix must've shown him your telegram, and mine. Now we have a real problem. How can we get a message to New York except by telegraph? D'you think we can risk sending one?'

'I don't know. Probably not.'

'That's just dandy! We've got to do something, and darned quick. You stay here. I'm going back to the mission to speak to the director. He may know someone else who could send a telegram, someone we can trust, not your Félix. You keep out of sight.'

'Okay. Be careful. Make sure you don't let Otto see you.'

*

Padre Mazzanti was in his study when Klara arrived.

'Ah, young lady. I was wondering where you'd got to. *Mamma mia!* You look unwell. Have you eaten? You found your friend, yes?'

'No. I'm worried, Padre. No sign of him anywhere.' She wondered how many Hail Marys would be the penance for lying to a Catholic priest.

'Oh dear. That's not good news. It's been a long time. I hope and pray that nothing bad has happened to him.

We must set up a proper search for him. Too late today. First thing in the morning, as soon as it gets light. Now, I insist you rest. I've spoken to Sister Vittoria and she'll look after you.'

'You're right. Better in the morning. I've been wondering if I ought to let Joszef's friends know he seems to be missing and tell them we're searching for him. Perhaps I can send a telegram. Would that be possible, Padre?'

'Telegram? Yes, I think so. There's a telegraphist in the village. He's called Félix. But wait until tomorrow, after you've had some sleep. You go and see Sister Vittoria now. You need…' He stopped and looked at her for a moment. 'Wait a minute. I was forgetting. I have a message for you. It arrived this morning, after you left to look for your friend Joszef. It must be very important.'

'Really? I'm surprised. A telegram for me, here? May I see it, please?'

'No, not a telegram. The message came by short-wave radio.'

Klara frowned. 'Short-wave radio? Not a telegram?'

'I was as surprised as you are. It came from the office of His Eminence the Cardinal Archbishop of New York. From his private short-wave transmitter.'

'What? Must be a mistake. I've never met the Cardinal. I know nothing about him. Are you sure?'

'I'm certain. His Eminence greeted me personally. I don't mind admitting, I was very gratified. Then someone called Eduardo spoke to me.'

'Eduardo! Yes, I know Eduardo.'

'This Eduardo person wanted to speak to you, most urgently. He told me they'd first tried to contact you at our sister mission in Tapurucuara, and the director there told them you were on your way here.'

'Please, Padre, what was the message?'

'I wrote it down like he spoke it.' He took a sheet of paper from his desk drawer. 'Here it is. It's puzzling. What can be so important about butterflies that requires the attention of His Eminence? Perhaps butterfly means something else. I hope *you* know what it means.'

As Klara read the message, her expression turned from shock to horror.

> *1. Major problem. LW attacked on way to gallery. Your telegram stolen from her so I not see. 2. We deduce telegram had critical information about rare butterfly. 3. Butterfly may fly to new location. Observe and report if you can. We will act as appropriate. 4. Your cover likely blown. Telegraphy network complicit.*

Klara's first thought was about Lily. Was she all right? Had she been injured? Jesus! Was she still alive? She remembered how that man in the black suit had been deliberately mowed down by a car on Fifth Avenue. She was tempted to telegraph Eduardo to find out, but, of course, now she couldn't trust the telegraphists, any of them.

Mazzanti saw her distress. 'My dear Miss Klara, you don't look at all well. Please, tell me what I can do to help. I'd like to know what all this is about.'

'Thank you, but I'm afraid there isn't much you can do. Not at the moment anyway.'

She was wondering whether it might be possible to contact Eduardo through the Cardinal's office, using the mission's short-wave radio, but that would probably mean letting the cat out of the bag as far as Mazzanti was concerned. She decided to change tack.

'Padre Mazzanti, I have to ask you something. It's about the man who does odd jobs for you. You know who I mean? I saw him earlier today when he was looking after the boys.'

'You mean Otto? Our handyman? Oh, you've met him, have you? Is he of interest to you for some reason? I wonder why. Your friend was also asking about him.'

'How long has he been working for you?' She could see that her questions were making him uncomfortable.

'A strange coincidence you should be asking about him today.'

'Coincidence? What d'you mean?'

'Well, Otto has been with us here for many years. A useful helper, especially with the children. Yet, just today, he told me one of his friends had been taken ill and he would have to leave us to go and look after him. Naturally, we're upset about losing him, but I'm sure it will all be for the best in the end. He asked me to give him the money we owed him, all the money he'd earned.'

Klara could hardly believe what she was hearing. 'You mean he's planning to leave Constância?'

'No. I thought I mentioned. He's already gone. Does it matter?'

Klara leant on the padre's desk for support. 'Gone?'

'As I said. But why does this bother you? He was just our handyman. You look so anxious.'

'Padre, where did he go? Please tell me. D'you know where he went... or where his sick friend is?' She had to restrain herself from taking Mazzanti by the shoulders and shaking him.

'No, I'm afraid I don't. I know nothing. He was no one of great importance, you must understand. The last time I saw him, he was walking towards the village, with his big duffle bag. Why are you two so interested in our Otto? Has he done something wrong?'

'Does he have a boat?'

'Yes, a little dugout. But forget Otto. Isn't it more important to find your missing friend? You must get some sleep now and we'll organise a search party in the morning. Sister Vittoria is expecting you.'

Klara hesitated then agreed. 'Yes, true enough. Please, excuse me now, Padre. I must go.'

But she didn't head for the sisters' quarters... this was no time for resting. She hurried to rejoin Joszef in the Indian's hut.

Joszef swore blue murder when he heard Klara's news. 'Fuck! What the devil made him run off like that so suddenly? Maybe your coming here scared him away.'

'No, I don't think so. He thought it would be easy to get rid of me.'

'So why? Do you think Mazzanti tipped him off?'

'Good question. It's a possibility. But here's another one. Maybe Otto assumed that I'd already told the New York people about him, so he thought our tough guys are already on their way here to get him. Could that be it?'

'Could be. Come on. If he's gone, there's no point my hiding here anymore. Let's go and search his hut. We're bound to find some proof that he's Schacht.'

Klara shook her head. 'No, it would be a waste of time. If Otto *is* Walther Schacht, he wouldn't leave anything incriminating behind, nothing useful, I can promise you that. He's managed to spend the last twenty years hiding from the world. He knows what he's doing.'

'Okay, you're probably right. Anyway, we can't waste another minute. Let's ask around in the village. Someone must've seen him. That's if you're up to it. You look exhausted.'

'Don't worry, I'm okay. We mustn't lose the trail now. So many places where he could hide. What if he headed for his canoe? He may be way up the river already... or down. Let's go.'

TWENTY

In the village, word spread quickly that two strangers were asking questions about the mission's handyman. Everyone they spoke to seemed reluctant to tell them anything. Many claimed they didn't know Otto at all, which was hardly credible given that he'd been living in the area for years.

It was getting dark. Joszef spotted a group of men engaged in an animated conversation. He overheard one of them mention the name Félix and approached with a friendly smile.

'*Olá, senhors.* What's this about Félix? How is my good friend?' His question was greeted with a nervous silence.

Klara joined him. She sensed something was wrong.

'Joszef, what's going on?'

'They're talking about that telegraphist I told you about.'

One of the men glanced at the others then spoke in a whisper. '*Senhor*, you know him, Félix?'

'Yes. The telegraphist. Good friend of mine. Why?'

The man lowered his eyes. 'He dead.'

'Dead? What do you mean? He can't be. I spoke to him just a few days ago.'

'*Senhor*, he dead. Bad man kill him. Today. Cut throat. Big mess. Plenty blood. Bad man steal all telegraph money.'

Joszef was stunned, but Klara was quick off the mark. 'What bad man? You know who did this?'

'No, no, *senhorita*. I not know who did it. Thief. No one know the man. You excuse me, please. I go now.' The rest of the group had already evaporated.

Klara turned to Joszef. 'Obviously, Schacht, as brutal as ever. Got rid of the man who knew too much. Come on, we've got to keep looking.'

A child, a boy of nine or ten, walked up to them. 'You look for man from mission, yes? White man? A bit fat?'

Joszef crouched down to the boy's level. 'Yes, that's right. Have you seen him?'

'I see him. I no like him. He always angry and shouting.'

'Yes, that's him. Have you seen him today? Please, think hard.'

'Yes, today. He told me he look for *Senhor* Vasques, and I take him to *Senhor* Vasques' house. You want I take you?'

'Who is *Senhor* Vasques?' Klara asked.

'He live over there, on river. Where all boats are. See? He hire boats. His are the best, everyone knows that. I take you. Not far.'

'So that's what he's up to,' Joszef said. 'Jesus! If he gets a fast boat, we'll lose him.'

Klara looked grim. 'Didn't I tell you? He knows what he's doing.'

They followed the boy along the riverbank as far as a broad wooden pier. A dozen run-down hovels were strung along its length. They stopped in front of one of them.

'*Senhor* Vasques, this his house,' the boy said, and without another word ran off into the darkness.

Two teenage girls were sitting on the doorstep, their faces illuminated by the glow from an oil lamp standing on the ground in front of them. Klara approached them.

'*Boa noite*,' she said. 'Does *Senhor* Vasques live here?'

'He is our father,' the older girl replied. She was smoking a cigarette. 'Who are you?'

'We'd like to talk to your father, please.'

'You not from here. Where you from?'

'A place far away.'

'Where?'

'America.'

'Is it nice there?' the younger one asked.

'Very nice.'

'Can we go there with you?'

'It would be difficult. But tell me, does your father have a boat we could hire?'

Her question sent the two girls into a fit of hysterical giggling. 'You as well,' the older one eventually managed to say. 'Just like that man. He asked us for a boat too.'

'Where is your father? We need to talk to him.'

'What about? He not hire boats, you know.'

'What? Your father? I thought he did.'

'Well, he doesn't. That's the other *Senhor* Vasques.' More giggling.

Joszef cut in. 'Will you please stop that. Take us to the *Senhor* Vasques who *does* hire boats. Now, at once.'

'You mean… where we took… the other man?'

'Yes, of course that's what I mean. Let's go. Now. We're in a hurry.'

The younger girl looked as if she was about to cry. Klara glared at Joszef then turned to the older girl. 'Please, we really would be very grateful if you'd take us to him.'

They followed the girls to the far end of the pier. A man in oil-stained overalls was hammering at something by the light of an electric torch. He looked at Joszef, then at Klara, and then at Joszef again.

'What you want? Surely not a boat, at this time of the night?'

'*Senhor* Vasques?'

'Yes, I'm *Senhor* Vasques.'

'*Boa noite, senhor*,' Joszef said. 'Yes, we do need a boat. We want to find our friend. I think he came to see you earlier today.'

'Ah, you mean Otto, the German workman from the mission. Yes, he come here. Ask for boat.'

'Did you have one for him?'

'He hire for two week. Pay me plenty. Fast boat with very good motor. You want one like that?'

'We have some important news for him,' Klara said. 'D'you know where he's going?'

'Well… not exactly.'

'We need to talk to him. It's very important.'

'Say he want go to Rio Tarapa. He no tell me why.'

'Where's that?'

'Tributary of main river, but long way upstream from here. My son, he know all these rivers. No need for you worry. He make sure your friend get there, no problem. They have plenty food. Everything.'

'You mean your son is with him?' Joszef asked.

'Yes, of course. I no hire boat without *motorista*. I need to make sure boat brought back here. Boat cost much money, you know. And the petrol engine. You know how much petrol engine cost?'

Klara and Joszef looked at each other. They were thinking the same thing. It was unlikely that *Senhor* Vasques would be seeing his boat, his petrol engine, or his son again.

'Look. If you want boat, I take you up river myself.' He hesitated. 'Er... if you have money to pay. Maybe American dollar? I give you good price.'

Klara rummaged in her rucksack. 'A moment please, *senhor*.' She pulled out a dog-eared map and studied it for a moment. 'Joszef, look. Here it is. River Tarapa. See? He must be heading for this place here, near the border with Colombia. What's it called? Can't read it.'

Vasques cut in. 'Jacaré. Tukano Indian village on Rio Tarapa. Is only place your friend could go. There's nothing after that. Just jungle. I never been to Jacaré, but I know is small mission there, just one old padre. Is very little place, not like Constância.'

Klara was frowning. 'How long will it take your son to reach that place, Jacaré?'

He jabbed a finger at the map. 'Well, you see how twisted is river. And he motor against current.'

'So how long?'

'Quite a few day, *senhorita*. You want boat?'

Joszef looked worried. 'Just a minute. Wait. We need to talk.' He took hold of Klara's arm and led her to the other side of the pier.

'What the hell are we doing, Klara? It's no good trying to catch him up. First of all, he has a good start. And he'd hear us coming, and hide somewhere, and then we'd never find him. Anyway, what would we do if we did get to him? He may have a gun.'

'Yes, I know all that. But we mustn't lose him. If we do, we're back to square one. Listen to me. We *must* find out where he ends up. Then, the New York people can arrange for him to be picked up. Game over.'

'So what? The question is, what do we do *now*? We don't even know for sure if he is heading for that Jacaré place, do we?'

'Okay, so what's *your* suggestion?'

'I haven't a clue… but wait a minute. Just a thought. What if we could find a way of getting there before he does? Maybe up a different river. Overtake him. We could wait and see if he turns up there. Keep out of his way, let him settle in, then get the details off to New York… somehow.'

'Yes, could be,' Klara said. 'Makes sense. We couldn't stay in the mission there. Heaven knows what he'd do if he found us.'

'Maybe we could stay with one of the Indians.'

She gave him a sardonic smile. 'Well, you'd know all about that, wouldn't you.'

'But what if we wait at that place for him and he never turns up?'

Senhor Vasques shouted to them. 'You want boat? Yes? No? You please make up mind. I have plenty work to do.'

Joszef shouted back. 'Yes, we want to go to Jacaré, but we want to get there before our friend does. Is there a faster way of getting there, maybe a different river?'

Vasques walked over to them. 'You no understand. Only one river. Your friend already on his way, and you no find anyone around here with boat as fast as my son's. If you want to get to Jacaré before he does, you'd have to fly.'

'Very funny,' Joszef retorted. 'As you can see, we don't have wings, do we. And Panair, they don't fly any further than Mercês. So, flying is out.'

'Not Panair, *senhor*. Military plane.'

'What military plane?'

'Air Force. They patrol border with Colombia and Venezuela. Quite often. Routine check.'

Klara's eyes lit up. 'Really?'

'Ah, that's interesting,' Joszef said. 'I thought I heard the sound of a plane once, far away, but it may have been a boat.'

'Well, believe me, is plane. The captain, he sometime give people ride if they want go where he make stop. Sometime, stop at Jacaré. Cost you much less than I charge you for boat. Maybe nothing.' He grinned. 'I lose business, but a good deal for you, eh?'

Klara beamed at him. 'That's incredible. D'you have any idea when the Air Force plane may be coming?'

'Soon, I think.'

'*Senhor* Vasques,' Joszef said, 'would you be able to take us down the river to Mercês, to meet the plane when it lands?'

Vasques laughed. 'No, no. Mercês for commercial plane... Panair Catalina... it land on river. Air Force plane is DC3, not flying boat. Land on military airstrip in jungle, few kilometres from here. They keep Jeep there. Sometime, drive to mission for meal. The padres, they may know. You go ask them.'

*

It was late when they got to the mission. Padre Mazzanti was about to go to bed. He was greatly relieved when he saw that Klara was accompanied by her missing friend. They told him a rather thin story about how Joszef had befriended a family in the village and had found it impossible to decline their offer of hospitality.

Mazzanti listened politely, but they could see he was far from convinced.

'What a pity you didn't let me know, Joszef. We were worried about you. But now, you must be hungry, and I can see how tired you both are. It's late, but I'll get *Clerico* Angelo to organise some food. Then you sleep. Miss Klara, Sister Vittoria has been wondering where you disappeared to. She'll be glad to see you. I must myself get some sleep now. Tomorrow, I have much to do, but perhaps in the evening you'd both be good enough to join me for supper, yes?'

TWENTY-ONE

'I'm not sure Mazzanti believed what we told him last night,' Klara said. They were eating breakfast in the *cantina*. 'I mean, about your going missing.'

'Probably not. He's no simpleton. Quite capable of putting two and two together. But I don't give a damn about that.'

'No, but that's not the point. I'm thinking about when we see him tonight. He's obviously got something on his mind. But whatever that is, it doesn't matter… we have to persuade him to find out about that Air Force plane, and we don't want any distractions.'

When they called on Mazzanti at suppertime, they found he'd arranged for the meal to be served in his study.

'I thought it would be better like this,' he explained. 'Just the three of us. We have a lot to talk about. *Buon appetito*.'

When they'd finished eating, a boy brought in a pot of coffee. As Mazzanti poured it, he asked them a question they hadn't been expecting.

'Something has been bothering me. Why are you two so interested in our handyman, Otto?'

'Otto?' Klara replied. 'We aren't especially interested in him. Just a bit curious.'

'More than that, I think. But why? He was just someone who helped around the mission, no one of any significance. I've told you truthfully what I know about him, yet I have a suspicion you haven't been quite honest with me about your real reason for coming here.'

'We've told you why we came here.'

'Yes, you told me something, but I believe the real purpose of your visit is something to do with Otto, not butterflies. Am I correct?' He put the coffee pot back down on the table.

The last thing Klara wanted was to get into a discussion about Otto. Her only agenda was to get Mazzanti to fix up a flight to Jacaré, somehow. 'Oh, that's all water under the bridge now, Padre Mazzanti. Otto's gone away. Let's leave it at that, shall we.'

'I don't think so. I would like you to tell me what you wanted with him. I suspect it's because of you two that he decide to leave us. A great pity. He's been our handyman for years, a good one, and the children liked him.'

'That may be so, Padre,' Joszef said, 'but how much do you know about his past?'

'His past? I know he's German, or perhaps Austrian. And I know Otto isn't his real name. I've already told you that, young man.'

Joszef responded bluntly. 'Yes, but did you know he was a Nazi?'

Mazzanti looked more embarrassed than shocked. 'Was he indeed.'

Klara tried again to draw them off the topic. 'Joszef, we don't need to worry about that now. He's gone. Padre, may I have another cup of coffee, please. I've been meaning to ask you: do you grow your own coffee here, or is the climate too humid?'

Joszef persisted. 'Padre Mazzanti, are you trying to tell me you really don't know what your handyman was involved in? Back in Europe, twenty years ago?'

'Well, now that you ask, yes, I have sometimes wondered.'

'You've sometimes wondered! Then it's time you knew. During the war, that old handyman of yours, Otto, as you call him, did some terrible things... cruel, vicious, unspeakable things.' Klara tried to intervene again, but Joszef ignored her. 'He was a murderer, over and over again. His real name is Walther Schacht. Well... we have good reason to think so.'

Mazzanti shook his head. 'What are you saying? Impossible! I know about Walther Schacht. Everybody does. A very wicked man, steeped in sin. But how could our Otto be him? You are mistaken, young man.'

'Then you must know that Schacht was condemned to death at the Nuremberg trials after the war. But he was never captured. He's been hiding all this time, most recently in your mission, right here. So, Padre Mazzanti, now you know why we came here. Walther Schacht must face justice, even after all those years.'

'Joszef, let me speak frankly. I've suspected for a long time that Otto may have been some sort of Nazi, but only a minor one. He couldn't possibly have done anything to merit a death sentence. I've seen no shred of wickedness in him in all the years he's been with us. He's nothing like Schacht. He wouldn't hurt a fly.'

Joszef glared at him. 'That's what you think! The son of a bitch tried to kill me. And now he's murdered the telegraphist.'

'Nonsense! Please, Joszef, let's not imagine things. And let's try to discuss this in a civilised way. No need for profanities. So you've heard about Félix, have you? Nothing to do with our Otto. The man who killed the telegraphist was a common thief. Took all the money. Anyway, even if Otto did behave badly in some way all those years ago, then for sure he has repented and is now a decent human being.'

'Padre Mazzanti, I can promise you, Otto has not repented. He's still a devout Nazi and a sadistic murderer.'

Mazzanti's frustration was beginning to show. His hands were shaking. 'My dear young man, you must try to understand. This man came to us in great distress. As Christians, we took him in and offered him succour. Didn't Our Lord preach the virtue of compassion? You must remember that our little life here on Earth is only a preparation for our eternal life with the Almighty. I have to remind the Tukano of that regularly, but I'm surprised I've had to remind you. In the end, it will be for the Almighty Himself to judge Otto, as He will surely judge us all.'

Joszef smirked. 'Oh, I suppose the Almighty keeps a special place in Heaven for the souls of Nazis, does he, after he's politely forgiven their sins?'

Mazzanti got up from the table and glared at Joszef. Klara was alarmed. She could tell he was about to order them out of his study. The discussion about Otto had completely overtaken the matter of the Air Force plane. She had to get Mazzanti back to the table, even if it meant lying through her teeth. She tried to sound conciliatory.

'Padre Mazzanti, it's obvious we'll get nowhere if we speak in anger. I must apologise, for both of us. Some of the things we said were badly out of order. I'm really very sorry, and I know my good friend Joszef is too.'

Joszef nodded but said nothing. He'd finally got the message.

Mazzanti stared at each of them in turn, then produced a long sigh and sat down. 'Miss Klara, I'm disappointed in you. Both of you. It's obvious you haven't thought carefully enough about what you've been trying to do here. I don't know who you're working for, or exactly what you intended to do, but in any case you were planning to take a man's life into your own hands, with no thought for the consequences. You speak of justice. I know exactly what you mean by that. Execution. Death.'

Klara had listened to him with her head bowed. Her expression was contrite. 'You make me feel ashamed. I have to admit, we came here with a single purpose, with our minds made up, but what you pointed out about the virtue of compassion has deeply affected me. And in any case, all the wicked things that happened in Europe… well, all that was so long ago.'

Mazzanti was looking less tense. 'Ah, you can see that, can you? That's something at least. Forgiveness always has greater merit than hate and vengeance. Perhaps you can convince your young friend of that, but I doubt it.'

'Whatever the rights and wrongs of the situation,' Klara continued, 'it's too late to do anything about it. Otto has gone away and we've got no idea where he is. We've done what we can, and we can't do any more.'

Mazzanti pursed his lips and fixed his eyes on hers. 'What are you actually saying, Miss Klara? Go on, tell me. I'm listening.'

'What I'm saying is that our business here seems to be over. We ought to go, as soon as we can.'

The padre's eyes twinkled. 'Ah, I see. You'll be leaving us and returning home. Is that what you're telling me?'

'Yes, there's nothing to keep us here anymore.'

'No, nothing,' Joszef agreed, 'but there's a problem. How do we get out of here?'

Mazzanti looked astonished. 'You mean to say you came here without making arrangements for getting back home? Remarkable. It shows just how utterly incompetent you two are.'

'I have to agree with you,' Joszef conceded. 'Bad planning. We didn't think it through properly. We need a plane to take us back to Manaus. All the way to Belém if possible. Is there some way you can help us with that?'

'Young man, you're not only incompetent… you're impudent. You expect *me* to help you get home, do you?' He looked up at the ceiling, shaking his head, then said, 'Well… I might, and I'll tell you why. I'll be glad to see the back of you two troublemakers; and the sooner the better.'

'Padre, we heard something about an Air Force plane.'

'So, Joszef, you know about that, do you? It's a

possibility. They usually let me know when they're planning to come here, but I've heard nothing from them recently. Perhaps tomorrow I'll make some enquiries. It's late now and I'm very tired. So good night. Please leave.'

As soon as they were on their own, Joszef said, 'What do you make of all that? Do you think he really believes we've given up on Otto?'

'Possibly not, but I don't think he cares, just so long as we get out of his hair. Did you see how pleased he was when we told him we wanted to leave? But, Joszef, you must try to be less confrontational. You almost torpedoed the whole goddamn thing.'

'Sorry, but I'd had enough of his preaching.'

'Even so, just cut it out, okay?'

*

They'd had breakfast and were enjoying a last cup of coffee when they saw Mazzanti approaching the *cantina*.

'I thought I'd find you two conspirators here,' he said. 'You'll soon be on your way, I'm glad to say. I radioed Panair. They have nothing scheduled, but the military told me a plane will be coming soon. One of their border security flights.'

'Oh, that's great news, isn't it, Joszef? When d'you think they'll come?'

'The day after tomorrow. They'll be coming here to the mission to eat something. I told them about you two… er… butterfly collectors, and they agreed to take you to Manaus. It appears that the good Lord hasn't completely forsaken you. Not yet anyway.'

'That's wonderful.'

'But wait. You'll have to put up with a long flight. They'll be flying further west to inspect Brazil's border with Colombia before they turn round. They land at a place called Jacaré. Our little mission there usually provides the crew with some refreshment before they head back to Manaus.'

'That's all right with us. We don't mind a long flight, do we, Joszef, just so long as we're on our way back home. Thank you, Padre.'

*

Two days later, just before midday, they heard the droning of a plane, first far away and then closer. They listened until they heard it land, somewhere close by. Half an hour later, a Jeep drew up at the mission. Mazzanti came out to greet his visitors, three men whose Air Force uniforms looked as if they'd seen better days. They were in good spirits, laughing and looking forward to some food. One of them, short and stocky, with his peaked cap clasped under his arm, turned to smile at Klara.

'Hello, hello. If you're looking for the main guy around here, that's me, the captain.' He saw the look of surprise on Klara's face. 'Yes, I speak English. Mine isn't as good as it should be, but theirs is worse.' He nodded at the man on his left. 'My navigator. Has a habit of getting us lost, but only once a week. And this is my radio operator.' Both men gave a mock salute. 'So, *senhorita*, you are the hunter of butterflies, yes?'

'No, no. You have that wrong. Joszef here is the butterfly hunter. I've been taking photos of the local animals for an American magazine.' She glanced at Mazzanti. His face had turned red. His hands were clasped together and he was gazing up at the sky.

Lunch was a hurried affair. As soon as they'd finished eating, the captain glanced at his watch and announced it was time to go. He turned to Joszef and Klara.

'You two are coming with us to Manaus, right?'

'Yes, that's right. We're grateful for the ride.'

'You ready? Got all your stuff?'

'Absolutely,' Joszef said. 'It's just our rucksacks. Oh, and my butterfly net.'

The captain winked at him. 'Mustn't forget that, eh? Padre Mazzanti, thanks for your hospitality. We have to get moving.'

'You and your crew are always welcome here, my dear captain. Miss Klara, and you, Joszef, you can be sure I won't forget your stay with us. I know you've made the right decision. I wish you both *buon viaggio*, and may God be with you.'

Klara gave him a warm smile. 'Padre Mazzanti, you've been most kind to us. Joszef and I would like to thank you, not only for your hospitality but also for your wise guidance. We'll remember your words, and you can rest assured that from now on we'll follow our consciences in everything we do. Now, we're looking forward to getting back home.'

Mazzanti looked gratified. He hadn't imagined that his words would have such a profound impact. But it wasn't only that. The smile that crossed his face betrayed a trace of triumph. He'd managed to get rid of them.

As they followed the crew to the Jeep, Joszef whispered to Klara, 'That was a bit much, wasn't it? What you just said to Mazzanti. But he seemed to buy it. I'm a bit surprised.'

'What I told him is what he wanted to hear. Look, the more the word gets around – and it will – that we're on our way back home, the better it will be for us.'

'Klara! You think of everything, and you lie far better than I do. I'm glad we're both on the same side in this.'

TWENTY-TWO

They were soon in the air. They watched the mission shrink until it was just a little white dot next to the wide black river. After a few minutes, the captain's voice crackled through the PA system, barely audible above the roar of the engines.

'Look down there. The river. I'm flying low to give you a good view.'

Joszef tapped Klara on the shoulder. 'That's where our friend is, somewhere down there.'

'And with poor Vasques Junior.'

The captain's voice again. 'It's easy to see why it takes so long to get anywhere by boat, isn't it. Look how the river wiggles its way through the jungle. The river's in no hurry. But we are, and we don't need to wiggle!' He laughed. 'But we can, if you like.' He banked the plane sharply to the right and then to the left, rocking his two passengers from one side to the other, then resumed his course. 'See? Ha ha!'

Joszef wasn't amused. 'Hell! He's got a weird sense of humour, this joker.'

Soon, they lost sight of the river. They were heading more to the north, and below them they could see a range of thickly forested mountains. The loudspeaker crackled again.

'That's Colombia over there, on the right. Those hills are the border. Looks peaceful enough from up here, doesn't it, but you wouldn't want to be down there. Take my word for it. That jungle's infested with wild Indians. Savages. They kill you as soon as they see you. Exciting, eh? If we run out of fuel now, we'll be joining them! Ha ha!'

Joszef whispered, 'I'll bet he's never seen a wild Indian in his life.'

The captain continued. 'And the drug gangs… that's another story. They're just across the border, in Colombia, growing their cocaine. If we spot a plantation on the Brazilian side, we report it. Then, our buddies drop in on them and set everything on fire.'

Joszef was thinking of something else. 'Look, how are we going to tell him we want to stay in Jacaré? He thinks we're going all the way to Manaus.'

'I'm not worried about that. We'll think of something. He'll think we're crazy, but so what?'

Half an hour later, they began to descend and the captain addressed them again. 'Right, boys and girls, we'll soon be landing at a little place called Jacaré. They usually bring us something to drink. Coffee, not beer, I'm afraid. Too bad. We'll just make sure everything's okay down there and we'll be on our way again. I'll get you to Manaus by about eight o'clock. Hope that's not too late for you.'

The airstrip was narrow and the DC3's wingtips barely cleared the trees on either side. Klara and Joszef held their breath as they made a bumpy landing.

The captain shouted to his two passengers. 'We'll be here for twenty minutes or so. Come down and have a cup of coffee... at least, that's what they call it.' He noticed they'd picked up their rucksacks. 'You can leave your stuff on board if you want.'

'Thanks,' Joszef answered. 'We'd rather take our things with us.'

A small crowd of Indians – half a dozen adults and twice that many children – had gathered around the plane. It was obvious from their scant clothing and general appearance that they'd been less influenced by the outside world than the Indians at Constância. The ground was still muddy from the morning's rain, and they were all squelching around in bare feet. A trestle table had been erected, and two stocky women with unkempt black hair were dispensing coffee from a clay jug.

Joszef approached the captain, who was holding a mug of coffee in one hand and a half-eaten banana in the other. 'Thanks for the ride, Captain.'

'You're welcome, but we've a long way to go yet. Coffee's over there if you want some.'

'I was thinking. This looks like a great place for butterflies. I wonder if...'

'Butterflies? Better not start chasing your butterflies now. We'll be taking off in a minute.'

'It's a pity we don't have a bit more time. Can't we stay here for an hour or two?'

'Are you kidding? You two may have all the time in the world, but we've got a job to do.'

Klara cut in. 'Joszef, haven't you caught enough of your goddamn butterflies already?'

'But they'll have different ones in this place. I can tell. Maybe we could stay here for a bit. A couple of days?'

The captain was shaking his head. 'Padre Mazzanti told me you wanted to go to Manaus. Do you or don't you?' He glanced at his watch. 'Hurry up and decide because we're leaving.'

Their conversation was interrupted by the arrival of a young man wearing a brown cassock.

The captain greeted him cordially. '*Clerico* Marcello! How good to see you again, and what a nice welcome from the villagers. Thanks for the coffee. And please thank the director for me, will you.' He pointed to his two passengers. 'Look, we've got a bit of a problem here. These two joined our flight at Constância and I agreed to give them a ride to Manaus. But now they're talking about staying here to catch butterflies. Butterflies! I kid you not. Actually, I don't think they know what they want. They don't seem to realise they may *never* get to Manaus if I leave them here.'

Clerico Marcello turned to Joszef. 'The captain is right. No scheduled flights. Or boats for that matter. If you don't go with him now, you may have to stay here for a long time.'

Klara gave the captain her sweetest smile. 'Perhaps you could collect us on your next border inspection?'

'You think so? That would be nice for you, *senhorita*, wouldn't it, but it doesn't work like that. I wouldn't bet on our coming back here anytime soon. Make up your mind. Will you come with us now, or are we going to leave you behind? Up to you.'

There was a pause, then Marcello said, '*Senhor, senhorita*, if you two really want to stay here, we'd be happy to look after you. We rarely have guests. It's only a small mission, not like Constância, but I'm sure we could put you up. If you like butterflies, you've come to the right place. But, as the captain said, it may have to be a long stay, so if you want to get to Manaus soon, better go with him now.'

'Really? Gee, thanks,' Klara said. 'That's really generous of you, isn't it, Joszef?' She turned to the captain. 'You see? All's well that ends well. *Clerico* Marcello has invited us to be his guests. It was very good of you to bring us here, Captain. I know it's a change of plan, but please don't worry about us. We'll be fine here.'

The captain looked at his watch again and started to walk to the plane with his two companions. 'You're making a big mistake, lady,' he called back over his shoulder, 'but it's your decision. Nothing to do with me. Good luck to you.'

They watched the DC3 taxi to the end of the runway, turn around and, with a deafening roar, make its take-off run. Once in the air, it circled to the right then disappeared over the trees.

Joszef gave Klara a triumphant grin. 'Well, here we are!'

Klara nodded. 'Yes, for better or for worse. Now we have to pray that Otto didn't get here before us.'

'I don't see how he could've, motoring against the current on that river. Anyway, we'll soon find out.'

It was a long trek to the mission, along a trail cut through the jungle. And it was hot. As they walked, Marcello explained that most of the Indians at Jacaré were Tukano. 'Many of them have been baptised, and then they wear a little Catholic medallion on a cord around their necks.'

'Yes, I noticed the medallions,' Joszef said. 'They all seem very friendly.'

'True, the Tukano are, but further up the river there's another tribe, the Kuru. You won't see any of them wearing medallions. They still live in their traditional way. Very dangerous to strangers, especially white men. They hardly ever come this far down the river, but now and again one of our Tukano will report seeing one or two of them. They're curious about what's going on here.' He nodded at Joszef's butterfly net. 'Butterflies. *Senhor*, you'll see plenty tomorrow morning, when the sun shines.'

They reached the river and followed a track running alongside it. The River Tarapa was very different from the wide Negro. In some places, it was so narrow that the trees on opposing banks mingled their branches with one other and the river appeared to be flowing through a green tunnel.

Eventually, they rounded a bend and Marcello pointed to a modest whitewashed building. 'That's it,' he said. 'We're home. I hope you're not too tired to meet the director. He'll be so surprised when he sees you two.'

'Yes, I'm sure he will,' Klara agreed, 'but I hope he won't be upset by our arriving out of the blue.'

'See, here he is. Good evening, Father. Look what the Air Force brought us.'

They were confronted by an old man in a cassock, bald except for a tiny wisp of white hair sprouting from each temple. He was small and looked frail, but his voice was strong.

'Who have we here now? Will you not be looking so surprised, you two. Yes, you're right, I'm Irish. Indeed I am. O'Connor's the name, Father Patrick O'Connor.'

'Good evening, Father,' Joszef said. 'I'm sorry. We didn't expect to find an Irishman out here in the middle of the jungle.'

'Will you just listen to that now! Won't you find Irishmen and Irishwomen all over the place, busy making the world go round?'

'That's true,' Klara said. 'I'm from New York, and I'm sure everything would come to a halt there if it weren't for the Irish.'

Father O'Connor surveyed the two newcomers then conferred with Marcello, pursing his lips and nodding his head. Then he turned to his guests again.

'So, welcome to our humble home. I understand you'll be staying with us for a while. You're the first guests we've had here in a long time. Only the two of us here; me and Marcello. It's a big responsibility, you know, looking after the eternal souls of all our people.'

'Thank you, Father. I hope our being here won't interfere with your important work. By the way, I'm Klara, and my friend here is Joszef.'

'Ah, Joszef, a good biblical name. Marcello here tells me you want to catch butterflies. Well, to be sure, this is a fine place for them.'

'I'm sure it is,' Joszef replied. 'Tell me, just you two here? No other Europeans around?' He glanced at Klara.

O'Connor seemed upset. 'Weren't you listening,

young man? Just us, as I said. We get a visit from the Air Force people from time to time, you know, but they never stay for longer than a few minutes.'

'I see. Do they drop in without warning, or do they let you know when they're coming?'

'What are you talking about? Of course they let us know. We've the short-wave radio. We rely on it. It's our only connection with the outside world.'

'Father, can the radio transmit, or does it just receive messages?'

O'Connor laughed. 'Away with you now! It seems to me you know nothing about radio. Of course we can transmit. What if there's an emergency? There's no telegraphist here. We have to use the short-wave.'

'It looks as if you're well organised.'

'Well enough. Usually, not much happens here, but we need to be ready for anything. A few months ago, we had some real trouble. Two Frenchies arrived here in their little boat. Photographers, they were. Wanted to take photos of the Indians further up the river.'

'The Kuru?'

'Yes, the Kuru. So you know about them, do you? You don't go up there, I told them. It's dangerous. But they laughed and went anyway. A few days later, one of them came back here, alone. He told us they'd been attacked by Kuru and his companion had been killed. You can't imagine how distressed he was, poor fella.'

'Father, that's awful,' Klara said. 'Tragic. Someone in Manaus told us a similar story. So, do you yourself ever go up there? I mean, where the Kuru live?'

'My goodness, no! Never been and never will. I

never go beyond the village where our Tukano live. It's dangerous to go too far into the jungle, even near the mission. Deadly snakes, you know, and, of course, jaguar. But never mind that. Now, we must find a place for you to stay. You both look tired. Don't you be expecting the Ritz, mind you. We live a simple life out here, you understand.'

Klara hesitated. 'Father, you mentioned an Indian village. Is it far away?'

'The Tukano village? No, not far. There's a trail through the jungle. Why?'

'This may sound a bit odd, but d'you think it might be possible to find a place for us to live there for a few days? I mean, with the Indians. It would be a wonderful experience for us, to find out how they live and how they think.'

O'Connor stared at Klara, clearly shocked by what he'd heard. 'Do you imagine the Tukano are so different from us, young lady? Not fully human, perhaps? No, the Tukano were created by God like the rest of us. When they die, their souls go to Heaven just like ours – if they've been baptised. You wouldn't be some sort of anthropologist, would you? Heaven forbid!'

'Of course not, Father. We understand what you are saying, but the Indians have more... er... more traditional ways of living than we do. Don't many of them live only on what they can find in the rainforest? It's a healthy way of living, and isn't it how God intended us to live? It would be useful for us to learn how they do that, wouldn't you agree?'

O'Connor stroked his chin. 'I see. Perhaps.' There was a long pause while he thought about it. 'If you *really* want to stay with the Tukano, then you'd better have a word with Nakuma.'

'Wonderful. Where can we find him? In the mission?'

'No, probably in their village – unless he's away hunting. He's an important man, the hereditary chief of the Tukano tribe. I'll write a note for you to take to him.'

Joszef was surprised. 'You mean he can read?'

'Of course he can read. I taught him when he was a boy, like many of the Tukano here. He can speak Portuguese, and even some words of English. They're not savages, you know.'

Klara looked crestfallen. 'Father, I'm sorry. We obviously have a lot to learn. Please, let us have a note for Chief Nakuma. Will you tell us how to get to the village?'

O'Connor chewed on his lower lip. 'Just you wait here now. I'll write the note.' He disappeared inside the mission.

Klara breathed a heavy sigh. 'That wasn't brilliant, was it,' she admitted to Joszef. 'Don't worry, we'll work something out. Anyway, we definitely can't stay in the mission. We'd scare Otto away the moment he arrives.'

'You mean *if* he arrives. What if he doesn't come?'

'Yes, I'm aware of that, Joszef. Thank you.'

O'Connor returned and handed Joszef a folded sheet of paper. 'Someone's waiting to take you to Chief Nakuma. That fella over there. You see? I hope everything works out for you. If not, well… I'm sure we can put you up here for a while.'

TWENTY-THREE

Without a word, their Tukano guide set off at a pace. Klara and Joszef, burdened by their heavy rucksacks, followed as best they could. After twenty minutes or so, they heard dogs barking and children shouting. In the failing light, they could just make out a circle of thatched huts. By some means, word had already reached the village that two white strangers were approaching. People appeared from everywhere and gawped at them. Some of the women held their children close, as if the Devil himself had arrived.

One man strode confidently towards them. '*Boa noite*,' he said. '*O que você quer?*'

Klara replied in English. 'Chief Nakuma, yes? We are honoured to meet you, sir.'

He gave them a broad smile. 'No, honour is for me. You arrive on Air Force plane today? You are welcome here. What I can do for you?'

He was wearing a pair of grey shorts. A Catholic medallion hung from a cord around his neck. He was short and muscular, with broad shoulders, strong calves and a headful of glossy black hair. His eyes were almost black, narrow, and slightly slanting upwards at the outer corners. In the flickering light from the fire, his skin glowed the colour of chestnut.

Klara handed him Father O'Connor's note. When he'd finished reading it, he looked at his two visitors and laughed. 'You catch butterfly? Very funny. Okay. You want live here with us? Live like Tukano in jungle?' He laughed again. 'You will find interesting. So will we!'

Klara smiled at him. 'Yes, that's what we want. Would that be possible?'

'Yes, possible. You from America, yes? America not like here. We show you how live in forest. You are sure?'

'Yes, Chief Nakuma, if it's agreeable to you.'

'Yes, agree. We find you house, for sleep. First, we drink. You thirsty.' He gestured to a young boy who'd been watching them. 'He my son,' Nakuma explained. He said something to the boy in the Tukano language and sent him away. Then, he spoke to a man who'd been standing nearby listening to them. They heard the man laugh as he walked off into the dusk.

Nakuma grinned. 'He is Tuco. I ask find house for you, so you live like Tukano. He think very funny. I think very funny. Ah, good, here is drink.'

His son had returned, carrying a woven basket containing three small clay pots and a shiny metal jug. He placed it on the ground at his father's feet. As Nakuma poured out the drinks, he noticed the furtive glance Klara gave Joszef.

'Please, you no worry. Water from river. River clean. And juice of fruit.'

Klara took a sip. 'It's lovely,' she said. 'What sort of fruit is it? Unusual.'

'We call *wirimá*. Grow wild in forest. I not know English name. You want learn speak Tukano?' He chuckled. 'Okay, I teach.' There was a twinkle in his eye.

'But very difficult, I think,' Klara said.

'No, very easy. You say *wirimá*.'

'*Wirimá*.'

'Good. You say *axkó*.'

'*Axkó*. What is *axkó*?'

'Water.'

'How you say butterfly?' Joszef asked.

'*Wa-owo*. See, now you speak Tukano!' He laughed. 'Now, we sit.'

Joszef looked puzzled. 'Where we sit? No chair.'

'We sit on ground, like this. You want to be like Tukano, yes? Then you sit on ground like Nakuma.'

They drank in silence. Eventually, Tuco returned and spoke to his chief. Nakuma turned to his guests. 'Is good. You go with Tuco. He take you to house. We say *wi'e*. Means house. Now is late. We speak again in morning. *Boa noite*.'

They followed Tuco through the village, accompanied by a gang of naked boys who were watching the two strangers with wide-eyed curiosity. Tuco waved his arms at them and shouted something. They scattered. He showed his guests into one of the huts and waited outside while they looked around.

Klara spoke under her breath. 'Well, what d'you think? Looks okay, doesn't it?'

'Just look at the floor. Bare earth. And the walls… made of dry leaves. I suppose we'll manage. I thought it would be like my Indian's hut in Constância. It wasn't like this, was it?'

'No, but a whole family was living there. This one looks as if it's been empty for years. The main thing is, we're far away from the mission. Otto will have no idea we're here.'

'If he ever turns up.'

Klara ignored his remark.

Tuco looked pleased when he saw Klara's approving look as they emerged from the hut. He spoke in halting Portuguese. 'Tukano sleep on earth, but Chief Nakuma, he give blanket to cover earth so you sleep good. Now you eat, then you sleep.'

They hadn't eaten anything for many hours. 'Eat would be nice,' Joszef said, 'but we have no food.'

'Food come.'

They saw a figure walking towards them. A woman. She hesitated when she saw the two strangers, and Tuco had to encourage her to come closer. She was carrying something bundled up in a cloth. She placed it on the ground and hurried away.

'Here food. Now you eat,' Tuco said. Then he left too.

They were famished, but even so Klara unwrapped the bundle with some trepidation. They were relieved to find that the contents looked edible: a bunch of ripe bananas and some cold roasted meat.

Joszef perked up. 'The chief's thought of everything, hasn't he. What sort of meat is it?' A look of horror crossed his face. 'My god, you don't think it could be monkey meat, do you?'

'Don't think so. Looks like river turtle to me. Remember? Like we saw in the market in Manaus.'

'Mmm! Not bad. If only we had some hot coffee. It's getting cold.'

'Joszef, I think we can manage without coffee for a few days, don't you?'

They ate without talking.

Joszef broke the silence. 'Klara, you look so nice tonight. Beautiful, like an angel.'

She hadn't expected this and wasn't sure how best to reply. 'I thought you didn't believe in angels. It must be the moon. You can never trust the moonlight, you know.'

'No, it's not the moonlight. It's you.'

'Well, that's nice, Joszef.'

They sat in silence again, then Klara said, 'Shouldn't we be turning in? We ought to get some sleep. You never know what we may have to face tomorrow.'

'Absolutely right. Let's go.'

Joszef led the way into the hut. It took a while before they could see anything. There wasn't much to see, just two rucksacks, a butterfly net and the blanket Nakuma had provided.

'We're supposed to sleep on that, aren't we?' Joszef asked. 'Or shall we use it on top, as a cover?'

'Probably better underneath. The floor looks hard.'

'Okay, let's try.'

They lay side by side for a while.

'Not so good without a pillow, is it,' Joszef said. Then, he whispered, 'Klara, you still look beautiful, even without the moon.'

She chuckled. 'Joszef, what are you talking about? You can't even see me in the dark.'

'No, but I remember. I will always remember.'

'What a lovely thing to say, Joszef.' There was a long silence, then she said, 'It's getting chilly, isn't it.'

'Yes. Shouldn't we put the blanket on top?'

'Joszef, I'm cold. Why don't you come over here and keep me warm.'

*

Klara woke early the next morning and went outside to watch the sunrise. The dark clouds drifting overhead were edged in pale gold as the sun's rays caught them. Wisps of smoke were rising from a nearby hut and there were sounds of food being prepared. Joszef ambled out to join her, yawning. She saw him gazing at her.

'Well, good morning, Joszef. How did you sleep?'

'I don't remember. I don't think I slept at all. How about you?'

'That's not true. You slept like a baby. I was watching you.'

'Were you?' A smile crept over his face. 'I had a wonderful dream. I remember that.'

'Really? Well, we're awake now and I'm hungry. Aren't you?'

'Very. Are there any more of those bananas?'

*

Later in the day, they made their way to Nakuma's hut. He greeted them with a grin.

'*Olá*. How are my two new Tukano this morning?'

'We're well, my chief,' Klara replied.

He smiled at them both. 'Yes, I think so.'

Klara stared at the ground. Joszef didn't know where to look.

'I wonder if you'd do us a big favour,' Klara said. 'You've been extremely kind, but there is one more thing.'

'Yes? You say.'

'Well, a friend of ours will be coming to join us here. Another white man.'

'He welcome. Also catch butterfly? No problem one more in your house. Big house, yes?'

'No, I'm sure he'd want to stay at the mission with Father O'Connor, not here.'

'I see. You want stay at mission with friend?'

Klara shook her head. 'No, we want to stay here with our Tukano friends. We won't be going back to the mission often, but it would be nice to know when our friend arrives. Don't some of your people call at the mission every day? I wonder if they would tell us when our friend gets there.'

'But Air Force plane, you hear when friend arrive, no?'

'No. He won't be coming by plane. Our friend is like an old-fashioned explorer. He'll be coming here on a small boat. He's got a good boat, with an outboard motor.'

'Ah, I see. But Tarapa not easy river.'

'No, but I think he's got that organised. He has an experienced *motorista* with him.'

'Ah, is good. He not go further than here. Very dangerous further for white man.'

'Yes, we've been told about the Kuru. I suppose they've had some bad experiences with white people. But are the Kuru aggressive to the Tukano people?'

'Our ancestors defeat them in battle. Hundred year ago. Now, they respect. But Kuru not good people. Bravos, wild people. Not civilised. They have big hut in jungle – a *maloca* – for everybody. All live together in *maloca*. Not house for one family like Tukano.'

Joszef was curious. 'Chief Nakuma, is it true they attack people with poisoned darts, shot from blowpipes?'

'Not true. Poison dart only for animal, for eat. Not for enemy. But bow and arrow very dangerous. Arrow not with poison, but big and sharp. Kill man, no problem. You keep away.'

'We certainly will,' Joszef said. 'I have another question. Do you always wear these clothes… shorts and T-shirts? Don't you have traditional Tukano things as well?'

Nakuma grinned. 'White man clothes are comfortable. But for important ceremony, yes, I have Tukano chief things. You want I wear for you? Maybe Miss Klara make picture.' He disappeared inside his hut and shortly afterwards emerged carrying a finely woven wicker box. 'Very old,' he said. 'Two hundred year. More, I think.'

A group of Tukano quickly gathered around them, curious to see their chief in his regalia.

Nakuma slowly and reverently began to take things out of the box, explaining what each item was, while his son helped him to put them on. He started with a colourful feathered headdress. Then armlets and anklets braided from monkey hair, and a loin cover fashioned from softened bark. His son handed him a massive bow, decorated with yellow feathers. Nakuma explained that it was the sacred war weapon used by his ancestors. Then, he struck a proud pose in front of his admirers and turned to Klara.

'You make picture now of Nakuma, Chief of Tukano.'

He looked magnificent, although the overall effect was somewhat marred because he'd kept his shorts on and they were clearly visible underneath the loin cover.

TWENTY-FOUR

A chorus of frantic shouts woke Joszef from his sleep. He peered through the hut's doorway. Several Tukano were scampering about in the half-light, screaming for Nakuma. He shook Klara awake.

'Klara! What the hell's going on out there? Look!'

Klara sat up. 'My god! Must be something dreadful. Maybe someone's been killed. Jaguar attack? Look, there's Nakuma. Why's he coming over here? Look at his face. What's he so angry about?'

The whole village had come to life. Nakuma had to yell to be heard above the din. 'You two. Quick! You come. Now!'

Klara shouted back. 'Chief Nakuma, what's happened? Can we help?'

'Now! You come with us to mission.'

Joszef grabbed Klara's arm. 'Let's go. This could be Otto.'

Dozens of excited Tukano were swarming around the mission's entrance and there were more inside. Father O'Connor was sitting on a bench next to the wall. He was as white as a sheet and his body was shaking pitifully. *Clerico* Marcello was standing by his side, trying to comfort him. The room looked as if it had been ravaged by a pack of wild animals.

An anguished cry burst from Nakuma as his eyes fell on the bodies of two of his people, lying together in a single pool of blood. He looked first at Joszef and then at Klara, his eyes just black slits. 'Your friend, the white man, he do this. Your friend. You look!'

Klara felt unsteady. She made her way over to O'Connor. He was in shock, unable to speak, so she turned to Marcello. 'Give him whisky, Marcello, rum… anything. You have?'

Marcello opened a drawer and showed her a bottle of something.

'Good, give him that.' Then she said, almost in a whisper, 'Father O'Connor, what's happened here? Can you tell me? Please try.'

O'Connor struggled to find his voice. 'White man… a stranger. Never saw the fella in my life. Told me he'd come up the river by boat.'

'I know that man,' Klara said. 'Please, go on.'

'You know him? How's that possible?' He took a gulp from the bottle. 'To be sure, I can't believe he's a friend of yours.' Another swig from the bottle.

Joszef was clenching his fists. 'So, it's him. He finally came. Come on, Klara. Let's go, before he gets away.'

'Then what? We don't know where he is, or why he did all this. Just wait. Father, what did this man want?'

'Said his boat ran out of petrol… had to paddle for days. In a bad way, he was. You should have seen his hands. Raw, they were. Sorry… wait a minute.' He shut his eyes and breathed a long sigh.

'Take your time, Father.'

O'Connor dabbed at his forehead with a handkerchief. 'A rubber tapper, he said he was.'

'He wanted you to give him petrol?'

'No, not petrol. Said he was hungry. Wanted food. Told me he'd done enough travelling on the river. Wanted a job here. Said he could help around the mission. Do odd jobs. That's what he said.'

'What did you say?'

'I told him I'd think about it. To tell you the truth, I didn't like the look of the fella. Wild-looking. I thought maybe running away from something… someone. To be sure, he looked the reckless sort. I didn't trust him. Told him I'd have to talk to my cleric.'

This was going too slowly for Joszef. 'This man. Was he with another man, a *Senhor* Vasques?'

'Another man? No, he was on his own. No one else. Why? Is *Senhor* Vasques also a friend of yours?'

Joszef looked at Klara and shrugged. Then he turned back to O'Connor. 'Father. Where is he now, this man? Still here?'

'No. At least, I hope not. I told him we had no room for him. I could see he didn't believe me, so I explained we already had two visitors, a young Britisher and an American lady. You two.'

Klara almost jumped out of her skin. 'You told him that? Oh my god! What did he say?'

O'Connor shook his head and looked down at the floor. 'I'll not forget it for the rest of my days. At first, the fella looked surprised. Shocked. Then he got angry. I didn't expect that at all. Then he… he… pulled out a gun. I couldn't believe my eyes. The fella looked completely different. Horrible. His mouth was dribbling. Like a mad dog, I tell you. What was it he said now? "Englander alive? Impossible. And that American…" Well, I won't repeat the word he used if you don't mind. He asked if we had a radio.'

'And he smashed it. I can see it over there.'

'No, not at first. That was later. Held me at gunpoint, he did, while he used the radio. He was an expert. That man was no rubber tapper, that's for sure. He got through to someone. No idea who it was, but I listened. Heard it through the loudspeaker. The man at the other end told him about you two flying here on a military aeroplane. Your friend swore like a trooper when he heard that.'

'What else did you hear?'

'Curse after curse after curse, that's what I heard. Oh yes, and he asked the fella at the other end whether some more people were coming to look for him. He said, "Make sure anyone like that is properly dealt with." Something like that anyway. What does it all mean? Are more of you coming here? I hope not.'

Klara took a deep breath but said nothing.

'So, will you be telling me what's going on? Who's that wicked fella who did all this? I really don't know who I can trust anymore.'

'Please, Father, tell me what happened after that.'

'The fella went completely off his rocker. Raving mad, he was. He smashed the radio with the handle of his gun then staggered around the room smashing everything within reach. Then…'

Klara saw the tears welling up in his eyes. 'Please, go on. We need to know. Try.'

'Then… then these two good brave men came in.' He pointed to the bodies lying on the floor. 'They'd heard the noise, you see. They tried to restrain the madman. But he… he…'

Klara said it for him. 'He shot them dead.'

'Yes, he did. It was like a nightmare. Horrible. Horrible. Then, he turned his gun on me. I felt certain I was about to meet my maker, but he looked at my rosary and laughed, and for some reason changed his mind. Would you believe that now? Then he left. I've no idea where he went, but I'm glad he's gone.'

Klara took the old man's hands in hers. 'This should never have happened. I'm so sorry.' She glanced at Nakuma. He was glaring at her. She glared back at him. 'Listen. Please, listen, everyone. The white man who did this is evil. No friend of ours. A dangerous murderer, a Nazi criminal who's been hiding out in Brazil for years. We've been searching for him. That's the real reason we came here.'

Marcello gave her an icy stare. 'So that's your story now, is it? That's not what you told us when you arrived here. Butterflies, you said.'

'I'm sorry, but we couldn't tell you, not then.'

'Oh, I see,' Marcello said. 'You've decided to tell us the truth now that the damage has been done. If that *is* the truth. Look what you've done. Look at the Father. Look at these two dead men. None of this would have happened if you'd never come here.'

'That's true, but we did come. The bastard who killed these two… well, murder means nothing to him. He's murdered many others. We have to find him, no matter what. You are angry. I can understand that. So are we.'

Marcello shook his head. 'So what? That's nothing to do with us. I've heard about those people, but it's all in the past now, and it all happened far away from here.'

'Marcello. It has *everything* to do with you, with all of us. He was living a comfortable life for years with your colleagues, your friends, in the mission at Constância until we rooted him out. Surely, you wouldn't want this killer, this monstrosity, to remain here living happily with you and your friends, would you?'

Marcello was silent.

Klara continued. 'This man must be caught and brought to justice. We're going after him. If we don't, then what sort of lesson would that leave for the future? We'd be letting the world believe it's perfectly okay for mass murderers to hide away, unpunished for their crimes. Can't you see that, for Chrissakes?'

O'Connor was shaking his head. He spoke slowly. 'I know what you're saying, for sure I do. And what he's done here today is monstrous. But God will decide on his punishment, not you. You want to find this fella, don't you, and get him hanged by the neck until he's dead. Like that Eichmann fella. That *is* what you want, isn't it? But think about it. Taking someone's life is no small matter. Okay, so this man has committed unconscionable crimes, but tell me now, can you be sure that executing him will prevent others from committing such crimes? No, you can't. Can you be certain that it will prevent even one single murder? No, you can't. I think what you're really after, young lady, is vengeance, not justice.'

A voice inside Klara's head was asking her if this was true. She couldn't deny there was some truth in it. Perhaps more than she was prepared to admit. 'At least,' she said, 'it would prevent *him* from killing anyone else.' She knew this wasn't a very convincing argument.

Nakuma had been listening. 'These Tukano dead. This white man and his woman, we no trust them anymore. They lie to us. Bad people. They no more friend. We Tukano catch murderer. Wherever he go, we find him. Then we deal with him in Tukano way. But first...' He pointed to the bodies lying on the floor and signalled to a group of young men. There was a hush as they lifted their two dead brothers. Nakuma accompanied them as they left the mission.

There was a shout. A Tukano youth was pushing his way through the crowd. He fell to his knees in front of O'Connor. 'Father, hear me. A woman... she try stop devil white man. I saw. He shoot her... she dead... she dead.' He started to sob.

O'Connor gasped. 'Shot a woman? Sweet Jesus! He must be mad. Mad. To shoot a woman! God in Heaven!'

'Wait!' Joszef cried. 'You saw him? The white man? The murderer? You know where he went?'

'Yes, I know. He go to river. His boat.'

'What? You didn't stop him? You let him get away?'

'But he has gun, *senhor*. Shot woman.'

'Which way he went on river?'

'He paddle upriver.'

Joszef glanced at Klara. 'Towards Colombia. If the son of a bitch gets that far, we've as good as lost him.'

Klara turned to O'Connor. 'Father, we've got no time to lose. We have to catch up with this murderer before he gets away. We need a boat. Can you help us?'

'What? Why should I help you kill somebody, will you tell me that now? You've lied to me. To all of us. Look at the trouble you've caused. Two... no... now three Tukano dead. Chasing after him won't bring them back to life, will it? And now you want to kill somebody else. No. Let Nakuma's people handle it their way. They know what to do.'

'But, Father, he has a gun. Listen, he'll murder more Tukano if they try to stop him. That mustn't happen. *We* must go after him, me and Joszef.'

'No. In any case, it's too dangerous. He's used his gun already and, to be sure, he'll use it again. And what about the Kuru people living up that river? You won't be able to see them hiding among the trees, but they'll see you. They kill white people. May even kill him, your friend the murderer. Will you just leave everything to Chief Nakuma? They'll find him. I've no doubt at all about that.'

Klara shook her head. 'No. It's *our* job. We'll have to take the risk.'

Joszef looked grim. 'No, Klara, you're wrong. It's *not* our job. What the hell are you thinking? All *we're* supposed to do is find out where he's hiding and tell the others. That's the plan, isn't it? Anyway, what could we do? He has a gun. He'd simply shoot us and get away. Father O'Connor is right.'

His words made no impact on Klara. 'Yes, that *was* the plan, but the situation has changed. For crying out loud, Joszef, we can't let him get away, just disappear, can we.'

Joszef scratched his head.

Klara thought for a moment. 'Okay, I'll go on my own if you don't want to come with me.'

Joszef gripped her arm. 'What are you talking about? How can you even think that! If you really must go, I go with you, even if it's madness. Jesus, Klara, surely you must know that.'

O'Connor breathed a heavy sigh. 'Look, Miss Klara. To be sure, you're a stubborn young woman. I think nothing will stop you. I've done my best to warn you. It's suicide. But will you listen to me now? If you two are going to chase after this murderer, I think it would be my duty, as a Christian, to help you… I mean… to keep you safe.'

'That's good of you, Father, but I don't see how you can help.'

'Wait. Just listen to me now. You said you wanted a boat. Well, we've got a boat. Just a little one, but with a good petrol motor.'

'What? You have? Just what we need. Where d'you keep it? What about fuel?'

'Don't you worry about that. We always keep the tank full… but I won't allow you to travel up the river on your own. I'll speak to Nakuma. He's a good *motorista*.'

Joszef looked doubtful. 'I dare say, but after what happened just now, I don't think he'll be in a great hurry to help us.'

'Will you just leave that to me, young man. To be sure, he'll understand you're all wanting the same thing.' He paused. 'No doubt you have a gun?'

Joszef shook his head.

'No gun! What on earth are you two thinking? What do you expect to do without a gun? You'd be dead in no time. Here, you'd better take mine.' He unlocked a cupboard and took out an old rifle and a box of cartridges. 'I don't like guns, not if they're used for killing. I use this now and again to scare off any jaguar prowling around after my chickens. You can use it to scare off the Kuru if there's any sign of them. Fire it into the air, mind you, not at them. Remember, they're not animals to be shot. They're as human as you and me.' He handed the weapon to Joszef.

'It looks ancient. Does it still work?'

'Does it work? Oh yes, it works fine. It may be old, but I keep it in tip-top condition. More to the point, young man, do you know how to use it?'

Joszef grinned. 'I don't like to boast, Father, but I'm a crack shot. I had plenty of practice in Hungary back in '56.'

'In that case, I wish you both good luck. I'll send someone to let Nakuma know. I'm sure he'll agree to help. I'll be praying for you.'

'Let's hope your prayers are well received,' Klara said.

'Are you two baptised? You should be. Then your souls will go straight to Heaven if, God forbid, something terrible happens to you. I can baptise you right now if you like, just as a precaution. It's very quick, you know.'

'That's more than kind of you, Father,' Klara replied, 'but I think our souls already know their destination.'

TWENTY-FIVE

When they got to the boat, they were surprised to find Nakuma already there, squatting in front of the outboard. His chest was bare and he'd removed his Catholic medallion. His cheeks, forehead and shoulders were striped with red *urucu* and he was wearing his monkey-hair armlets and anklets. They were even more alarmed to see his huge ceremonial bow and several arrows lying by his feet, and, next to them, poorly concealed by a tangle of ropes, a large knife. He glowered at them but said nothing.

Klara tried to greet him civilly, but he remained silent. She decided to take a different approach.

'Listen, Nakuma, I've told you how sorry I am for what's happened, and I'd be happy to visit every single one of your people and apologise to each of them personally. But, at least for now, you and I and Joszef must work together to do something about this killer. That's why you've come, isn't it? Unless you mean to kill *us*?'

Nakuma gave a sharp tug on the pull-rope to get the engine started. 'We go.'

It was a solidly built boat, with a wooden canopy to provide shade from the sun. They had to proceed slowly because the jungle on both banks of the river was dense and it was hard to see further than the next bend. Klara was keeping an eye on Nakuma. She sensed he wasn't familiar with this part of the river. He seemed nervous and was constantly scouring the forest around them. Perhaps he was looking out for the Kuru, although she doubted they'd got as far as their territory yet.

The heat and humidity were stifling. They knew there was no point in trying to wipe the sweat off their faces. It just kept coming, as did the myriads of tiny flies which followed them everywhere, *piums*, whose painful bites left little black spots on their skin.

They motored on uneasily for some hours, with hardly a word spoken. Then, Nakuma switched off the engine and the boat began to drift. He was listening for something. For what, Klara wondered. Hostile Indians? The splash of Otto's paddling? Wasn't it obvious that if Otto was anywhere near them he'd have heard the noise of their engine? On the other hand, it was difficult to hear anything above the continuous chittering of a million cicadas. Nakuma restarted the motor and they continued upstream.

The river narrowed, and the jungle on both banks closed in on them. Giant trees soared skywards, their massive trunks dappled with patches of orange lichen. Everything was entwined by a network of creepers. Drops of water on the leaves, left by the morning's rain, sparkled like diamonds wherever a shaft of sunlight managed to penetrate the forest's dense canopy.

They knew that the further they went up the river, the more likely they were to meet the Kuru, so it wasn't surprising that they were on edge.

They were alerted by a rustling sound. Joszef spotted something moving among the trees. If it was the Kuru, they could expect an attack any second. He picked up O'Connor's rifle and took aim at a dark shape half hidden by foliage. Klara covered her ears.

Nakuma shouted, 'No, not gun!', but his warning came too late. Joszef pulled the trigger. An orange flame spurted from the rifle's muzzle and the explosion resounded into the distance, sending innumerable birds squawking into the air. There was an eruption of jabbering and shrieking. The trees shook wildly as a gang of terrified monkeys leapt about in every direction. One of them came crashing down through the branches and hit the ground with a thud.

Nakuma threw Joszef a reproachful look. 'You too quick with gun. Noise warn killer man.' Joszef ignored him. He reloaded the rifle and put it down.

Klara was beginning to wonder whether their decision to follow Otto upriver was a mistake. Anything could happen. First, there was Otto. He was clever, no doubt capable of turning the tables on them and shooting them all dead before they even knew what was happening. Then there were the Kuru somewhere in this dense forest, and they wouldn't hesitate to kill intruders. And there was Nakuma. What was his game? He'd have to be watched. Maybe none of them would get out of this alive. She tried to dismiss the thought, but she couldn't.

They progressed slowly, rounding bend after bend, straining to stay alert, looking for any tell-tale movement in the jungle. They watched a family of capybara cavorting on the riverbank. They saw parrots and toucans and monkeys – and blue butterflies – but no Indians. And no Otto. The heat was overwhelming. Little by little, drowsiness was setting in, and their concentration was beginning to lapse. Klara found herself musing about this supposedly dangerous Kuru tribe. Where were they? They'd seen no sign of them. Perhaps Kuru was just a Tukano word for, say, evil spirit of the forest. Maybe the whole thing was a myth. Did the Kuru really exist?

Suddenly Joszef stiffened. 'Look! Over there. Something moving.' He pointed to their left and at the same time grabbed the rifle. At first, they saw nothing, but a few seconds later they could make out a brown-skinned figure, almost naked, hiding in the dense foliage.

'Kuru!' Nakuma hissed.

They saw more of them. Four… no… a dozen at least. An arrow whizzed over their heads and landed in the water. They existed all right! Joszef fired the rifle, aiming high. The explosion was deafening, but it made no impact on the attackers. Arrows began to fly. Most of them missed the target, but one embedded itself in the boat's wooden canopy with a heavy clunk. 'We're sitting ducks,' Joszef yelled. 'Let's get out of here!'

Nakuma had already increased speed and was steering the boat towards the opposite bank. They sped along until it felt safe to ease the throttle. Only then did they realise they were shaking. All three of them.

Joszef's heart was thumping. 'Klara. You all right?'

'My god! That was really something. Don't worry, I'm okay.'

'We were lucky to get away.' He stretched upwards to examine the arrow lodged in the canopy. It was over a metre long, with a wickedly barbed tip. Nakuma stood up and grasped it, but he couldn't pull it out. He broke off the shaft and tossed it into the river. 'There will be more,' he said. 'Kuru no go away.'

The light was beginning to fail. The river was wider at that point and the water was almost standing still. Joszef pointed to what looked like a pair of green golf balls floating on the surface.

'Alligator,' Nakuma explained. 'Plenty here. Only see eyes. That one very big. He watch us.' Klara shuddered. Nakuma looked up at the sky. 'Dark soon. We look for place and stop for night. Tomorrow, go further.'

Joszef was apprehensive. 'What about the Kuru?'

Klara had already considered that. 'We'll take turns on watch. First sign of them and we fire the gun. In the air if that works, but fire right at them if the noise doesn't scare them off.'

Something attracted Joszef's attention. 'What's that? There on the left.'

The others saw it too. They slowed down and Nakuma steered towards the bank. It was a small boat. No one was in it.

Nakuma switched off the engine and used the paddle to get closer. Something was stencilled on the boat's side: *VASQUES 3 CONSTÂNCIA*.

'Otto's boat!' Joszef said.

Klara put a finger to her lips. 'Shh! Quiet!'

'Where the hell is he?'

'Must be resting. All that paddling. Probably asleep for the night, let's hope.'

'Where's the motor? Vasques told us it had an outboard.'

'Ran out of fuel, remember? A motor's heavy if you're paddling. Must've chucked it out somewhere.'

'Together with young Vasques, I expect. What do we do now?'

Klara thought for a moment. 'Get the rifle. We'll hold him at gunpoint and tie him up. I'll get those ropes.'

'Ropes? Are you serious? Have you ever tied anybody up before?'

'You don't want to turn around and go back, do you?'

'But what about his gun?'

'Won't have time to use it. We'll tie him up good and take him back to Jacaré. Lock him up in the mission. Nakuma's people will guard him until we get help. They'll make sure he doesn't get away.'

'They'll probably kill the bastard first.'

'We'll have to take that chance.'

Nakuma said nothing. He was lashing the boat to a tree. Klara threw him a concerned look.

'Please, Nakuma, listen to me. You stay here in the boat. He's a dangerous killer and we only have this old gun. We don't want you to get shot. We've already caused your people enough grief. Please, you stay here and wait for us, okay?'

The river's bank was steep and slippery. It was a difficult climb, especially with Joszef carrying the heavy rifle and Klara loaded with an armful of rope. They made their way as quietly as they could. When they reached the top of the slope, they crouched in the undergrowth and looked around to get their bearings. It was almost dark. In the stillness, they could hear each other's breathing. Joszef wondered if Klara was feeling the same as he was – almost overwhelmed by a combination of breathless excitement and sheer terror. He sniffed the air. Something smelled rancid. It was the smell of his own sweat.

'No sign of Otto,' he whispered. 'Maybe the Kuru got him.'

'Just what he deserves. I wonder what they do to their captives.'

'Let's get moving. We'll find the bastard, dead or alive.'

They followed a narrow path by the side of the river, with Joszef in the lead, gun at the ready.

'Must be an Indian track,' Klara said. 'Keep your eyes open, they can't be far away. May even be watching us.' They came to a clearing. 'Shh! Quiet… he's got to be around here somewhere.'

Joszef moved forward, slowly. At first, he could see nothing out of the ordinary. Then, he stopped and held his breath. He signalled to Klara and pointed to something lying in the long grass some twenty metres away, barely visible in the gloom.

Klara saw what he was pointing to. She was trembling. 'Yes, yes. That's him, the son of a bitch, getting his beauty sleep. Give me the rifle.'

'What? Are you sure? Better if I—'

'Give me the goddamn gun! This is something I've got to do myself.'

She took a deep breath and inched closer, with Joszef just behind her. She raised the rifle, pressed the butt to her shoulder and positioned her index finger on the trigger.

'Okay, you bastard,' she called out, 'it's time to get up and face the world. Up! Slowly. Hands above your head.' She felt a surge of triumph. It was a strange feeling. At last, after twenty years, she'd got him.

There was no response. 'Up, you dirty bastard! Get up or you'll feel this!' She rushed forward and jabbed savagely with the muzzle of the gun. There was still no response. She saw why. It wasn't Otto. It wasn't anybody. Just an old bag, a sort of duffle bag made of dark green cloth, faded and frayed.

'It's got to be his,' Joszef said, 'but where the hell is he?'

They heard a metallic click behind them, then a voice. 'Welcome, my friends. We play hide-and-seek no longer.'

Klara swung round. There he was, Otto, pointing a pistol at them. Her knees went weak.

'*Fräulein*, you better drop that old gun before you hurt yourself with it. Yes, that's good. Now, put your hands up, both of you. And you, Engländer... still alive? Not drowned? You disappoint me.'

Joszef made a headlong rush at him, his eyes gleaming. 'I'll fucking kill you!'

Otto took a quick step backwards and levelled the pistol at him. 'Back where you were. I don't want to have to shoot you. Not yet anyway.' His face twisted into a smirk. 'So, you think I'm an idiot, do you? Of course you would follow me. Why you think I left my boat there where you would see it? Fucking amateurs. You think I didn't know what you two were up to? Butterfly hunter! Thought you'd catch *me* in your net, did you?'

'Wait, Otto,' Klara said, 'you've got it all wrong. We followed you to… to tell you… Padre Mazzanti wants you to come back. He needs you there, Otto. And the children.' She was looking at the rifle lying on the ground where she'd dropped it, a couple of metres away, wondering if she could get to it before he had time to shoot.

'The rifle? Forget it, *Fräulein*. And why you still call me Otto? That's not my name. You know who I am, don't you? Of course you do. Look at me.'

Klara's blood was boiling. 'Of course I know who you are. We've known from the start, you scumbag.'

'How clever of you, *Fräulein* Weber. But it won't do you any good. You'll still end up like your father. Colonel Hans Weber used to be a friend of mine, but then he started to think he was better than the rest of us. Big mistake. We liquidated the lot of them. But no matter, that's all over now. And you, *Fräulein*, you'll soon be joining your father in the great unknown. Doesn't that make you happy?' He laughed.

'You must be mad. You'll never get away with this. Surely, you know that?'

'No? *Fräulein*, you must be dreaming. Ah, I see you have your camera with you. You took some interesting photographs, did you? The camera, please. Throw it over here. *Schnell!*'

She didn't have any choice. He must have seen her taking those photos of him after their confrontation in Constância.

'Here, take it!' She tossed the camera over. It landed at his feet and in a couple of seconds he'd smashed it to bits with one mighty stamp of his boot.

'So, now we get down to business. You, *Fräulein*. An attractive young woman like you should be enjoying yourself, living the glamorous life in New York. Night clubs… champagne. But no, you have this insane ambition to finish what your father failed to finish. And this foolish young man… blindly infatuated with you, completely out of his depth. I think he would do anything for you, *Fräulein* Weber. You took unfair advantage of him. You should be ashamed of yourself.'

She glanced at Joszef. His eyes flicked over to the rifle and then to her. She shook her head.

Otto smiled. 'Good decision, *Fräulein*. I can see you're not in a hurry to die. Unfortunately, death doesn't always come when you expect it. You should remember that. Now, Joszef… that is your name, isn't it? I want you to tell me something.'

'I don't care what the hell you want,' Joszef roared. 'You must be crazy. The others are coming for you. Didn't you know that? You thought it was just us two?'

'Ah! Thank you, Engländer, that's what I wanted to know. There are always others. I know how you people operate. I want you to tell me more about these agents. Every detail.'

'Why should I, you fucking maniac.'

'That's not very nice, Joszef. I'll show you why. You leave me no choice.' He trained his gun on Klara. '*Fräulein*, come over here.'

'You go to hell!'

'Come here! Or you want me to shoot your friend?'

She took a tentative step forward. Otto grunted, grasped her arm and dragged her towards him. She screamed and made a grab at his hair. There was a brief struggle, then he threw her to the ground.

She glared up at him, eyes burning with hatred. 'Bastard! Don't you touch me!'

Joszef was shaking with rage. 'You… you—'

Otto leered at him. 'So, Joszef, you ready to talk now? Or you want I shoot her?' He placed the toe of his boot against Klara's ribs and pushed her over onto her front, then held her down with his boot pressed into the small of her back. He grinned like a big-game hunter posing for a photograph with his trophy. 'Now, I want you to tell me how many people are coming for me, and where they are stationed. Speak up, or *Fräulein* Weber here will suffer more than you would care to witness.'

'Bastard! You just leave her alone. I'm not telling you anything.'

'I warn you, don't you try to play games with me. Talk! Your time is running out. This is your last warning.' He angled his pistol downwards, pointing it at the back of Klara's head. 'Now, you tell me. Those agents. How many are there? *Schnell*!'

'Okay, okay. How many? Three.'

'Only three? That's pathetic. They wouldn't be able to find me even if there were ten of them. Not where I'm going. Okay, now their names.'

'You're joking. No one knows their names, so how can I tell you?'

'I see. That's very clever of them, isn't it. So, where are they, these agents of yours? You know that, don't you?'

'Where? Oh yes, I know that. Tapurucuara… two of them are based there. You know where that is? It's a missionary settlement on—'

'Stop wasting my time. What about the other one? I'll know if you're lying, and if you are…' He jerked his boot down harder on Klara's spine. She uttered a short cry then kept quiet.

'Okay, okay. I get it. The other one… Manaus, but you don't understand. It's too late. They're already on their way here.'

'You think so? That's very interesting, because it just so happens I have friends in Tapurucuara, and in Manaus, and I've given them clear instructions. They know what they have to do, so it's likely your people are already dead. If not, no matter, they soon will be. All very satisfactory, no?' He looked down at Klara. 'Now, *Fräulein* Weber, stand up. It's time to complete unfinished business.'

Joszef was desperate. 'You're a fucking idiot if you think you can get away with this. If you're clever, you'll let us go and get yourself as far away from here as you can. We won't follow you. I promise. I guarantee it. Okay? It's your only chance. Otherwise, you're as good as dead. We'll all die if we don't get out of here. The Kuru. They'll kill us all. Is it a deal?'

'Leave you two alive? That's very funny. What kind of fool do you think you're dealing with? Now, *Fräulein* Weber, get over there. You will die quickly… not like your father. Colonel Weber was a traitor to the Reich and to the Führer. You too are a traitor, so please think of this as your official execution if it makes you feel any better. Stand over there.' He indicated a spot where the ground sloped steeply down to the river. 'Yes, that's good. We don't want to leave anything unpleasant behind, do we. Goodbye, *mein Fräulein. Auf Nimmerwiedersehen.*'

He was pointing his pistol at the centre of Klara's forehead, his finger on the trigger. Klara was focusing her eyes on the little black hole from which the fatal bullet would emerge and crash into her skull. Her instinct told her to duck, to run, but she couldn't move. She could already see her body lying dead on the ground, sprawled out like the body of that murdered young woman she'd seen in Manaus. One anguished thought kept running through her head: her death would be the end of the line for the Weber family, all of them murdered at the hands of this evil man, and she couldn't do a goddamn thing about it. She opened her mouth to curse him, but before she could utter a sound everything was thrown into confusion. As Otto squeezed the trigger, he grunted and lurched forward and the bullet missed. At first, she thought he'd tripped over something… a rock or a tree root. But then she saw the massive arrow that had lodged itself in the middle of his back.

Joszef reacted instantly. 'Klara! The Indians! The Kuru! They're back. Get down!'

But no more arrows came. Standing at the other side of the clearing, dimly visible in the half-light, they saw Nakuma, his face contorted with rage, his huge bow clenched in his fist. His arrow had found its mark. Otto was groaning in pain, still on his feet and still grasping his pistol. Despite the arrow in his back, again he took aim at Klara, screaming, 'Die, you bitch.' It was now or never for

Joszef. O'Connor's rifle was lying on the ground between him and Otto. Joszef leapt forward and managed to grab it by its barrel. Then, with a ferocious swing, he smashed the rifle's heavy butt into Otto's head. Otto's eyeballs curled upwards in their sockets. His mouth fell open and there was a hideous gurgling sound, followed by a flood of dark blood. He staggered about like a madman performing some sort of *dance macabre* until a second arrow from Nakuma put an end to it. It struck Otto in the chest. He managed to stay upright for a second or two then keeled over. He tumbled down the steep bank and hit the river with a splash. For a few moments, he floated, face down. Then, as they watched, he quietly sank below the surface, leaving a little cluster of bubbles where he'd gone down.

At that moment, a band of Kuru burst from the forest, howling like a pack of wolves. They'd seen the brave Tukano warrior attack the white intruders and wanted to finish the job. Nakuma waved his arms about and roared at them to stop, but they ignored him. There was a hail of arrows. Joszef leapt in front of Klara to try to shield her, and at the same time pressed the rifle's butt against his shoulder and squeezed the trigger. He heard one of the Indians scream and fall to the ground. The others fled back into the jungle. There was a sharp cry behind him. Klara was on the ground, groaning. An arrow had pierced right through her arm. Joszef dropped the rifle and crouched down beside her, too shocked to do or say anything.

Nakuma saw what had happened. With his great bow slung over his shoulder, he rushed across to them and examined Klara's arm. 'Arrow in flesh,' he said, 'not hit bone. Is good. I take out.'

Without waiting for any sort of response, he grasped Klara's arm in one hand and with his other hand snapped off the arrowhead. She winced. So did Joszef. Then, he gently pulled out the arrow's shaft from its feathered end.

Klara had started to shiver. Her eyes were closed and her voice was weak. 'What's happening?' she asked.

'Don't worry. We got the arrow out,' Joszef explained.

'She lose blood,' Nakuma said.

The wound was bleeding heavily. Joszef pulled off his shirt, ripped off one of the sleeves at the seam and tied it over the wound. Then, he ripped off the other sleeve and used it as a tourniquet, tying it tightly around Klara's arm just below the shoulder. He kissed her gently on the cheek and tried to reassure her. 'It's not so bad, but we have to get you out of here and back to the mission.'

'Yes, but what about Otto?'

'Don't worry. He's dead.'

'Yes, I know, but… we must find him… even dead. His body. Don't you see? For the New York people. They'll send someone to identify him.'

'But he practically admitted he was Walther Schacht.'

'You think they'll believe us, just like that? No. We have to find his body.'

Nakuma was listening and shook his head. 'Plenty alligator. Plenty piranha. Body all gone very quick. We go now. Kuru come back. Many. We go quick.'

Joszef grimaced. 'Fuck! If we can't find his body, how can we prove he's Schacht? Or dead, for that matter. I thought we were going to take him back to Jacaré with us, not kill him. We've really messed things up.'

'We didn't have much choice, did we?' Klara said. 'But we must find his body. We have to search the river.'

'Okay, but first we have to get you to the boat.'

'No. I'm all right.'

'No, not all right,' Nakuma said. 'We take you to boat.'

Between them, they raised Klara to her feet and helped her down the slope. She was obviously in pain but she cried out only once. As they lowered her into the boat, she caught hold of Joszef's wrist.

'Now, go and look for his body. I'm all right.'

'Okay, I'll look.' He peered through the darkness. 'Jesus Christ! Can't see a thing. Nakuma, we can search better if you get this darned boat moving.'

They heard a twang from somewhere in the trees and an arrow whizzed past them and plunged into the water.

Nakuma grabbed the pull-rope, but before he could start the engine Joszef leapt out of the boat. 'The bag! Otto's bag!' He clambered back up the slope and disappeared. Nakuma cursed. Then, Joszef reappeared and scrambled down again. He flung the duffle bag and O'Connor's rifle into the boat. 'Right. Let's get going.'

The noise of the engine resounded across the water and they were off. Several more arrows flew by, all wide of the mark. Nakuma was crouching in the stern, steering the boat through the darkness, following the river's twists and turns. Joszef sat on the floor next to Klara. She'd stopped shivering and was almost asleep. He bent down and pressed his lips to her brow. He felt her hand squeeze his, and when she opened her eyes for a moment he saw tears in them.

TWENTY-SIX

They reached Jacaré early the next morning. The sound of the engine brought a horde of Tukano down to the river. Nakuma waved to them like a triumphant monarch acknowledging his people. He climbed out of the boat and stood erect, his bow held aloft, and addressed the crowd in their own language. When they heard what he had to say, the air was filled with a chorus of wild whooping and shouting.

Father O'Connor arrived. He threw up his hands in horror when he learnt that Otto had been killed. Then, he caught sight of Klara lying in the boat with her eyes closed, with Joszef squatting at her side.

'Oh, my goodness!' he gasped, almost falling to his knees. 'Whatever's happened here?'

The sound of his voice reached Klara. She opened her eyes and managed a faint smile.

O'Connor clasped his hands together and looked up at the sky. 'Oh, thank God! Thank God! I thought…' Then he turned to Joszef. 'Satisfied now, are you, young man? Happy about all this? What am I to say to you? You told me you were going to capture the fella. You didn't say you were going to kill him. That's doesn't sound like justice to me. More like an execution.'

'Father, I'm afraid you don't understand. It wasn't what we'd planned, but we had to do something. He was about to shoot us. It was self-defence. We'd all be dead if it hadn't been for Nakuma.'

'Self-defence, was it now? That's why you killed him? So you say. Even so, you wilfully ended this fella's God-given life. There's only one thing for you two to do now. You must get down on your knees and pray to the Almighty. Beg for forgiveness. And you'd better be giving me back my rifle now before you kill anybody else.'

'Okay, okay. But, Father, look at Klara. I'm very worried about her. She was hit by an arrow. From the Kuru. We've got to see to her. It's urgent. She's not well.'

'My goodness! The Kuru. That's terrible, terrible. We need to get her inside. I'll get Marcello to fetch a hammock.'

They rolled Klara onto the hammock, carried her into the mission and lay her on a mattress. Marcello seemed to know what he was doing. He removed the improvised tourniquet and replaced the temporary bandage with a proper dressing smelling of antiseptic. Klara whispered her thanks.

At last, she was alone with Joszef. She looked at him anxiously. 'We have to tell New York what's happened. They need to know.' She tried to sit up but couldn't.

'Listen to me, Klara. New York can wait. Otto's dead, so what's the hurry? Anyway, there's no telegraphist here. No radio. Otto made sure of that. So forget about it. What you need now is plenty of rest. The main thing is to get you better, then we'll see about getting back.'

'I suppose you're right. You always are, aren't you. Well, nearly always. But my arm feels awful. Worse than before.' Her eyelids were beginning to droop. 'Joszef, I'm tired. Let me try to sleep now, okay? We'll talk later.'

Joszef didn't leave Klara's side while she slept. He could see she wasn't getting any better. By early evening, she was hot, and sweating profusely. He could only assume that the wound in her arm had become infected. He got Father O'Connor to look at her.

'Oh, dear, dear. It doesn't look good, young man, not good at all. I think you're right. Infected, and if she gets blood poisoning…' He shook his head. 'We must pray to God she doesn't get any worse. I'm not sure what more we can do. You make sure she drinks plenty of water.'

Nakuma must have heard about Klara's deteriorating condition, because the following morning he turned up with a clay pot containing some sort of medicinal potion.

'This for her,' he said. 'She drink. Make better.'

Joszef sniffed it. 'What is it? That smell!'

'Smell bad, but is very good. She drink.'

Klara had been dozing, but now she opened her eyes and gave Nakuma a smile. He poured some of the liquid into a mug, raised her head, and put it to her lips. 'You drink.'

Her voice was weak. 'Nakuma… you brought that for me? Tukano medicine, yes?' She took a sip and pulled a face. 'It's vile. That taste! And the smell!'

Nakuma grinned. 'Good medicine for Tukano white woman. You drink all.'

'My chief, d'you think the Kuru arrow was poisoned? Is that why I'm so ill? Tell me the truth.'

'No, not poison. If arrow with poison, you not ill. You dead.'

'Gee, that makes me feel a whole lot better. Thanks.'

Later, Father O'Connor came to see Klara again. He placed his hand on her forehead. 'Dear lady, will you not listen to me now. The infection seems to be getting worse. I don't like the look of it at all. What you need is antibiotic, but we have none here. We must get you to the mission at Constância as soon as we can. The sisters there are very capable. Our radio is broken, impossible to mend, so there's no chance of getting a plane. You'll be taking our boat again. I'll speak to Nakuma. He'll get you there.'

Joszef agreed. 'I think that's the only thing we can do. But how long will it take?'

'It's downstream so you'll be helped by the current. And it's a fast boat. Full speed, maybe three days. If Nakuma brings one of his friends along, you'll be able to keep going through the night.'

*

They set off at dawn the next morning. They'd put a mattress in the bottom of the boat for Klara to lie on, and a blanket to keep her warm at night. Marcello had provided a basket stocked with bread, cooked fish and bananas, and a clay pot full of boiled manioc. Nakuma and his friend had brought their own food, wrapped in a cloth.

Klara slept for most of the voyage, but her frequent periods of delirium worried Joszef. He watched over her constantly, sometimes succeeding in getting her to take a spoonful of the manioc concoction. Only occasionally did he allow himself to doze off for a few minutes, resting his head on Otto's duffle bag.

When at last they arrived at Constância, word quickly reached Padre Mazzanti that the people who'd caused him so much trouble had returned. He found this difficult to believe – until Joszef showed up in his study.

'*Mamma mia!* So it's true. I thought we'd got rid of you two for good. I don't understand... the Air Force plane—'

Joszef interrupted him. 'Listen, Padre, never mind about that now. Klara's been wounded. She's very sick and she's not getting any better. Worse, I think.'

'What? What are talking about?'

'Please, you must come to the boat and see for yourself. She needs antibiotic, urgently.'

Mazzanti followed Joszef down to the river and saw immediately that Klara was in trouble. She was barely conscious and her breathing was shallow.

'She doesn't look at all well,' he said, clasping his hands together in front of him, 'but don't worry. Sister Vittoria will look after her. Let's get her to the clinic. They have antibiotic. Then you must tell me what happened.'

Sister Vittoria knew exactly what to do, and in no time she'd set up an intravenous drip to deliver the antibiotic. Once Joszef was satisfied that he was leaving Klara in good hands, he hurried back to Mazzanti's study. He was surprised to find him with Nakuma. From the look of sheer horror on his face, it was obvious that Nakuma had told him everything. Mazzanti sprang from his chair and waved his fists about in a very unpriestly way.

'You lied to me! You had no intention of going home, did you? Not until you and your Indian friend here had murdered our Otto. It was all lies, you wicked, wicked man.'

'But, Padre, hasn't Chief Nakuma told you what Otto did to three of his people? He shot them dead, all three of them.'

'Yes, yes, but those three would still be alive today and none of this would have happened if you and your lady friend hadn't come here in the first place with your mischief and lies. What you have done is unforgivable, from start to finish.'

Joszef was undaunted. 'Unforgivable? In this world, perhaps, but I understand God will forgive us in the next. Isn't that right, Padre?'

Mazzanti glared at him, then, without another word, strode out of his study, leaving Joszef and Nakuma looking blankly at each other. Joszef began to wonder what had made him say the very thing he knew would most upset Mazzanti. Why had he behaved like a fucking adolescent? The whole thing was beginning to feel unreal. A bad dream. He was tired out and needed to sleep.

*

Klara responded well to the antibiotic and after five days in the clinic was feeling much better. She dismissed Joszef's suggestion she should rest for a few more days.

'We've got a lot to do, Joszef. I've been thinking about Otto's duffle bag. You still have it, I hope.'

'Don't worry, I've got it. Already looked at it. Big disappointment. There's nothing of any use. The son of a bitch got rid of anything that could've identified him. Even the jacket from his uniform… I thought that would tell us something, but he'd removed everything. No name, no initials, no insignia, not even a number.'

'Are you telling me he'd risked keeping his SS uniform for twenty years? Hell, he must've been very proud of it. So, we're no further forward, are we?'

'Ah, but wait. There is something.'

'What? Don't tell me there's some good news after all.'

'Listen. When I jumped off the boat to get Otto's bag, I found his gun. Sheer luck. It was on the ground where he'd dropped it.'

'His pistol? That's fantastic! Aren't you clever! Where is it?'

'I've got it here. Look.'

'Let me see. Ah, I know that gun. My father had one just like it. It's a Mauser, standard Wehrmacht issue during the war.'

'Look. What's this? A serial number or something stamped into the grip. I hadn't noticed that before. Won't that tell us who the owner was? I mean Schacht?'

Klara's eyes lit up with excitement. 'My god, you're right. Now we're beginning to get somewhere. We'll get the New York people onto it as soon as we get back. Top priority. Keep it in the duffle bag. We'll take everything back with us.'

'Back to civilisation! I've almost forgotten what it's like. But we've got the same problem as before – how the hell are we going to get out of here? Transport, I mean.'

'Yes, we've got to get that sorted.'

'I'll have to go and talk to Mazzanti, won't I? That's if he's willing to talk to me. We're not on the best of terms at the moment.'

'Wait, Joszef. I'm coming with you.'

Mazzanti wasn't in his study. They found him in conversation with *Clerico* Angelo in the quadrangle. 'See, Angelo, here he comes again. More trouble, no doubt. What do you want from me this time, young man? Ah, Miss Klara, I didn't see you there. Did Sister Vittoria say you could leave the clinic?'

'Padre, I feel well enough. I'm very grateful for the way you and the sisters looked after me. They were wonderful. They saved my life. But now it's time we left. We've troubled you for long enough.'

'You certainly have. More than enough, and we don't need your sort of trouble. So, now you are leaving? Good. I hope this time you've made the necessary arrangements.'

Joszef cut in. 'That's just it, Padre. We think there may be a plane coming here. Do you know of anything? A plane to take us to Manaus?'

'What? Haven't I heard that before? I can hardly believe it. What a couple of… never mind. So, here we go again. How do I know…'

Klara threw him a broad smile. 'Padre, we'd be enormously grateful if you could help us with this.'

'Very well, I'll see what I can do. The sooner you two get out of my hair, the better. Go home. Go anywhere, as far away from here as possible. Just leave us. And don't you dare come back here again. Ever.'

*

A few days later, they climbed into the canoe that was to take them to Mercês to meet the Panair plane. Before they set off, Klara had one last word with the mission's director.

'Padre Mazzanti, I don't think it's right for us to part on such bad terms. You're a good man, and maybe in God's good time you'll be able to think better of us. But please understand, we *had* to do what we did. We had no choice.'

'Miss Klara, it doesn't matter how you look at it, you've caused the death of a human being… well, several, in fact. I know you think what you've done is right. You are certain of it, yes? You have no doubts. People like you weigh such things against practical criteria. You live by the rules set out by your fellow men. But you and I are different. I try to look at things as I think God our Creator might see them, at least to the best of my ability. But, unlike you, I am not always certain. I confess as much. I suggest we leave it at that.'

It was obvious to Klara that Mazzanti was completely impervious to her way of thinking. His logic worked in a different way from hers. It was based on the faith he'd been born into, the faith he was living with, the faith he'd die with. His views on right and wrong, virtue and sin, sprang from an ancient tradition, where the rules were formulated by a divine being and had little to do with the worldly concepts of crime, justice and punishment. For him, justice would be dished out in the next life… including, where appropriate, eternal torment in fire and brimstone. She knew that nothing she could say to him would change that.

*

It was around 7pm when they looked out of the Catalina's porthole and marvelled at the lights of Manaus sparkling below them. Half an hour later, they were in a taxi on the way to town. After living among the tiny settlements of the Upper River Negro for so long, it took them a while to get used to the scale of the city, with its crowds, its traffic, its bright lights and loud music. Now, to them, the River Palace Hotel seemed genuinely palatial. Even so, they hadn't forgotten their first – and only – experience of its restaurant and decided to have dinner at the Hotel Amazonas. They were in high spirits and celebrated their return to civilisation with a bottle of champagne… at least, what's what was printed on the label.

After they'd eaten, Joszef reminded Klara that she needed to let the New York people know what had happened.

'We should also give Wolfgang Müller the news,' Klara said. 'Let's go and see him tomorrow. That's if he's not away on one of his hunting trips. About New York. I was going to tell you about that. I've already spoken to Eduardo on the phone. Told him everything. He listened, but I couldn't make out what he was thinking. Sounded disappointed. Thanked me and said we'd talk when we get back there. He's arranging a meeting with the whole group. To tell you the truth, I'm not looking forward to it.'

'I'm not surprised he wasn't over the moon. It wasn't the news he'd been hoping for, was it. They wanted to capture Schacht alive.'

'Joszef, I'm well aware of that. Yes, they wanted him alive so they could give him a thorough hearing. I know that. But they also wanted him dead. Look, because of what we did, he *is* dead, not living out his days peacefully among the priests in Constância. Not bad for a couple of amateurs, is it? Don't be so negative.'

TWENTY-SEVEN

Just over a week later, their Pan Am flight from São Paulo touched down at Idlewild. It was mid-February and neither of them was dressed for the chilly New York weather. The blast of cold air which hit them the second they stepped out of the plane made them shiver. They went straight to Carmine Street.

Klara wasn't surprised to find herself bombarded with a million questions from Lily. She was able to deflect most of them, even those concerning her scuffle with the bag snatcher on Fifth Avenue. It was more difficult to convince her that she'd jumped to the wrong conclusion about the nature of her relationship with the young Hungarian she'd brought back with her.

Although it was Joszef's first visit to New York, the idea of doing any serious sightseeing was out of the question. All their thoughts were focused on the forthcoming meeting at the 89th Street art gallery. When that day arrived, they found Eduardo waiting for them in the foyer, no longer in a gaudy blue uniform but wearing a dark grey suit, and there was no sign of a moustache. He said hello to Klara, then turned to Joszef.

'So, you are Joszef Poganyi, the famous butterfly hunter, right?'

Joszef grinned. 'And you are Eduardo, the famous doorman, Klara's controller, right?'

'Wrong. I don't think anyone could control Miss Brandt. She's a woman who follows her instincts. Welcome to New York, Joszef. I know you took some serious risks down there, chasing that big red butterfly. I must thank you for what you've done for us.'

'What we did had to be done, I guess. Er… these people we're going to meet here. I'm hoping they're okay with… I mean, with the way things turned out.'

'That remains to be seen.' He turned to Klara. 'Miss Brandt, I've already given them the gist of what you reported on the phone from Brazil. I have to warn you, they didn't look too happy with the news so don't expect it to be plain sailing. Okay, let's go up.'

Klara recognised the same gloomy room and the same group of people, including the elderly man in the baggy tweed jacket, still puffing on his pipe, and the woman with the blue-rinse hair. In addition, there was someone she hadn't seen before: a chubby man in his forties, wearing a black three-piece suit. Judging from the way he greeted Eduardo, it looked as if they were old friends.

She saw the old man approaching her. He greeted her without even a hint of a welcoming smile.

'Hello, Miss Brandt. I expect you're very glad to be back in the USA. I was sorry to hear about your arm.'

'Oh, Eduardo told you about that, did he? Much better, thanks. Stiff, but I'm sure a bit of physio will sort it out.'

'No doubt.' He rapped on the table with his pipe. 'Okay, everybody, do please sit down and let's get started. There's coffee if you want it. Miss Brandt, I'm sure you know that Eduardo has already briefed us about your efforts. It didn't go quite as we'd hoped, I'm afraid. Not as we'd planned it. Still, we need to hear about it directly from you. Tell us. Go right ahead.'

They listened in silence as Klara related the salient details. Their reaction was subdued. There were no questions, no discussion. Their disappointment was palpable. Klara could understand. For them, the failure to capture Walther Schacht alive must have felt like the death of a dream.

The old man said a few formal words to thank her for her account then turned to Joszef. 'Now, Mr Poganyi, from what we've been told, you played an important part in this. You deserve our grateful thanks. Do you have anything you'd like to tell us?'

Joszef stood up and bowed. 'I can tell you for sure that what Miss Brandt just told you is exactly what happened. I don't really need to add anything, except to assure you that Miss Brandt did everything she possibly could to fulfil her mission, and at great risk to her personal safety.' He sat down.

The woman with the blue-rinse hair spoke. 'Mr Poganyi. Miss Brandt. I must congratulate you, both of you. A most remarkable story. Nevertheless, in my opinion, we ought to have some way of corroborating what you've told us. Who was this Otto of yours? You say he admitted to being Walther Schacht, but that's just hearsay, isn't it. And how can we be certain he is really dead? It seems to me that—'

The man with the pipe stopped her. 'Before we go any further, I think Eduardo has something to say about that.'

Eduardo rose to his feet. 'Yes, I have. What Miss Brandt told me when she phoned from Brazil gave me a lot to think about. Like you, ma'am, I also felt some sort of corroboration was needed, so I asked the Cardinal Archbishop to let me use his short-wave equipment again. We eventually managed to get through to the Catholic priest in charge of the mission at Constância.'

Klara was wide-eyed with astonishment and didn't try to hide her indignation. 'You mean you didn't believe me? For crying out loud, you thought I was making it all up?'

'Miss Brandt, whether I personally believed you or not is unimportant. I needed an independent voice and, you'll be glad to hear, I got one. Now, to continue. The priest was furious with Miss Brandt. He told me she'd betrayed his trust, and her underhand activities had resulted in the death of the mission's odd-job man, an elderly German they'd named Otto—'

Klara interrupted him again. 'Yes, it's true. He couldn't forgive me for what I'd done. But so what? He knew all along he was harbouring a goddamn Nazi, and I had a job to do.'

'Will you please let me finish? What I wanted to say was that the priest told me he'd learnt all about Otto's death directly from the chief of an Indian tribe.

The Indian's account was identical to what we've just heard from Miss Brandt. As far as I'm concerned, that's corroboration.'

The man with the pipe turned to the blue-rinse lady. 'I think that's what you wanted, yes?'

'As far as it goes.' She gave Klara a polite smile. 'Miss Brandt, I'm impressed. You're a very brave, clever, determined young lady. You and your friend here seem to have rid the world of a loathsome barbarian.' She had to pause while the others voiced their agreement. 'However, we don't know whether this man was SS-Gruppenführer Walther Ludwig Schacht or some lesser official, do we, Miss Brandt? You failed to carry out the agreed plan, and because of that we don't have either him or his dead body. If we had, it's likely we'd be able to identify him from his dental records. Mr Eduardo, you've examined the duffle bag Miss Brandt brought back with her, and all the items in it, yes? I understand your people found nothing to tell us about the identity of its owner. Isn't that right?'

'I'm afraid that's true. Our forensics specialists tried everything. Infrared, ultraviolet, all the latest technology. They found nothing of any use.'

Joszef jumped to his feet. 'What about Otto's gun, the Mauser? It had a serial number.'

'No good. It wasn't even a genuine Mauser. Our experts identified it as a copy made by a factory in Paraguay. Churned out thousands of them in the '40s and '50s. And I'm afraid it wasn't a proper serial number. Apparently, they were all stamped the same, to make them difficult to trace.'

'Wait!' Klara called out. 'The photos of Otto I took in Constância. Didn't you get those films processed?'

The man with the pipe looked puzzled. 'Photos, Miss Brandt? But didn't you tell us he smashed your camera?'

'He did, but I had more rolls of film in my rucksack. I'd left them at the mission when we followed Otto upriver. Come on, Eduardo... did you find any pictures of him?'

'I did, and here they are.' He took two large prints out of his case and placed them on the table. 'Disappointing, I'm afraid. The focus is poor. Take a look.'

Klara sighed. 'I see what you mean. To tell you the truth, I'm not surprised. I wasn't quite myself when I took them. I think I was running away from him.'

A heavily built man – she remembered him from the first meeting – picked up one of the photos and screwed up his eyes to scrutinise it more closely. 'You know, this really could be that motherfucker. He was a lot younger when I met him, but it could be him.'

The woman with the blue-rinse hair shook her head. 'That's just wishful thinking. You can't tell anything from these photos. They prove nothing. The man in these pictures could be almost anybody.'

Klara was beginning to show her frustration. 'I *know* Otto was Schacht. That's apart from the fact that he practically told me he was. Look, if he wasn't, then who was he? Definitely a lousy Nazi. A fanatic. A cold-blooded killer. Clever, determined, well organised and ruthless. He was the right age for Schacht – he told Joszef he was sixty-eight – and had all the right physical characteristics. He'd persuaded – probably bullied – a whole network of telegraphists to look after his interests. Sounds typical of Schacht from what I've learnt about the way he operated. It looks as if he was able to organise, at very short notice, an attack on my roommate, Lily Wang, right here in New York. Eduardo witnessed that directly.' Eduardo nodded. 'That means Otto's network extended over thousands of miles. Why would someone so clever, with that level of organisational ability, put up with the monotonous and demeaning sort of life he was enduring in that far-flung backwater? I'll tell you why. Because he was Walther Schacht. He knew exactly what Nuremberg had decreed, and he knew he'd be hanged by the neck if he was ever found. That's why.'

Eduardo stroked his chin. 'Miss Brandt, you make a good point. Really, I know of no one else who fits that picture, and believe you me, we know them all.'

The blue-rinse lady was unconvinced. 'You may know them all, Mr Eduardo, or think you do, but that's not proof. It's only an opinion. Unsatisfactory.' She turned to the man with the pipe. 'I'm not sure we can go much further with this.'

No one said a word.

The silence was broken by the sound of approaching footsteps, followed by a knock on the door. Eduardo's colleague in the black suit strolled over to open it. He mumbled a couple of words to whoever was out there, shut the door, and handed Eduardo an oversized envelope.

Eduardo looked apologetic. 'Sorry about this. It's from the forensics people. I'd better take a quick look.' He slit open the envelope with his pocket knife and fished out a handwritten note. As he read it, a surprised expression crossed his face. He read it again, out loud.

'Listen to this.

> *'We found fingerprints all over the fake Mauser. Likely most of them belong to the guys who found it. Too bad. They should have been more careful. It's a real mess. Still, it's possible there may be prints from the gun's owner as well, whoever he was. Enlargements enclosed. Hope this doesn't lead you on a wild goose chase. Good luck!*

'Well, what d'you know! I hadn't expected this. We'd better take a look.' He shook the envelope and a shower of photographs landed on the table, each one bearing the magnified image of a single fingerprint. 'Okay, let's see what we've got here.'

Klara could hardly contain herself. 'My god, fingerprints! Probably mine and Joszef's, most of them. Could there be some of Otto's among them, d'you think? Is that possible, after all that pistol's been through?'

'We'll have to see,' Eduardo said, then turned to his black-suited friend. 'Hey, come and take a look at these.'

'Sure thing,' his friend replied, and started to flick through the photos. 'Let's see. Gee, it looks as if most of 'em are junk. But hang on... maybe a few of 'em are okay.'

Klara looked puzzled. 'I don't get it. Even if some of the prints are Otto's... Schacht's, I mean... we won't be able to tell, will we? How will we know? We've got nothing to compare them with.'

The man examining the photos grinned and extracted a small plastic folder from the inside pocket of his jacket. He slid its contents onto the table: two cards, each the size of a picture postcard. 'Miss Brandt, I been carrying these darned things around with me forever. Come and take a look. They're the real McCoy.'

Klara leant forward. One card was marked *Linke* and the other *Rechte*. Each bore a set of four fingerprints and a thumbprint. At the bottom of each card there was a name and a date, inscribed in ink, faded with time but still legible: *Walther Ludwig Schacht, Freiwilliger, 1922*.

'I don't believe it! How on earth did you…'

'Wasn't easy, ma'am. Took a long time and a helluva lot of shoe leather, but we knew darned well there had to be his prints someplace. We started at Landsberg Prison. That's in Bavaria, ma'am. Schacht was jailed there back in 1924. Spooky place, I can tell you. There were fingerprint records of inmates by the hundred, but did we find Walther's? Nope. Must've had 'em destroyed as soon as he became a big shot.'

'So, where *did* you find them?'

'The *Kyffhäuser* archive in Rüdesheim. Tell you the truth, we should've looked there first. They've got records of everyone and everything stored in there, including stuff on every darned Freikorps member from way back when. Our Walther Schacht had been a member. Either he forgot to have his details destroyed or he figured his service with the Freikorps would look good on his résumé. *Freiwilliger*… it means volunteer.'

'Yes, I know what it means.'

The old man with the pipe was shaking with excitement. 'So, get on with it, will you. You have a magnifying glass?'

'Sure thing. Sherlock Holmes at your service.'

The room fell quiet as he began to examine the prints, switching his attention from one to another. He dismissed some of them in a couple of seconds, while others held his gaze for longer. But each time his verdict was the same. 'No... no... nope... hell, no. Nothing. Tell you the truth, I'm not surprised. Looks like a lotta guys got their paws on that gun.'

Several long minutes later, it was the same. 'Still nothing doing, folks. This could take quite a while. You got dozens of prints here from that pistol and I gotta compare every one of 'em that's decent with Schacht's on these cards here. We got nothing so far. It ain't gonna be easy.'

The old man was watching eagerly. 'Just take your time... and don't miss anything. We can wait here all day if necessary.'

'You may need to. Wait. Hold your horses... here's something... maybe. Not sure. Eduardo, come and take a look at this.'

Klara grabbed Joszef's arm and squeezed it so hard that he cried out.

Eduardo took the magnifying glass. 'Yes, I see what you mean. Similar to this print here on the card, isn't it? Middle finger of his right hand. But you're the expert. Are they identical?'

'Can't say. Could be, but it's smudged. And it's not complete. Half of it's missing. Where was it? On the gun, I mean.'

Eduardo peered at something scrawled on the back of the photograph. 'Let's see. It was on the front edge of the grip. That makes sense, doesn't it? There must be others. Go on, see if you can find any more.'

'You bet!'

The next few minutes passed slowly.

'Sorry, folks. Nothing else so far. But never mind, there's plenty more to look at, so we ain't done yet.' He took a deep breath then resumed the search. 'This one? No. This one? No... er... no. Maybe this one, let's see... no. Wait. Hang on... I mean... *yes*! This one here. Look, it matches his pinkie. I think. And it's a good print, nice and clean.' He glanced at the scribble on the other side of the photo. 'This one was also on the pistol's grip, just below the other one. Wait. I gotta make sure. Bring that lamp over here. Ah, that's better.' He bent low over his magnifying glass and appeared to be talking to himself.

They were all watching, looking for any twitch of his face that might indicate success or failure. After a while, he quietly put the glass down on the table and smiled mischievously but said nothing.

'Well?' Eduardo asked. 'Are you going to tell us?'

'Ah, I thought you might want to know. Guess what? A perfect match!'

Klara couldn't wait. 'My god! Does that mean—'

The lady with the blue-rinse hair interrupted her. 'Yes, what exactly *does* it mean? Are you trying to tell me that just because of that little smudge, you think the gun may have belonged to Walther Schacht? Well, I call that pie in the sky.'

'Ma'am,' Eduardo replied rather tersely, 'can you please tell me how that little smudge, undoubtedly made by the little finger of Walther Schacht's right hand, got there if it wasn't his pistol?'

Klara's face was flushed with excitement. It seemed too good to be true. She addressed the fingerprint man directly. 'Are you certain? D'you think it could be some sort of coincidence?'

'Coincidence? Forget it. Not a chance. I'll say it again: that's Walther Schacht's fingerprint on that darned gun. I'd stake my life on it.'

Klara persisted. 'You're sure?'

'Ma'am, sure I'm sure, one hundred percent sure. That's his print, and there's gotta be more of 'em. We'll check out the whole enchilada when we get back to the office. But in any case, that pistol belonged to Schacht. He's the guy. Not a smitch of doubt about it.' He pulled a pack of Philip Morris from one pocket and a cigarette lighter from the other and lit up. 'So there ya go.'

Klara couldn't stop herself from shouting, 'What did I tell you? You see? I knew it was him.'

The room was filled with the buzz of feverish conversation. Faces beamed with excitement and relief. Only the woman with the blue-rinse hair still looked doubtful.

The old man with the pipe limped over to Klara and grasped her wrist. With his other hand he took hold of Joszef's arm and drew the pair close to him. He was smiling, but Klara could see tears forming in his eyes. She couldn't tell whether they were tears of relief or joy or what, but she could see he was struggling to overcome a flood of emotion. It took him a while to settle down.

He wiped his eyes with the back of his hand. 'My friends, you are all witnesses to what I'm about to say. On this day, here in New York City, I pronounce that the convicted war criminal SS-Gruppenführer Walther Ludwig Schacht is dead. The sentence of death passed on him *in absentia* at Nuremberg almost twenty years ago, for crimes against humanity, has at last been carried out.' He looked around the room. Someone was sobbing. It was the heavily built man who'd thought he recognised Schacht from one of Klara's photos.

The man with the pipe continued. 'Well, that's how I look at it, and that's how we should all look at it. We must remember that millions have grown old waiting for this news, and many have died still hoping for it. I hope now we may be able to draw a line under all those years of anguish. I will arrange for a press release to be prepared, and in a day or two the entire world will know.' He stopped, as if he'd finished, but then carried on. 'Ideally, we'd have preferred to capture Schacht alive. Then, we'd have found out what he had to say about those evil bandits at the helm of the Third Reich. But we'll just have to get along without that. And I think I'm right in saying that all of us in this room would have derived some particular satisfaction if we'd had the opportunity to confront the murderer in person, yes?' This last comment drew a surprisingly subdued chorus of unintelligible murmurs from his audience. 'I see. Never mind. Miss Brandt, you've done an extraordinarily good job. Very satisfactory from our point of view.' He raised an eyebrow. 'And I think I'm safe in assuming, from your personal perspective also, yes?'

Klara nodded. 'Yes, indeed. Most satisfactory.'

In his excitement, he'd let his pipe go out. He stared at it for a moment, muttered something under his breath, and stuffed it into his pocket. 'Well then,' he said, 'I think we can all go home.'

*

They were back on Fifth Avenue. It had started to snow, and the trees in Central Park were beginning to turn white.

Joszef was rubbing his hands together. 'I'm freezing. It's like being in the Arctic. Funny, just a couple of weeks ago we were sweltering in the jungle. I wish we were back there now, just for an hour or two, to warm us up.'

Klara pulled her coat more tightly around her shoulders and lit a cigarette. 'Forget it. I've had my fill of the jungle for one lifetime. But cheer up. I remember a little place along here where we can get a decent cup of coffee. That'll warm us up.'

'Good. And something a bit stronger, I hope. I'm cold.'

'I thought you didn't approve of alcohol this early in the day, or have you changed your views about that?'

'Yes, about that and many other things. Anyway, we have a good reason to celebrate properly now, don't we.'

'Absolutely right. We do and we will.'

They walked on in silence until Joszef said, 'Klara, I have to talk to you. I'm going back to London, to my job at the school. I have to, I promised them.'

'Ah, I thought that was on the cards. Good for you. I'm sure you're a marvellous teacher. But you're not planning to leave just yet, though, are you?'

'Soon. Next week, in fact. I've booked on the *Queen Mary*.'

'So soon? That doesn't give us much time to show you the town.'

'I suppose not, but I can't stay any longer. By now, they'll be wondering if I'm ever going to come back. But what about you? What are you going to do now?'

'Me? I'm going to pick up my life where I left off, as a journalist. To tell you the truth, I've been toying with the idea of doing a piece on the demise of Walther Schacht. Still haven't decided, but I think it would make a great story.'

'Absolutely. It'll probably win you a Pulitzer.'

'Some hope!'

'Klara... you know, I'm going to miss you when I get back to London. But I think you won't miss me much, will you. Anyway, you'll be busy with your work.'

'Why, of course I'll miss you, Joszef, after everything we've been through together. Of course I will.'

'I suppose so. A little bit, anyway. I've been thinking. Maybe I come back here in summer vacation and we meet again... if you haven't forgotten me completely by then. Maybe we can see around the USA together. What you think?'

'I don't know. Let's wait and see. Look, here's that coffee place I mentioned. Let's go in. The snow's getting heavier.'

Joszef looked up at the sky, opened his mouth, and caught a falling snowflake on the tip of his tongue. 'Okay,' he said.